Elastic Girl

OLIVIA RANA

© 2017 Olivia Rana
All rights reserved.

ISBN: 1976170605
ISBN-13: 9781976170607

This book is dedicated to the memory of my father, with love.

PROLOGUE

My mother prayed for the miracle of a boy, but again and again sharp pains gripped her body as she lost the child she was carrying. 'God does not wish it,' grandmother said. 'It will come soon.' When the nausea returned and my mother's back began to curve with the weight of her stomach, everyone said, 'This is it.'

I arrived in December, and unlike my older sisters, Safa and Belli, I was a puny little girl. 'She has a face like a pearl,' my mother said. 'We'll call her Muthu.'

My father would not look at me for days, no matter how hard I cried, for while I suckled on my mother's breast, a storm was raging all around us. It tore through the Tikaram family, pitching us out of our home in Kallikuppam and into hardship and disgrace.

'She is cursed,' grandmother said. 'It is all her fault.'

From the beginning my fate was written.

1

We settled in the town of Ambattur, on the bed of the dried-up Puzhal Lake. Our new home was in a housing tenement, built by the government when the reservoir was declared out of use. It was the same as almost every other house around us, with walls of sun-baked bricks and a slate pitched roof, and every corner of the two small rooms was crammed with all the things my parents had taken from Kallikuppam, including rosewood chairs and a folding table covered with a white embroidered cloth. An array of glistening brass vessels lined the shelves, and on a makeshift temple in the corner of the room sat a gold-framed picture of the elephant god, Ganesh, and a photograph of my grandfather, the great Samir Tushar; he was dressed in his green police uniform and peaked cap, his mouth open slightly as if he'd been about to speak.

Every day I followed my sisters as they made their way to Sri Ramaswami Secondary School. They were both dressed in crisp blue and white checked uniforms, Safa with a blue dupatta draped across both shoulders and Belli a white one.

My parents had decided that two educated girls were more than enough.

As I skipped behind them across the bridge, Belli's duppata slipped down onto the ground, and before she could reach it, I ran forwards and whipped it up into the air. *'Even today, a gust of wind surely lifts the locks of your hair,*' I sang, twirling the scarf up into the air and imagining myself as Aishwarya Rai in my favourite film of all time, *Hum Dil De Chuke Sanam.*

Belli scrambled to tear her dupatta from my hands, but jumping up onto the wall of the bridge, I began to dance. A small gathering of children stopped to have a look, and a passing truck honked its horn.

'Even today, your hair must still be adorned with flowers,' I continued to sing.

'Tell her to stop,' Belli wailed at Safa. 'She's making us look like fools.'

Turning my back, I waved the dupatta up over my head, and then suddenly Belli and Safa grabbed me by the arms and held me out so that I was dangling over the bridge.

'It will carry you all the way down to Chennai,' Belli said. 'Then you won't be so clever anymore.'

Behind me one of the children began to cry, even though the riverbed was as dry as the back of a rock lizard.

'I'll tell Ammachi!' I screamed.

'Then don't follow us,' Safa said, and they set me down and carried on ahead to school, matching leather satchels swinging by their sides.

Smoothing down my skirt and gathering up the parcel of rotis from the ground, I made my way to the narrow end of the bridge. My job was to sell amma's soft, flaky bread to workers who were hurrying on their way to Ambattur Industrial Estate.

Maheesh was waiting for me there: the best chai wallah in the town and my only friend. He gave me a gap-toothed smile and shook his wild head of hair from side to side. 'Muthu, you'll be a great movie star one day.' He nodded down the bridge to where I'd just performed. 'So much better than Zinta and Kajol.'

'But not so pretty.' Unlike their heart-shaped faces, mine was as curved as a handi pot, my eyes big and round like a tree frog, and at ten years of age, I was no taller than a Kanni dog. But when Maheesh and I went to Rakki cinema and sat in the dark, I could imagine myself looking like any one of them, my thick, wiry hair tamed into a slick wave of curls.

Maheesh and I shared a love for Bollywood, and it was he who had figured out a way of sneaking in through the roof of the cinema, allowing us to watch every film through the cracks in the floorboards of the ceiling. We knew every song by heart, and, unlike Safa and Belli, Maheesh had not laughed when I told him I was going to be a star. Maheesh understood.

On the bridge, children and adults from the lake gathered, carrying bundles of firewood on their heads, baskets of curry leaves, and plates of bright-orange, sugary jalebis. Together we waited until they came: patched-up buses shouldered their way across the bridge, sprouting arms and legs like centipedes; yellow hooded rickshaws; rumbling Tata lorries from the city; and cyclists flitting past us like flies, the owners' scarves flying in the wind, their wives and sisters balancing on the frames.

'Breakfast,' we called over the din of honking traffic. 'Don't forget your breakfast.'

As things reached gridlock, some of the passengers began to reach out and click their fingers. Delivering roti into the palm of their hands, Maheesh worked his way along behind me, sieve held high in the air as he poured a stream of liquid from his tea pan into small clay cups.

'Faster,' I told him. 'They're starting to move.'

The two of us had a system—for every five cups of chai Maheesh sold, he gave me the price of one. 'Without roti to dry the mouth, there's no need for tea,' I told him. 'It's only fair.'

As the morning rush hour tailed off and the rotis dried up, we slid down the banks, hop-skipping over rubbish-filled trenches, squeezing our way through the long queues of half-clad men at the public taps. On one patch of the lake were the remains of a military bungalow with a windmill, pump house, and small swimming pool. 'Souvenirs from British rule,' my father called them.

We swung off the crumbling blades on the windmill and climbed up into the rafters of the pump house, ducking and diving under the swoop of the blue rock pigeons.

'No eggs.' Maheesh peered into their nests.

He had sold four already, passing them off as the eggs of a yellow-throated bulbul. 'That boy has no scruples,' amma had said when she heard of the scam.

We took it in turns to dive through the porthole windows on a rope swing, flying across the mound of rotting waste lying in the black sludge of the swimming pool below.

'Let's pretend you are Saajan in *Baaghi*,' I called out to him as he swung across the pool. 'And I'm Kaajal, so you must save me.'

Swinging back onto the ledge, he pulled me out with him onto the rope swing. 'I'll tell my parents we are to be married,' he said in his serious Bollywood voice, and we swung back together over the pool.

'That looks like a perfectly good bicycle.' I pointed to the upturned frame of a Zippo in the pool below us. The handlebars poked up into the air like the curved black antennae of a leaf beetle.

'Just think where we could go with that.'

'Or better still, we could clean it up and sell it: five hundred rupee at least.'

'Muthu, that bicycle is stuck as fast as a boot,' Maheesh laughed. 'You would need an elephant to draw it out.'

'You should be more positive,' I told him, scrambling down into the bowels of the pump house, which, like the pool, was filled with unwanted odds and ends: a rusting oil barrel, a torn mattress, and a box filled with shards of cracked pots.

'Here, this will do.'

Maheesh helped me fetch up an old reel of fishing wire and a mis-shapen wheel trim, all the while singing 'Chunari Chunari.'

'*What would I do without you? Take pity on my youth.*' He sang as though he was holding his nose, but he could remember lines like no one else and sang it right through until we had gathered up everything we needed onto the ledge of the pool.

'Sush is the most beautiful woman in the universe,' Maheesh said. 'A real hottie.'

'She wouldn't look at you,' I snapped, and then we sat on the floorboards of the pump house and fashioned ourselves a lasso.

'You're the strongest, so you must stay here, Maheesh, then you can pull me in on the swing.'

'You're too small; you'll never reach.'

Not listening, I began to tie the wire around my waist, handing one end to Maheesh before swinging out over the pool.

'You're a fool,' he called out to me.

'Better a fool than a coward.' I lowered my end of the wire with the wheel trim attached.

Again and again the lasso slipped off, and the bicycle sank a little farther out of view.

'It's no good,' Maheesh called. 'Leave it, heh?'

Just then the wheel trim caught on the end of the brake handle.

'Lean back!'

Maheesh heaved on the wire, pulling it tight against my middle. As I was caught in a tug-of-war between Maheesh and the bicycle, which wouldn't budge an inch, my hands began to burn, and suddenly the wire attached to my waist snapped and whipped up into the air, the bicycle pulling me down into the pool.

Maheesh was leaning out through the window. 'Muthu, hold on!' he called, the end of the wire still dangling in his hands. Grabbing onto a length of wood, I tried to pull myself up, but it gave way below me and disappeared, my arms and legs thrashing about wildly as I tried to find something else to hold me up.

'Dadi!' I screamed. 'Dadi!'

Above me Maheesh was trying to untangle the remainder of the wire. 'I'll get you,' he said, but it was useless, because down I went under the murky sea, being pulled farther and farther by a tangle of metal reeds. Up once, twice, three times, gagging and choking into the air, my heart pounding in my ears, and looking up one last time, I saw that Maheesh was gone, and there was nothing, only the perfect blue arch of sky above the pump house.

Everything was very still as my body slipped down like a golden mahseer onto a silky seagrass bed. This was what it felt like to be dead, but then my dress caught tight on the edge of something, and the life was sucked back into me, pulling and tugging, as thick, vile water filled up my nose and my throat, and the pressure inside my head ached for release. It was the gentle sound of a whistle that reached me, and then suddenly my dress came free, and I disappeared from the pool completely.

This place where I found myself was no bigger than the width of a watermelon and blacker than the himej seeds my mother crushed to powder when we had stomach cramps. I crouched down onto my elbows, my chin touching off a metal floor; the smell stuck to my skin and formed a mucus inside my mouth, making me retch again. As I crawled along on my belly, it crossed my mind that this was the depths of narakam, the hell for evil-doers and cursed souls, and that maybe grandmother had been right about me all along.

My cries of fear and pain bounced off the thin metal walls, and I knew that my torn knees and elbows were bleeding, but I kept on moving through the darkness, praying to Shiva, and then a prick of light appeared before me, and as I reached it, the sun burst down on me as I fell like a stone from the end of a pipe, spluttering and coughing. Kneeling there on the ground, my body began to shake as sobs broke through me.

'It's a ghost,' someone said.

Looking up, I saw there was a group of bewildered women sitting in a circle beyond me, their knitting needles crisscrossed in the air. As they rushed forward, my body collapsed, burying itself into the earth.

Half a dozen men carried me on a broken door across the lake, stopping every so often to press an ear to my chest and rapping at doors with a stick, to ask the owners if they knew who this child belonged to. Faces came and went over me in a haze, until I recognized amma.

She scooped me up into her arms, and without any sound, the tears slipped down her face. 'We thought she was dead,' she said.

Inside the house the furniture was quickly rearranged to make way for the door, and then they laid me down in the centre of the room. 'That boy, he came and said she had fallen into the pool.' Amma's hands ran circles over my face and down my arms. 'The men fished everything out, but she was gone. Everyone said she was dead inside the pump, that it couldn't be possible.'

'It's a miracle,' one of the men said as they made to leave, my mother pressing some coins into their hands. When they had gone, I noticed for the first time that the room was filled with neighbours, standing and sitting around the walls like pieces of furniture.

While amma busied herself with cleaning my cuts and making up a remedy, they came and touched my feet, some of them tucking money into the tattered folds of my skirt. 'You've defeated evil,' one of the women said. 'You are blessed.'

When amma held a glass to my lips, the smell of the ginger and jeera warmed me, and something in her face made me cry. 'There, there,' she soothed, brushing the palm of her hand across my head, and then she began to bathe my wounds and sprinkle them with powdered mehndi.

By the time Belli and Safa arrived home from school, I was tucked up in bed, but the neighbours had not yet moved, some of them keeping vigil by my bedside. They could not believe that I'd crawled inside the vent to escape the pool. 'It's impossible,' they said. 'Tell us again.'

And in telling my story, the greater it grew. 'It was like a monster clawing on my heels; it dragged my body and then my head.' I placed a hand on my throat.

'Keep going.'

'My breath stopped, and everything went black as soot.'

'Was it like dying?' Belli asked.

'I *was* dead, but then I came back to life.'

The women gasped.

'My dress caught on the edge of the vent, and as I pulled, it opened up like a trap. It whistled at me.'

'Lord Krishna!' Mrs. Gupta said. 'He was leading you to safety with his flute.'

When my father arrived home from work, the neighbours crowded around him.

'Your daughter survived a fate of death,' Mr. Kapoor told him.

'It was that boy with the hair,' Mrs. Gupta said. 'He was the one who pushed her in.'

'Where is Maheesh?' I'd forgotten about Maheesh.

'You'll never see that boy again,' amma said. 'He's nothing but trouble.'

'Is it true?' dadi asked, coming to me and putting his hand on top of mine. He looked as if he had just climbed out of bed, his eyelids drooping underneath a thick mop of tousled hair. 'I'll kill him,' he said, in an unlikely fit of rage, and amma jumped up from her chair like a spring, catching him by the arm.

Everyone fell quiet, their gaze shifting awkwardly about the room.

It was then I should have defended Maheesh, but instead I said nothing.

'How are they all in one piece?' Mrs. Nadar asked, breaking the silence. She leaned over and poked at my legs and arms. 'Not one broken bone.'

'She's like the goddess Durga, the invincible one,' Mrs. Gupta said.

My mother slowly hushed them all away, telling them I needed to rest.

'She is a rubber doll,' Mrs. Nadar said, as she made her way to the door. 'Able to squeeze into such a small space.'

'No, like elastic,' Mr. Kapoor said. 'She is the Elastic Girl.'

2

Maheesh disappeared from the bridge, and it was several weeks later when I saw him standing outside the railway station, selling chai to thirsty passengers. He'd been beaten black and blue.

When I returned to the house, amma reached into my pouch and counted out the takings, sliding each coin out on the table before her and forming a neat silver line. 'Is that all? Where is the rest?'

'Without Maheesh the roti won't sell.'

'Too much talking and not enough selling—that's your problem, Elastic Girl.'

Mr. Kapoor's new name for me had stuck, and my mother was right, for instead of selling roti on the bridge, most of my day was spent entertaining children from the lake with tales of my survival from the pool. They wanted to see the gash up the length of my arm and hear about how the rats scampered across my back while I'd crawled through the pipe. To them, my story was one of the most exciting things to have ever happened on the lake.

But at home the sympathy had quickly vanished, and when I complained about pains in my legs, they just shook it off.

'Self-pity is a bad habit,' amma said, and she took to serving up leftover roti again with the dinner instead of bowls of spiced kidney beans and sweet rice.

And instead of dadi sitting by my side, he resumed his position at the head of the table, Safa and Belli flanking him on either side, leaning in every so often to tell him bits and pieces of news from school.

'Lajita's Dadi works for the government,' Safa told him. 'She said that they call us encroachers.'

'Is that right?' Dadi tore off a corner of his roti and spooned some subji into his mouth. He ate with his mouth open, washing the roti down with a glass of milk.

'She said that they want to reopen the lake,' Safa continued.

'All they are concerned about is quenching the thirst of the bloody Chennaiites,' he said.

'They won't do it,' amma soothed. 'Not with the elections coming up.'

Everyone in Ambattur was talking about it. The government wanted to capture the rainwater that flowed down from Red Hills during monsoon. They wanted to put us out of our homes.

'Mr. Chaudhari says it's the alluvial soil,' Safa said. 'It makes it suitable for water retention.'

'Well, it is most *unsuitable* for us,' dadi snapped. 'Tell Mr. Chaudhari that.'

'We could go back to Kallikuppam,' Belli said brightly.

'That's enough!' My father brought his fist down onto the table. 'We're going nowhere.'

Everyone ate in silence, Belli sobbing quietly onto her plate until dadi leaned over and kissed her head. 'This business has unsettled everyone,' he said. 'It is better to leave it alone.'

After dinner Belli and Safa stayed at the table, their homework books spread out before them, and dadi settled himself for the evening in the high-back chair, his belly resting like a baby in his arms. Having cleared away the dishes and helped amma with the pots, I went to him with a handful of porcelain cowrie shells.

'A game of pachisi?'

'Not now.' He waved me away.

'What about the tanks, Dadi?' I asked, kneeling on a cushion by his feet.

Every morning my father rose at five and cycled to Avadi, a Bombay Fashions bag and transistor radio hanging off the handlebars. He worked in the Heavy Vehicles Factory, producing military tanks. He called himself a combat vehicle mechanical engineer, and I knew that above all things, dadi liked to talk about this very important job.

'We have an urgent defence contract with Russia,' he said. 'One hundred and twenty-five Arjun tanks.'

He described to me the hull, the armour, and the turret, and he complained about the delay on the power packs being bought from abroad. 'They're fifty-eight tonnes each—a beast,' he said.

'Two months and you have not been paid.' Amma swept around us with a broom. 'Our rent is due by the end of the week.'

'There's been a delay on the contract.' I could feel his foul mood returning as he held on tightly to the arms of the chair. 'These things take time.'

My mother stopped sweeping and pointed the end of the broom handle at him. 'Well, if you don't have the money by the end of the week, then the government won't be the ones tossing us out.'

Belli and Safa looked up from the table as our father rose from his chair and left the house. We knew that he would be gone to Kumar's to drink toddy until it made him sing, and that in the morning he would be late leaving the house, and amma would stay cross all day long.

It was my mother I blamed for driving him to it with her spiteful tongue, and in defiance the following day, I went to see Maheesh at the station.

■ ■ ■

'I'll drop my cut of your takings; we can be equal partners instead.'

'They said to keep away from you,' Maheesh said quietly. As he turned away, I could see a scar above his eye that had still not healed.

'We won't tell them. We can pretend that we are Arjun and Pooja in *Achanak*, pretend that we are on the run.'

Maheesh smiled. '*Is Arjun a victim of fate or the target of a conspiracy?*' He quoted from the movie's trailer.

'You'll come then?' I asked, and Maheesh linked his arm in mine and began to sing again.

'*I am the first, I am the last. None other have I ever known. I am the wisest of them all. Bulleh! Do I stand alone?*

'You are famous now?' he said, as we made our way along the bridge, boys and girls skipping along beside us.

'Tell us about the flute, Elastic Girl,' one of them asked.

'It's a good name, *Elastic Girl*, a stage name you could call it,' Maheesh said.

'Did *he* do it?' one of the boys asked, pointing at Maheesh. 'Is he the one who pushed you in?'

'It was an accident; that's all.' I pulled Maheesh away.

They would not leave us alone, calling Maheesh names and shouting for me to come away. 'We'll break his legs,' one of the older boys said. 'He won't do it again.'

Maheesh stood quietly in the middle of the enclosing circle waiting for them to attack.

'It was a lie. I wasn't pushed.'

The boys dropped their fists to their sides, and some of the girls began to whisper among themselves. 'But I escaped through the pipe; that *is* true, and it was Krishna playing the flute.'

But they began to walk away slowly, some of them shaking their heads.

Maheesh was smiling at me. 'You like me after all, heh?'

'Let's go to the cinema; they're showing *Vaastav* with Sanjay Dutt.'

The following day we fell back into rhythm, Maheesh clinking his way along behind me, filling cups with bubbling froth. 'A nice cup of chai with your roti?' he asked. 'It will set you up for the day.'

A broken-down lorry caused a tailback, giving us the best run of business we ever had, and my worries about us not being able to pay the rent began to slide away as we wove in and out amongst the traffic, serving up roti and tea to upset passengers.

Neither of us noticed what was happening on the lake.

'Look, look,' one of the passengers shouted, pointing out through the opening of a rickshaw and towards the lake. 'They are finally moving them on.'

When we stepped up onto the wall, we could see them: four lean lorries with bulldozers on the back, waiting like gunners. People came from their houses, scuttling down through the lanes like an army of ants, surrounding the lorries until the drivers were unable to move.

'The government has come!' I shouted as Maheesh and I raced down the dry banks. 'Safa said it would happen.'

'Have pity,' someone shouted at the drivers as we made our way into the crowd. 'We've got nowhere else to go.' But the bulldozers tracked their way off the lorries and into position, blades lowered like griddle-scrapers to the ground.

People raised their arms in the air, some holding sticks and metal rods, and then above the crowd a figure appeared, draped in a long white kurta. It was Mr. Mody, perching on the top of a ladder. Mr. Mody was the varuna of Ambattur, the keeper of divine order. He had a head of wispy grey hair, a matching beard, and heavy bags under his eyes like a man who never slept.

'Let's not get carried away,' he pleaded through a megaphone. 'This can all be resolved without violence. Anger will only drive them on.'

'It's our home!' someone shouted. 'Those dogs have no right.'

Mr. Mody raised his hand and began to speak again, but the bulldozers roared to life, drowning out his words so that he could do nothing but look on in desperation as men continued to close in on the rumbling lorries.

'I can't see,' I said, standing on my toes, but Maheesh was gone. I climbed back up the banks until I could see him joining the surge of men as they rushed forward, some of them making their way up onto the roof of the lorries to bang their fists against the windows. Inside, drivers stared straight ahead, their hands gripped tight to the wheel. If the police did not arrive soon, the crowd would tear them apart.

At the house, amma was planted in the doorway, facing a department official. In her hands she carried containers with sprigs of omum and mint, and her face was turned to the side, as if she could not quite hear what was being said.

'Here is the money for the rent.' I began pulling the roti money from my pocket and held it out to him.

The man glanced in my direction for only a second, and then his gaze returned to my mother. 'Your husband had prior notice about the demolition. You need to go to Tahsildar's office to get resettlement tokens.'

'I was just going to plant these.' Amma looked down at the pots in her hands. 'It's that time of year.'

'You have one hour, tops,' the man said, and he raised his eyes upwards as he walked away.

'There must be enough.' I slid past her into the house and set down the money on the table. 'Look here, amma.'

'It's the government; they want us off the lake,' she said.

'They will flatten the houses? Just like that?'

'We'll pack a few things.' She put the plants down carefully in the windowsill. 'Just in case.'

We hurried about packing what we could into two orange crates. 'My jewellery box!' amma called. 'The blue pottery from Rajasthan.' As we worked, she grew more frantic, piling things one on top of the other and dragging pieces of furniture out into the lane. Everyone around us was doing the same, and soon the lane looked as though it was set for a grand party, the tables laden with plates and pots and pans. My mother sat outside with Mrs. Gupta.

'They will have to kill me before I leave this place,' Mrs Gupta said.

Back at the bridge, the police had moved in and were using their lathis to drive the crowd back. 'Protestors will be arrested,' they announced over speakers.

When some of the men refused to move, they were dragged by their feet across the dust and piled into waiting vans. Two rows of housing had already been flattened into the earth, and I could taste the dust in the air.

Right then, with the roar of desperate voices and grind of engines, I wanted to be curled up inside the pump again, but then Lata Singh, president of the Women Workers' Union appeared just on the curve of the hill. She was accompanied by a photographer and had handcuffed herself to a fence. 'This is a breach of human rights,' she shouted up over the crowd. 'This dislocation will destroy their livelihood, especially for the children!' Lata would be able to help, I thought, pushing my way towards her, through the barricade of people trying to block the lane, but when I reached the place where she had been, there was no sign of her, only the handcuffs left dangling from the fence.

We were on our own. Men and women rushed about carrying belongings over their heads, and when I spotted Mr. Mody in the distance, he was bent over the limp body of a man, his white kurta stained with blood. Mr. Mody had lived on the lake for over twenty years, and he had told me once that there was nowhere safer than the lake. 'In all my time, no one has ever come to any great harm,' he had said.

By the time I made it back to the house, through the growing mound of rubble, Belli and Safa were there, and the police had beaten a path for the bulldozers right up through the lane. Everything in their wake had been crushed to dust, families left staring blankly into empty space.

Our house was next in line.

My mother was still sitting in the doorway, the framed picture of Ganesh in her lap.

'Move aside,' the official called over the rumble of the lorries. 'Or we will have you removed.'

'You've no right,' my mother spat at him. 'This is our home.' And she pressed the tips of her fingers against her eyes.

'It's not our problem; you need to speak to the Public Works Department,' he said, and then he turned to the police officers behind him and nodded. They moved forwards as Safa and Belli rushed towards our mother and pulled her up from her chair, the picture of Ganesh falling away from her hands.

Mrs. Thevar held my mother in her arms as we watched a bulldozer knock through our door with one clean sweep. The rest of the house gave in easily, falling in on top of itself. Belongings and debris were scattered through the air, covering us in a thick layer of dust. Beside me Safa and Belli were both shaking, and Belli's thick, glossy hair was stuck to the tears on her face.

When it was all finished, the bulldozers rested momentarily behind a mound of rubble, and everything was very still. We walked together towards the ruins, and when we reached it, amma leaned down and lifted up the container of omum, which was lying unharmed amongst the debris.

'I forgot to plant it,' she said in a voice that was barely there.

The bulldozers continued to work their way neatly through over one thousand houses, until there was nothing left on the lake but wreckage. We sat on the hill and watched people wandering about through the haze of dust, like wounded soldiers, and then when the bulldozers had gone, a piercing silence settled over everything.

∎ ∎ ∎

By the time dadi returned from the tank factory and found his way to us, we were pitched up under a flimsy tent of blankets and rice sacks, waiting for the kettle to boil on the little gas stove. He stood beside his bicycle looking at us and then down towards the lake, one hand pressed flat against his head. When amma saw him, she reached in under the pile of belongings, pulled out a pitcher, and hurled it at his head.

He fell to his knees, clutching at his ear, and began to moan.

'You knew, you knew,' she wailed, but dadi continued to lie there, staring into the rubble.

'They did not tell us,' I heard him whisper. 'There was no letter.'

∎ ∎ ∎

The following day the men of Ambattur Lake gathered on the bridge to survey the damage.

Maheesh and I sat close by as they went through the list of injured and arrested, shaking their heads and spitting on the ground in turn. 'Mr. Chari is dead,' Mr. Mody said. 'His wife is expecting their first child next month.'

Some of the families had already relocated to the farmers market and to the streets around Ambattur, but most of them had moved back among the rubble and debris of their demolished homes.

'We will rebuild the houses,' Mr. Mody said finally. 'We'll show the government that they can't treat us this way.' A cheer rose up from the little crowd that had gathered.

The men organised themselves into groups, some foraging through the rubble for pieces of timber, others laying out bricks to dry in the sun, and the department officials, who drove up and down the road in their cars each day, did not try to intervene.

'Our efforts have scared them off,' my father said. 'They know we are made of stronger stuff.'

But the officials were simply biding their time, for out on the Bay of Bengal, winds were spawning a storm that would drive us out like rats.

Before the thunderstorms began to crack overhead, we could taste it in the sticky June air. Sandbags were passed out among the houses and drains cleared of debris, but when the rain came, it flooded down from the Red Hills, surging through the reopened dam. It waterlogged the drains and ravaged the earth under our feet, turning our homes into a stinking, muddy bath.

For three days the monsoon swept across Ambattur, washing away everything we owned, severing road links, and flattening crops. We had no choice but to go.

We waded through knee-high water to reach the bridge, me hoisted on dadi's shoulders, Belli in our mother's arms. In the week since our house had been demolished, Belli had developed a fever, and her arms were covered in insect bites. We could not afford the doctor's fees, not now that our only valuable possessions had been washed away in the floods.

We watched from the roadside while my father and other men floated to and fro on rubber tubes and improvised boats, trying to save what they could, and every so often, Belli whimpered like a dog by my side.

'This will cheer you up.' I began to sing Dhoom Dhoom Luck Luck. *'Dhoom again, and run away with me on a roller-coaster ride; Dhoom again, and see your wildest dreams slowly come alive. Dhoom again, we gotta break the rules and party all the time.'*

Belli cried all the louder, and amma pulled me down onto the ground. 'You would sing about celebrations? When we are in the middle of all this?' she swept her hand across the breadth of the lake. 'What kind of child are you?'

■ ■ ■

While the government worked to rebuild dams and pump out flood waters, we settled into a new home at the side of the Chennai Central railway line. Musty platforms became crammed with hundreds of families and lopsided houses that were made from sheets of plastic and corrugated metal. Rain gushed from the overhang on the platform, streaming in through every break in our cover, drumming against the bottom of pots and pans, and children combed through rubbish that ran the length of the station, crisscrossing through the overflowing sewers.

If grandmother was right, it was me who had brought us into this hopeless place.

Belli's health grew worse, forcing my parents to borrow some money so that they could pay for medicine, Safa was unable to go to school because their uniforms lay in tatters on the lake, and my mother and father stopped talking altogether. So when amma told me to go to Tahsildar's office and join the queue for resettlement tokens, I couldn't have been more relieved, even though it meant standing in the rain, with water funneling down the back of my neck.

'Where are they?' amma asked, when I returned empty-handed to the platform, my clothes dripping a line across the bare ground.

'They said come back tomorrow. The line never moved an inch.'

She *tut*ted and returned to combing Belli's waist-length hair.

So each day, instead of selling roti, I returned to the queue that never seemed to move, while amma took Safa and Belli to the library on Venkatapuram Road to catch up on their studies. Belli was due to take her CBSE exams, and without a certificate, she would be unable to follow Safa into senior class.

'No one will have them,' my mother complained to dadi. 'Every good boy wants to marry an educated girl these days.'

'I will sort it out,' dadi said. 'I'm working on a plan.'

'If it doesn't happen soon, we will all end up on the steps.' Amma motioned towards the front of the station.

The steps of the station had become choked with boneless-looking men, begging tins set out before them. Wandering towards them, I thought about Maheesh, expecting to see him there with his pot of chai in his hand. When he wasn't there, I walked up and down the platforms calling his name, suddenly desperate to find my only friend. The pump house had been destroyed, the cinema closed because of flooding. His family must have taken off to Chennai, because he wasn't anywhere to be found, and standing at the front of the station, I began to cry, big, thick tears streaking down my face as commuters moved around me, some jostling me out of their way.

More and more families began to leave, farming children out to relatives in other parts of the county. Then dadi had an idea.

'It's all arranged,' he said. 'Tomorrow you are going to stay at Aunt Gounder's house in Tiruvallur. She even sent the fare.'

Aunt Gounder was a widow and had no children of her own. Instead she had a seamstress business that employed two women, and each year for Diwali she sent us a package with three cotton lengha cholis. My mother would run her hand over the seams. 'Machine stitches,' she would *tut*. 'They won't last.'

Belli whooped and jumped in the air, and I joined in, too.

'It's for *their* exams,' my father said, looking at me. '*You* are needed here.'

In the middle of the night, I unpacked everything from their case, including the bag of chaats amma had prepared for them to eat. Hiding all of it underneath my blanket, I then curled myself inside the case. It was dark, like the inside of the pump, and for a few moments, my heart quickened. It crossed my mind to get out, but then the rise and fall of my chest settled, and even though the bottom of my spine began to pinch, the small space was comforting, and my mind stilled.

My father woke me when he hoisted the case up above his head, telling Safa and Belli that they had overpacked. By now my arms and legs were numb, and only my neck ached as he jolted me around in the air.

'Muthu?' Safa asked.

'Leave her be,' amma said. 'She would only make a fuss.'

The train was late, and Belli began to get restless. 'I'm hungry,' she complained. 'I want some chaat.' She popped the lid open on the case and let out a scream, falling back onto the ground.

Inside the case I sucked at the air, my lungs stinging with every breath.

'Stupid girl,' dadi spat, as I untangled my arms and legs and dragged myself out onto the platform.

'Now we will be late for Auntie,' Belli cried. 'It will be all your fault.'

My father made me run back with the case to collect their belongings.

By good fortune my mother was washing clothes at the edge of the track. She did not see me lugging the case back up to where my father was standing with his hands on his hips, the train now whistling by his side.

As they climbed on board, only Safa said goodbye.

3

Each day I continued to queue outside Tahsildar's office. Most of the men and women passed the time recounting their eviction; some had not been given enough time to save any possessions, others had been badly beaten, and most of them had now lost their jobs. 'When the house came down, my husband's heart broke in two and he died,' one woman said. 'How will I support my daughter and my grandchild? I've lost everything.'

Some of the children formed teams and played Kabaddi, tagging and wrestling one another to the ground. 'You're too small,' they said when I asked to join in. 'You would not make it.' So I continued to stand in the heat and the rain for hours, listening to their excited shouts as they scrambled for points in the dust.

Play stopped when the guard appeared and blew his whistle. 'The tokens are not ready,' he announced. 'Come back tomorrow.' Any complaints from the crowd were silenced with a swipe of his lathi, and the women cried helplessly into their hands as they shuffled away wondering how they would make ends meet.

We were the lucky ones, it seemed, because unlike most of the men at the station who had lost their jobs, my father continued to travel to Avadi each day, hitching a ride on the roof of the train. But as the days turned into weeks, he came back later each day, always with a downturned face.

'No pay?' amma asked.

'It's because of the delay on the tanks,' he said. 'We have to finish the contract, and then I'll be paid handsomely.'

My mother couldn't afford to wait around any longer, so with what little money we had, she went to Farm Bazaar each morning and then stood at the front of the station with baskets full of fruits, vegetables, and sweets. She earned enough to keep us fed.

'I could get a job as a tiffin carrier, Amma, or washing pots; there are always pots to be washed somewhere.'

'Your place is in that queue,' she reminded me. 'If we miss those tokens, my life will be over.'

It continued that way for three more weeks, and when talk of the eviction had worn itself out, some of the women turned to knitting blankets and scarves, and a handful of devout Brahmins chose to recite prayers in the hope that it would advance the distribution of tokens, but most of those in the queue were crippled with boredom, and before long several of the men decided that they couldn't wait anymore and abandoned the queue in search of work. 'This government won't feed us, so surely they won't put a roof over our heads; this whole thing is a gimmick,' they said. If it was true, then we were all ruined, and with the same thought, men and women all around me grew lightheaded and fearful.

Right then I would have given anything to be on the bridge, singing with Maheesh and serving up amma's warm rotis, and each day I prayed to Brahma that it would come true and that everything could be just as it was before.

Somewhere, the god of creation was listening.

'It's her—the Elastic Girl,' the man behind me said one day. It was Mrs. Patel's husband. He told the man beside him about my escape from the pool. 'It was the size of your fist,' he said of the vent. 'She must have curled up like a ball.'

'Show us,' the other man said. 'Show us how you did it.'

Sitting down on the hard ground, I wrapped myself up like a hedgehog so that my legs were curled right around my head. After a few moments, my elbows began to ache and the blood pumped in my ears, but everything around me went quiet until Mr. Patel and the other man began to clap, and then others were peering over their shoulders, jostling to have a look.

'She has legs like ropes,' someone said. 'Such talent!'

As I unfolded myself, a shiver of happiness ran through my body, and then the crowd coaxed me into doing it again. Up and down the length of the queue I went, bent right back like a crab. The crowd closed in, people blinking into the light and scratching at their heads, as if they had only just woken up, and then when I was finished, they began to clap, like rain beating down on a tin roof.

The queue outside Tahsildar's office became my audience, and after that first performance, people began to call me Elastic Girl again. 'Ah, she is here,' they said when I arrived in the morning, and then they waited patiently for me to begin, watching as I sang, danced, and tied myself in knots.

'Sing something by Karthik,' one lady asked.

'What about Alka Yagnik? Her songs are much better,' another said, and everyone forgot about their misfortune for a while.

Even the guard who patrolled the line did not tell me to stop. 'Can you sing anything from *Hum dil Chuke Sanam*?' he asked, adding his own request.

Maheesh had taken me to see the film, and we both knew *Tadap tadap ke* by heart. '*This lifeless heart, this lifeless heart, your love has brought it alive*,' I sang, the guard swaying his hips from side to side like Salman Khan. Seeing how he had lightened up, others joined in, singing and dancing, but it was one voice that caught my attention—the high-pitched tone of Maheesh. He danced up, waving his arm in the air and looping in and out amongst the crowd, who whooped with joy at his dazzling moves. He carried a plastic bag in one hand, his clothes were filthy, and his thick hair had been cut away so that his head looked like the prickled end of a wire brush, but his smile was still there, stretched across his face.

'*I have been completely looted in your love*,' we sang together, and when the song had ended, the crowd wanted more, but Maheesh waved them away, and the guard quickly began tapping people into place again with his lathi.

'I thought you were dead, that you had been drowned in the lake.'

'Can't I swim like a rat?' he said.

Maheesh told me that his family had been living on the street, in a shelter at the side of Ponnu market. 'It's not so bad,' he said. 'Plenty of vegetables that nobody wants.'

'You can get vouchers for a house in Morai,' I told him. 'We could be neighbours.'

'They say there are no houses, that it's all a government trick to get votes.'

'They have to put us somewhere,' I snapped. 'And if I miss the tokens, my mother will whip me all the way to Cuddalore.'

'They have put you here.' He laughed, motioning at the queue that stretched out behind us.

'Then why did you come?'

'Because I've discovered that queuing is thirsty business.' He lifted out a teapot from the bag he was carrying. 'There is money to be made at times like this, and *your* pockets must be lined with gold.'

'I don't sell roti anymore.'

'Not *roti* money, money for performing,' he said. 'They must pay to see such a star?'

'How can I charge to perform to people who have nothing?'

'People will pay their last rupee for happiness.' He wandered off and began to light a little stove for boiling his tea.

The idea had been planted, and the following day, Maheesh returned, and together we began performing hits from all the films we had seen, and I learned how to squeeze myself inside a small concrete pipe that we found discarded at the back of the office. At first people grumbled that they should not have to pay to see such things. 'This is not Kalakshetra,' one woman sniffed. 'If we want to pay for dancing, we will go there.'

But when the boredom began to press down on them again, they came to us with requests. 'Five rupee for the pipe and two dances,' Maheesh offered, and eventually they began to give in. Maheesh was right; there was a price for happiness, it seemed.

With the money, we returned to the cinema. The monsoon had prompted the owners to mend the roof so that we could no longer sneak inside, but with our earnings, we were now able to enter through the foyer as paying customers, and while the rain pelted the streets outside and the vigil continued at Tahsildar's office, Maheesh and I sat in the front row of the auditorium eating pani puri.

All was well again in Ambattur, and for three weeks it continued, Maheesh and I performing each day and returning to the cinema three times to watch *Raincoat*, starring my heroine, Aishwarya Rai. It was possible to see it, me sitting opposite Ajay Devgan, my chin resting in the crook of my hand as he talked to me, and then us going to the Crystal Globe awards to accept the 'best actress' trophy.

Maheesh nudged me. 'You are in the land of dreams,' he said.

I noticed that the credits on the screen had stopped rolling. 'We need to get back to the queue.' But I continued to sit there, staring up at the screen because something inside of me knew that when I returned to the queue that day, it would all be over.

Later that afternoon, when we returned to Tahsildar's office, amma paid me a visit.

'Good things always come to an end,' Maheesh said when he saw her coming towards us from the direction of Kamalam stadium.

Her face appeared through the opening in the pipe, like a monsoon storm. And before I could pull myself out onto the ground, she had grabbed Maheesh by the ear and was twisting it like a wet rag.

'We told you to keep away!' she shouted at him. 'Do these ears not work?'

Maheesh wrenched his way out of her grasp, and peeping over the edge of the pipe, I could see him scamper away like a frightened dog, his teapot and tin pan clattering as he dragged them along behind him in his plastic bag. 'If you ever come near her again, you'll be sorry!' my mother called out after him.

If I had known then that it was the last I would ever see of Maheesh, I would have called out, run after him, begged him not to go, but by the time I had finally clambered my way out from the pipe, he was gone.

'After all I have gone through.' Amma was standing over me with her hands on her hips. 'After all that has been done for you.'

'You've done nothing!' I shouted, thinking of Safa and Belli, who were still comfortably settled in Aunt Gounder's home. 'You've never done anything for *me*.'

Her eyes closed, and her face moved to the side as if she had just been slapped, and the thought struck me that she might cry, like when our house was knocked down. But she simply walked away, me following along reluctantly behind her.

When we arrived back at the platform, Mrs. Patel was waiting for us outside the tent. 'Your head is like an empty well.' She tapped me on the back of the skull. 'Did you ask her about the money?'

My mother did not answer but took me behind the covering of our home and shook me so much that I thought she would never stop. Then she made me kneel on the hard ground and recite aarti, the prayer of surrender, again and again, while she sat in the corner and wrapped herself in a maroon-and-green Jamawar shawl. It had been a wedding gift from her parents, and after she had married my father, she had never seen them again. 'That's just the way it was,' she had told me once. 'When a woman marries, your ties with your parents are over.'

I thought about marrying Maheesh and never seeing them again. 'I'm sorry, Amma. Sorry for everything.'

Amma started to cry, pulling the shawl closer around her so that I could barely see her face at all.

By the time my father returned home, she was busy washing pots out over the edge of the track, and I was still kneeling on the floor.

'What are you doing down there?' he asked me, the stale smell of alcohol on his breath.

'I'm being punished.'

'Ah, I see.' He turned away from me and looked out to where amma was, before deflating down onto his chair. There were wet patches under the arms of his shirt, and he placed his hands on his knees, as if he was waiting for something. Soon his eyes closed and his head nodded forward.

'Exhausted from a hard day in the factory?' My mother shook him from his sleep.

My father looked up at her and smiled, like she had just asked him if he would like some tea.

'Ah good, drinking too,' she said coldly. 'That must mean you've finally been paid.'

'Next week,' my father said. 'The contract is coming next week.'

'You take me for a fool.' Amma set down the pots she had been carrying in her arms and waved a ladle in front of his face. 'You think I don't know the truth of it.'

My father pulled himself up in his chair and held his hands out before her. 'It is the truth. The contract is going well.'

'I'm cursed.' She banged the ladle down on the floor. 'Mrs. Gupta saw you in Avadi, and she saw what you were doing as well.'

My father's mouth sprang open, but nothing came out.

'A shoeshine man and an elastic girl, that is what I have.'

My father and I looked at each other, and he shook his head. 'Nonsense,' he said, but it was now too late. My mother reached for the Bombay Fashions bag, which was resting at the foot of my father's chair. 'Not like this.' He tried to stop her, pulling at her hands. 'I can explain.'

My legs and feet tingled as I rose from the floor, prayers of arti now forgotten as amma reached into the bag for a wooden box. She set it down on the folding table and like a magician, reached in and pulled out two cans of Nylace shoe polish, two horsehair brushes, a polishing cloth, and two sponge applicators. She laid them all out carefully on the floor.

'What about the tanks?' I asked him.

He would not look up from the floor, continuing to stare at the shoeshine kit, as if he had never seen it before.

'There are *no* tanks,' my mother shouted. 'Don't you understand? Your father shines shoes for a living; that is what he does.'

'They had to let us go,' he said, still not raising his head. 'The contract fell through.'

'This family is poisoned with lies,' amma said. She turned her back on us and walked back out to the edge of the line.

'I'll find the answer,' my father called after her, but she did not move, continuing to stand there looking down at the tracks with the stillness of a Bengal fox.

Each day my father continued to shine shoes in Avadi, and each evening he told amma that he almost had the answer to our problems, and then one day he did. It was on his way home from Avadi that he found it—on a billboard for The Great Raman Circus of Chennai.

4

When our housing began to fall apart with the rain, Mrs. Patel and my mother took it upon themselves to organise a demonstration, inviting some of the other women at the station to join them under the sagging roof of our house. Hiding inside the small wooden sideboard my father had rescued from the floods, I watched as five of them pressed in together, cross-legged on the floor, rolls of flesh spilling out from underneath their cholis. Mrs. Patel sat on my father's chair, her legs tucked up underneath her, and my mother busied herself with passing out cups of sweet tea. 'I didn't have time to prepare breakfast,' she said. 'Next time you come, I'll make gobhi paratha.' A couple of the women shook their heads, and my mother turned towards the dwindling jars of lentils and flour propped up beside our gas stove. 'Maybe I could make a few roti?' She bit down then on the edge of her lip.

'There's no time for eating in such a crisis,' Mrs. Patel waved her hand in the air. 'It's been one whole month since we came here, and the men have done nothing.'

'Yes, we must organise a march.' My mother rested the teapot on the ground and breathed out noisily through her nose.

'You are too full of modern ideas,' Mrs. Gupta complained.

'India is changing,' Mrs. Patel told them. 'Manorama has shown us with her protests in Karnataka that women have choices.'

'My husband calls her a firecracker,' Mrs. Nadar said.

'That woman does not practise pati-paramesvara,' Mrs. Gupta complained. 'We would be disrespecting our husbands to follow her example.'

'No water, no electric, no toilet,' Mrs. Patel continued, counting each item out on her fingers. 'How can we let our families suffer like this? It's our *duty* as mothers and wives to act.'

Mrs. Nadar and my mother clapped their hands together. 'We will give that firecracker a run for her money,' Mrs. Nadar said.

They all agreed on a protest to Konnur East, where the district official was scheduled to open the new post office. 'That will show them,' my mother said. Never had I seen her face so full of life.

They did not waste any time, because the following day instead of sending me to queue for tokens, amma pulled me along to Mani's Café in the station, where she convinced one of the ladies to provide her with cardboard boxes. When we returned to the house, she showed me how to turn the cardboard into placards with strips of wood.

'We'll need plenty of banners for a march.' She bound the placards with string and tested their strength by raising each one up over her head and waving it up and down. When she was satisfied that they were sturdy enough, she took the placards with her, bunched up under her arm, and made her way back to the station, me tagging along behind.

On the steps she stopped one of the railway guards and tapped him on the shoulder. 'What is it?' he asked, hooking up the arm of his jacket and looking at his watch.

'You're from the lake,' my mother said to him. 'You are the son of Mrs. Verma.'

'They moved.' He went to walk on.

Amma caught him by his sleeve. 'These are for our demonstration against the government.' She held out the placards up for him to see. 'We want you to write some slogans for us.'

'*We* don't support such demonstrations.' He looked around him, tipping his cap down over his eyes.

'Then I will tell your boss that your father was a rickshaw-puller and that your sister had an affair with a Muslim from Hasan,' amma said.

From behind her I had to cover my mouth to stop the laughter.

The guard turned around and raised a hand in the air. 'Auntie, there is no need to be so cross.'

'Write '*Are we animals or humans?*'' my mother told him, 'and '*Boycott the Lok Sabha elections.*''

The guard took the placards, telling her to return that afternoon and they would be done, and my mother walked back to the house, her lips pinched in a tight little smile.

Ordered to return to the queue, I was restless all afternoon, wondering what else amma was stirring up. 'There's going to be a march,' I told those around me. 'It's going to put a stop to all this waiting.'

'It's time something was done,' one man said. 'If we stand here much longer we will disappear into the dust.'

'My mother is leading a demonstration.'

'When is it happening?' They asked.

'At the opening of the new post office at Konnur East; the district official will be there.'

When I returned home that evening, amma had received the placards back from the guard, the cardboard now covered in thick black lettering.

'When do we go?' I asked her. 'Is it tomorrow?'

'*You* will stay here,' amma said. 'There can't be any trouble.'

'Amma, I promise to be good,' I pleaded, but she would not listen and set about tearing an old blue dupatta into strips.

'What's this?' my father asked, stooping his way into the room and picking up one of the placards.

'The women are taking action,' she said. 'We are going to get this mess sorted.'

My father rested the placard back down on the floor. 'They don't listen,' he said.

'Maybe *we* don't shout loudly enough.'

'Tell her to let me go, Dadi,' I said. 'Someone can hold my place in the queue.'

'No. Once they get word of our march, the doors could be opened straightaway,' she said. 'You must not leave the queue.'

■ ■ ■

In the morning the women set off down the platform, the strips of blue dupatta tied tightly around their upper arms. Mrs. Patel and my mother marched up front, a dozen other women behind them as they made their way out from the station and towards Konnur East. From the front steps, people watched as they waved their placards in the air and sang 'Vande Mataram,' children chasing alongside the procession as they passed.

'They're disgracing themselves with such behaviour,' someone beside me said. 'Anyone who follows them is a fool.' But I didn't listen, for despite amma's warning, I was all set to follow them like a langur monkey.

But just then my father pulled in alongside the station steps on his bicycle. 'Hop on,' he said. He propped me up on the bar of his bicycle and we wove our way through the traffic, zipping in and out of gaps like a toothpick, my heart pounding with excitement. Then he turned away in the opposite direction to Konnur East and the post office.

'Aren't you following the march, Dadi?'

'We're going to the cinema hall; there's something that I want you to see.'

'*Jodhaa-Akbar*?' I asked, leaning back into him as he swerved his way around a bullock cart.

'That film is a crime against history,' my father snapped. 'Bollywood has no respect for such things as the Mogul Empire.'

Every day my father listened to the film reviews on Aahaa FM. Amma said it was like reading *Bhagavad Gita* to a buffalo. 'You listen to things you have no knowledge about,' she told him. My father had never been to the cinema in his life, and now, when it seemed most unlikely, this was where he was taking me.

A crowd had gathered outside Rakki cinema. Children clambered up onto shoulders; women rose unsteadily on their toes, and a wave of cheers and applause rolled over them. My father chained his bicycle up on the opposite side of the street, and we pressed our way to the front, until we were standing at the edge of a white sheet. In the centre of the sheet, cycling around on a bicycle was a chimpanzee.

We were not going to see Jodhaa-Akbar.

'Let's give Raja a cheer,' called a man, and he stepped forwards and delivered Raja a nut. Raja thrust his lips out, and the nut promptly disappeared. He then climbed down from the bicycle and took a bow, his bald head touching the ground.

The man held his hands in the air to hush the crowd, who were cheering and whistling with excitement. 'I am Mr. Prem,' he called out. He had big fat eyebrows and a horseshoe mustache. 'I am from The Great Raman Circus of Chennai; we are looking for a star.'

My heart leapt inside my chest, and I looked up at my father, who was staring straight ahead, one hand raised to his chin.

'They want a star.'

'That's why I brought *you* here,' he said, without looking down.

One by one, parents pushed their children forwards onto the sheet. 'Dance,' they called from the sidelines. 'Recite 'The Gift,' by Tagore.' Some of the children simply burst into tears, and the audience booed and hissed until Mr. Prem waved them away and called the next child forward. One girl stood on her head and rolled a ball on her feet; two boys performed with a scruffy dog, making it jump through a hoop.

The good ones were given a lime drop by Mr. Prem and directed to sit on the steps.

'Next,' Mr. Prem called, and my father stepped forward, pulling me with him onto the sheet.

'But, they're all looking.' I could feel the weight of a hundred eyes on me.

'Pretend you are on the bridge,' he said, backing away.

'Shall I sing *'Haan Main Tumhara Ho'* or maybe *'Mehbooba Dilrub'*?' I whispered over to him, and several people around me laughed.

'No singing.' My father came forwards again with the Bombay Fashions bag he had been carrying and removed a wooden container, not much bigger than his shoeshine box. 'Show him what you can do.' He removed the lid. 'Show him how you can curl up into a ball.'

I looked down inside the empty box. 'It's too small.' The space was smaller than Safa and Belli's suitcase and smaller than the pipe under the swimming pool. A trickle of sweat worked its way down my back as dadi disappeared.

'We have to hurry along.' Mr. Prem clapped his hands together twice.

Someone in the crowd coughed, music played in the distance, and my heart raced. If I had walked away then, everything would have been different, but it was my chance to be a star.

I lowered myself into the empty wooden case and onto my knees. I twisted my feet in behind my back, folded my body over, and tucked my head in tight. Someone closed the lid and I was in complete darkness. 'Ek, do teen, char,' I counted, and then the lid came off again and the crowd burst into applause.

'A contortionist!' Mr. Prem said, as I pulled myself back out.

'She's called Elastic Girl,' my father announced, coming forwards to help me from the box.

Mr. Prem reached into his pocket, handed me a lime drop, and directed us towards the cinema steps. The only available space was beside Raja. His long arms hung loose by his sides as he drew circles with his knuckles on the ground, and as we watched the remainder of the acts, the lime drop rolled about on my tongue, filling my mouth with a delicious syrupy juice.

When everyone had finished and the unpicked children had sulked their way back out into the streets, Mr. Prem descended from the steps and paced before us, hands clasped tight behind his back. 'The Great Raman Circus is the most famous circus in India,' he said. 'Our show is full of fire, passion, thrills, and excitement. We need only the best performers for our daredevil acts.'

'Like the Wheel of Death?' one of the girls asked, and all the mothers drew a breath.

'In all my time in the circus, I have never witnessed a death,' Mr. Prem said. 'There is more danger of dying right here on the streets of Ambattur.'

The mothers nodded. One recalled the story about the boy who got stuck in the mud during monsoon last year and drowned. Another told about the accident under the elevated highway. 'The poor man was simply passing by on his motorbike when iron rods came crashing down on him. It was an accident waiting to happen.'

They were all agreed: in comparison to Ambattur, the circus was a very safe place indeed.

'Stand,' Mr. Prem ordered, pointing at me, and my father nudged me forward. 'There is a contortionist in the Russian circus called Albana; she can shoot a bow and arrow with her feet,' he said. 'It's a very neat trick indeed.'

'Muthu is full of promise,' my father said. 'I'm sure she can be just as good.'

'I'm sure.' Mr. Prem circled around me. 'But girls are becoming expensive. They want good soap and coconut hair oil.'

'She's fair,' my father said, pulling up the sleeve of my choli so that Mr. Prem could see.

The last sliver of lime drop cracked under my tongue. 'Can you really make us into stars? Like Aishwarya Rai?' I asked.

Mr. Prem laughed. 'That's my very business. I've made them all: the great magician Upendra Thakur and Hopi the clown—he has his own TV show, you know.'

'There's a boy I know who's a very good dancer.'

'Anyone can dance, even a hippo,' he said.

Above us, the clouds closed in, and the sky opened up on us, lashing against the steps, pinning the white sheet to the ground. We drew in under the canopy of the cinema, watching as the streets turned into a lagoon.

'I'll call you one by one.' Mr. Prem dashed off through the rain with Raja clinging to his back. They disappeared into the circus van, where Mr. Prem then opened up a hatch on the side and popped his head out.

'The juggler,' he shouted.

A girl with the clubs ran through the puddles with her mother, both of them stepping up into the van.

One by one he called them, and then it was our turn. When we stepped inside the van, we were soaking wet. Raja was reclining like a Buddha across the front seat, head resting in the palm of his hand and Mr. Prem sat behind a table, a stack of cards before him and a picture of the Shimla Mountains hanging on the wall.

'Sit, sit.' He motioned to two plastic chairs. 'If she performs well, we will pay two hundred rupees per month,' Mr. Prem said. 'I will send you the money.'

My father leant forwards on the edge of his seat. 'Do you beat them?' he asked in a lowered voice.

'We raise them like our own children,' Mr. Prem said. 'I have so much love for each and every one.'

'And we can see her if we want?'

'Whenever you want; the circus is a place for family, after all.'

'I've every trust in you.' My father settled himself back in the chair.

'And what about you, Elastic Girl?' Mr. Prem turned to me. 'Are you happy to join us?'

'Yes, sir, I've always wanted to be a star.'

Mr. Prem slapped his hand off the table. 'That's the spirit,' he said. 'You will fit right in.' He flicked a card from the top of his pile and handed it to my father. 'Bring her on Tuesday, and we can begin.'

My father shook Mr. Prem's hand, and then we were off on the bicycle again, the rain now reduced to a fine mist.

'If I don't want to stay, can I come back home, Dadi?'

'Of course, beti, you can come back whenever you want.'

As we arrived back at the station, my body felt light with excitement. I was going to escape from the damp, cramped space at the railway station and from the boredom of waiting in the queue outside Tahsildar's office; I was going to be the Elastic Girl.

5

My father had to wait for my mother's mood to settle. She had returned from Konnur East like a wasp, telling us that the district official hadn't turned up. 'He sent a driver with his apologies and a box of coconut burfi for the post office workers,' she told us. 'He said it was because of the rain.'

'You'll get another chance,' my father told her.

'He must have found out what we were planning; that dog of a guard must have snitched on us.'

I turned away from her, thinking of all the people I had told about the march, about how I had brought amma misfortune once again.

Despite itself, their effort paid off, for two days later, Mrs. Patel came screeching down the platform, waving a newspaper above her head. 'We did it,' she shouted, slapping the paper down in front of my mother.

'Ambattur Lake evictees living on the streets,' my father read. *'It is unfortunate that a government scheme meant to improve the lives of the urban poor is being used to impoverish them.'*

'That will do it,' Mrs. Patel said. 'We have put the government's nose well and truly out of joint.'

The women embraced each other. 'Victory, victory,' they shouted up and down the platform.

'It's only a matter of time before we are all moved on,' amma said. She wasted no time in beginning to pack, placing our stainless-steel tumblers, idli plates, and brass pots into a cardboard box.

'Does it mean that I can't go?' I whispered to my father, worried that my chances with The Great Raman Circus had just disappeared into thin air.

'Nothing has changed,' he said, waving a hand at me. 'I'll tell her after dinner.'

■ ■ ■

That evening amma cooked up a thick vegetable kootu and crisp appalams. She stirred the subji with a hum on her lips.

'The circus is a dying art form.' My father's voice was stiff. 'They say its decline is a consequence of modern India.'

'This matka has a crack in it.' Amma nodded towards the earthen pot resting at the top of the box. 'We'll need to buy a new one when we reach Morai.'

'It's a good life,' my father continued. 'It would teach her discipline and strength of mind.'

Amma continued to stir, as if she had not heard a word he had said.

From behind my father's chair, I nudged him, urging him to continue. He coughed loudly and stood up. 'Muthu could earn two hundred rupees a month; that's what the troupe master said.'

'What is it you are talking about?' Amma raised the spoon to her mouth and tasted the kootu.

'The circus: The Great Raman Circus of Chennai has offered Muthu a job.'

My mother lowered the spoon back into the pot. 'The circus? You want to send our daughter to the circus?'

'It's the answer; it will keep things afloat until I get a job, and you said it yourself; she can't sell roti all her life.'

'Mr. Prem said that I could be a star,' I said. 'Sunita Sen owns three houses; think about that, Amma.'

Amma snorted. 'You have filled her head with nonsense, you fool.' A lump of thick yellow kootu dripped from the spoon she was holding out before him and onto the floor.

'She would be like part of the family,' my father continued, his voice now wavering.

Amma poked a finger firmly against her chest. '*We* are her family,' she said.

'It's what Muthu wants.' When dadi looked at me, I nodded my head.

'No, it's what your mother wants,' amma said. 'It's what that woman has always wanted!'

'Shush now.' Dadi held his hands up in the air. 'This has come as a surprise; it will all make sense in the morning.'

'There is no sense to such an idea, and I can tell you now that she will not go.'

My father sat back into his chair, and amma returned to the subji, swiping a diced green chili into the pan. We ate in silence, and after dinner she told my father to travel to Avadi the following day and ask every employer if they were hiring. 'Don't come back without a job,' she told him. 'I won't have you.'

In the morning she instructed me to go to Tahsildar's office. 'They will be opening up the doors soon, and we can't afford to miss out on the tokens,' she said, as we walked together to the front of the station. Amma was carrying a basket of bruised mango and guava fruit over her head, and when we reached the steps, she lowered the basket to the ground and reached out to grasp my arm. 'Forget these notions of the circus,' she said. 'And if I hear of you performing like a clown, I will take you straight to Aashiana.'

Then she climbed up the steps and offered fruits to passengers as they hurried past her. 'If I can't be a star, then take me to Aashiana now!' I called out after her, but she couldn't hear me under the scrape and hiss of a train as it hauled its way into the station.

Aashiana was the psychiatric hospital in Anna Nagar where my grandfather ended up before I was born. He had been a constable in Ambattur, tipped to become a senior police officer earning ten thousand rupees per month, but then one day he killed a man. Standing at the station, I remembered my grandfather's uniform; for years it had lain folded up inside a wooden trunk that sat at the end of my parents' bed. It had two chevron points and gold stripes on the shoulder, and the smell of aniseed and tobacco was still fresh in my memory even though grandmother had taken the uniform with her when she went to live with our uncle in Pondicherry. It was me who had driven her out.

'I can't look at her anymore,' she had said, as I had stood knee high in the doorway. 'She has brought us all this shame.'

I'd always known that grandmother hated me, but I didn't know why, and every time I tried to figure it out, my head began to pound. By the time I reached the queue and people asked me to perform, there was nothing but anger inside me. 'Go away!' I shouted at them. 'Can't you just leave me alone?'

'Useless girl, after all that we have paid you.'

'They will pay me better in the circus!' Sitting on the ground, I watched the veil of rain shifting over the hills, working its way in to calm the muggy July heat and the morning workers plodding their way along Thiruvalluvar Street and into the TI Cycles factory; none of them looked our way. We were nothing but grain weevils, scuttling along in the dust.

Not anymore. My mind floated off into a glittering big-top as I imagined myself standing inside a ring, and then the rain began to splatter the ground around me, and it was a moment before I noticed the shift in the queue. 'Get a move on!' one of the men behind me shouted. 'They have opened up the doors.'

In the rush, some people were pushed to the ground, and a pregnant woman fainted in the struggle. The guard appeared from the office and beat them back. 'If there's any further disturbance, we'll close it up again,' he shouted. 'No tickets will be issued.'

Everyone pulled in tight behind one another like a beaded necklace, and there were cheers from the front as, one by one, people began to emerge from the office to stand on the steps and hold their tokens in the air. By the time I'd reached the door, the rain was coming down in sheets, and the path we were standing in had turned into a gully. Dripping my way across the floor, the guard worked quickly with a mop to clear up behind me, and then there in the middle of the room was a desk with a squat little man seated behind it. A copperplated namebarrel rested before him, with *Mr. Vishwakararma, District Official* printed in thick black lettering. The guard mopped me forward, forcing me in front of the desk.

'Name?' Mr. Vishwakararma asked without looking up from his desk.

'Muthu Tikaram.'

'Tikaram.' He ran a finger down a list before him and hovered over a line. 'Mr. Devesh, Pavan Tikaram?'

'My father.'

He reached into a drawer under the desk and pulled out a voucher, handing it over to me. 'Plot 209, Morai.' He waved me away with a flick of his hand.

In the entrance I held the voucher up to the light. It was nothing more than a thin slip of blotting paper, with the plot number printed in the middle and an official stamp embossed in red at the bottom left-hand corner, but in that moment it was enough.

Tucking the paper into the folds of my skirt, I splashed and jumped my way through the streets of Ambattur, singing '209, Morai 209' as I went. Neighbours came from their houses to see what all the commotion was about, to see me waving the voucher in the air. 'It's a ticket for Morai,' someone said. 'Shiva, Shiva; we are saved.' And they began to dance up and down the line.

When I reached our watery home, amma was bent over on the floor. 'Didn't you hear me, Amma?' She failed to move, her eyes fixed on the photograph in her lap, a photograph from my parents' wedding day. In the picture her face was soft and round, her eyes like almonds, and she had a sharp, chiselled nose, clipped at the end with a maroon-and-white nose ring. The gold-threaded end of her sari was draped across the back of her head, releasing a few stray wisps of hair. There was no doubt that she was beautiful then, and nothing like the frail, greying face of my mother.

'I got it, Amma!' I put my hand on her shoulder. 'The voucher for Morai.'

She swivelled around on the floor, her eyes all red, and when she reached out to take it from my hand, I could see that the thick gold wedding band was missing from her finger. 'It had to be sold,' she said.

She took the piece of paper from my hand and examined it, turning it over in her hand. When she stood up, she reached out to press her hands against my shoulders and then planted a kiss on my head. 'Now everything will be OK.' Something lifted in her face, like the day when they had marched to Konnur East.

■ ■ ■

When my father returned that evening, she did not ask him about the job, and he did not ask her about the missing ring. Instead they began to re-pack the orange crates, my mother humming 'Haan Main Tumhara Hoon'; 'You're the One for Me.'

'We can grow vegetables,' my father said. 'Maybe get some chickens.'

'Okra and eggplant,' amma said. 'They grow well.'

They whispered in the dark, under the glow of the gasoline lamp, the sound folding itself around me.

That is the moment I wish I had frozen, right there.

6

When the vouchers for Morai ran out, there was uproar. The crowd left stranded outside the office smashed the windows on the district official's car as he drove away, and later that evening, a crowd of masked men set light to the office of the public water department. We could see the thick black smoke billow its way over the roof of the station.

'These goons are determined to make havoc,' my father said. 'They've already blocked some of the roads.'

'Didn't they know how many houses were needed?' amma asked. 'How could they run out so soon?'

'They say some crooks from Porur got their hands on the last of the vouchers; they'll sell them up for a handsome amount.'

Amma looked about her, then reached up to the tea caddy and removed the lid. 'Shanti, Shanti.' She clutched the tin to her chest.

The voucher was still where she had hidden it, but soon the unrest had moved into the streets around the station, and my parents decided that we would leave the following morning.

'Better to reach the safety of Morai and our new home as soon as possible,' my father said. 'Soon they will have stopped all the trains and buses out of this place.'

Shouts and protests rang up and down the line all night, broken now and then by the sound of firecrackers. In my dreams Maheesh and I were standing on the roof of the house, setting off crackers for Diwali. They soared up into the sky, whistling and exploding into fountains of red and blue. 'Don't stand so close,' I warned him, but he was laughing, and then the firecracker exploded in his hand, and he was covering his eyes and falling to the ground.

By morning my parents had finished all of the packing, and as I dressed, my father quickly began to tie up my bedding like a dosa roll.

'What about Maheesh, Dadi? We never got to say goodbye.'

'No time for goodbyes,' my father said.

'He was my only friend, and now who will I have?'

'There will be new friends in Morai, good people,' amma said. 'You have no need for that boy anymore.'

But, I was going to the circus. Amma couldn't have known what kind of people lived there.

'I could have left some of our things with Mrs. Patel or Nadar auntie,' she said. 'We can't carry it all.'

'Just leave them,' my father told her. 'No need to rub their noses in it.'

None of the ladies who marched that day with my mother had received a voucher, and as we left the platform, the clatter of our pots and pans echoed against the walls, ringing out our departure so that amma kept her eyes firmly on the ground. It was only when we had passed by the scorched remains of a cart at the front of the station that she began to cry, the crate she was carrying on her head shaking.

'They will be OK.' My father reached up to steady her load. 'Mrs. Patel will not take it lying down.'

At the depot my father clambered up onto the roof of the bus to secure our few pieces of furniture and boxes of belongings. Most of what we had owned in Ambattur had been swept away by the floods; some we had left behind at the station. It seemed that with every move, our lives shrank, so that now it could be bundled up and carried in our arms.

'The bus is filling up,' amma called to us, and she pulled me up onto the steps, craning her neck to see who was already there. 'All strangers,' she said. 'Not one from the lake.'

After we had secured the last seat on the bus, the driver continued to hand out tickets. All around us, passengers crammed into the aisles, depositing sleeping children like baggage on overhead racks, while others hung like monkeys off the grab handles. Behind us a dispute broke out over a seat.

'You have had too many ladoos,' a man complained. 'You're taking up the space of an entire family.'

'Your breath smells of onions,' the woman replied, pulling her sari down over her fleshy folds.

A cluster of men, including my father, were packed in tightly to the front compartment of the bus and had drawn the driver into a discussion over cricket. Their arms flapped wildly in the air as they argued about whether India could beat Australia in their own backyard.

The bus had not yet moved, and the women were passing out puris and parathas wrapped in paper. One of them leant across the aisle and offered one to my mother, who waved it away.

'Don't insult me.' The woman pressed the puri into my mother's lap.

As the bus made its way out of Ambattur, the acrid smell of breaking wind wafted down the bus, and everyone was in an excellent mood. Even my mother's shoulders began to fall a little as she pointed out to me the buffalos sitting in muddy ponds and workers bent over in the paddy fields, planting winter seedlings into the soft-clay earth.

Every so often the bus swerved slightly as the driver took his hands off the wheel and ran a comb through his slick of dark hair. 'Idiot!' amma tutted. 'Fancies himself, like Salman Khan.' And she nudged me gently in the side.

When we reached the outskirts of Morai, the men at the front began to bargain with the driver to take us up the narrow road. They dipped into pockets and bags, producing paan, a medicine bottle filled with hooch, and a half-used pot of Fantasia hair oil, which the driver turned over in his hand to examine and then slid neatly into his pocket.

Everyone gripped their seats as the bus rattled its way down a rutted track, and then the wheels began to spin helplessly in the dirt. 'It's no good!' the driver shouted over his shoulder. 'It's stuck.'

Several of the men at the front went out onto the road with the driver. We watched from the windows as they scratched at their heads and kicked at the wheels.

'Everyone off,' the driver shouted, returning to the front. 'There's too much weight.'

By the time we had made it out onto the muddy ground, some of the men were using spades they had found among the belongings on the roof to try to release the wheels. 'Try again!' they shouted in at the driver, and he started up the engine. The wheels continued whirling away at the mud, splattering the men who were pushing from behind. 'He's ruined his good shirt.' Amma nodded to where my father was bent over with his hands pressed against the back of the bus.

On the fourth attempt, the bus jolted forwards and onto harder ground. Everyone cheered, and the women congratulated their men on a job well done, some offering handkerchiefs for them to clean their mud-speckled faces. 'Better than a herd of bullocks,' one woman said, and we all laughed, making our way back towards the bus.

Standing in the doorway, the driver had his arms outstretched, blocking our entrance. 'I'm not going any farther,' he said. 'There's a gap up ahead big enough for me to turn around, and then I will take her back to the depot.'

'We've paid you,' the men complained. 'You have to take us.'

'The track is too narrow. I'll lose my job if I fail to get the bus back in one piece.'

'We saved your bus,' one man said, pulling at his dirty shirt. 'You owe us a lift.'

The driver refused to give in, closing the door with a hiss.

From the lane we watched as he removed all the items of luggage that had remained inside, pitching them out the windows to the crowd. 'Remove your luggage from the roof, or I'll take it with me,' he shouted out.

One by one men climbed up and began to untie the ropes, passing items to those down below.

'Sister fucker,' they shouted. 'Stupid donkey.' If they had been able to get their hands on the driver, they would have killed him there and then.

When the men had finished removing all the belongings, the bus shook back into life again and slowly reversed into the gap up ahead. We could hear the overgrown hedges scratching against the windows, and as it trundled past us again, the wheels sent another spray of mud out in every direction. I laughed out loud, until my mother's hand swiped the back of my head.

'We will come and find you!' one of the men shouted after the bus. 'We will tear you to pieces for such a crime!'

'That bastard dog kept my hair oil,' another man complained.

We waited until the bus had disappeared back out onto the road, and then everyone began pulling together all the grubby belongings that were strewn along the ground, women dabbing helplessly at their ruined saris.

'It's better that we left some of those things behind after all,' I said to my mother. She released a hopeless little laugh, pressing the end of a cloth against her pink-and-yellow skirt.

'Just think of what's lying ahead,' my father said, joining us. 'We need to hurry if we want to get there first.' He tucked a roll of bedding under my arm, secured a bag with clothes to my back, and handed me a cloth sack carrying our gasoline stove.

Amma hoisted a crate onto her head, and as we set forwards on our journey up the lane, we must have looked like a group of hardworking mules carrying bricks from the kilns, everyone bent over with the weight of their burdens, the clatter of kitchen pots the only sound. Every so often I had to stop to set the stove down on the ground, and each time, amma huffed at me to hurry up. 'The sooner we can get there, the sooner we can rest.'

'They have three rooms and an indoor toilet,' one woman beside us said.

'And underground drains,' her husband added.

Everyone began to make suggestions about what the houses would look like, some claiming that they were already furnished with beds, a sideboard, and set of chairs. The air around us bristled with excitement, and it was the hope of what lay ahead that spurred us on when we began to grow tired.

Amma stopped to wipe her forehead with the back of her hand. 'It's in the middle of nowhere,' she said. 'Why would they put us away out here?'

'See, it's just up ahead.' Dadi pointed at a huge sign that rose up into the air. 'SRR Housing Development,' he read. The sign had a picture of a fair-skinned family huddled together, and as we grew closer, we could see that the father was holding a key in his hand.

'A gated entrance!' someone exclaimed. 'They've thought of everything.'

Excited chatter rose in the air. 'To have a bed to lie on, that's all I want,' one woman said, and amma nodded her head in agreement.

As the distance closed in, we could see beyond the huge sign, to where knots of people were woven across the landscape, dogs and children darting in and out between tired-looking shelters. We gathered at the gate in silence, our eyes scanning across the brown fields stretching out into the distance.

Amma lowered her crate onto the ground and stepped forwards to rest a hand on the gate. 'Where are they?' she asked. 'The houses with three rooms and indoor toilets; where are they?'

'I will make some enquiries.' My father lifted the latch and proceeding through the gate. 'We must have missed a different entrance.'

Everyone followed him through and waited at the edge of the field. Among the group of men he approached was Mr. Mody, our old neighbour from Ambattur Lake. He embraced my father, and when he stood back, I could see that his face was shrunken like an empty balloon. They spoke for a moment, and then my father reached into the breast pocket of his shirt and held out our voucher to Mr. Mody, who shook his head. Behind me amma took a sharp breath.

Mr. Mody returned with my father. 'There are no houses,' he said. 'A scrap of land; that is all we get.'

Men and women began to produce their vouchers, just as my father had done, waving them in the air before Mr. Mody. 'They're useless,' he said. 'They have dumped us in this wasteland with no basic facilities, no safe drinking water. You're better to turn and go back to Ambattur.' And he waved his hand in the direction of the lane before walking away.

Women began to wail and lament into the ends of their saris, and amma collapsed onto her crate and began to sob, shrugging away my father when he reached out to touch her.

Running after Mr. Mody, I tugged at the end of his kurta. 'Where are the houses, Mr. Mody? Our ticket says plot 209.'

'The houses are yet to be built; it's best to forget about that now.'

'Maheesh said it was all a scam; he said that the government was just playing us for fools.'

'Maheesh is a wise boy; you should listen to him more often.' And Mr. Mody left me there.

With nothing else to do and the sky over us starting to grey, everyone set about finding their plots, but amma still refused to budge from the gates. 'Build me a pyre right now,' she moaned. 'I want to leave this body.'

'We will sort it out tomorrow,' my father told her

We left her there, tracking across the vast field until we found what we were after.

The ground had been marked out with wire—an irregular rectangle, no bigger than the huts at the station, and there was a little flag poking up out of the earth with number 209 written in green letters. 'Where will we sleep?' I asked him, my body beginning to shake.

'It's a dry night,' my father said. 'We'll set everything out, and then you can go and fetch your mother.'

She was still lying on the crate at the entrance of the grounds, with one of the women coaxing her to drink from a pitcher of water, but she would not look at me when I knelt down beside her and asked her to come.

'Tomorrow is Tuesday, and Mr. Prem is still expecting me at the circus; there is still time.'

'Is that what he told you to say?' She raised her head. 'That is his answer once again?'

'No, I *want* to go, and then I will make enough money to get us all out of here, to build a proper house.'

She put her hand out for me to help her up, and then together we carried the crate across the field to where my father was boiling tea. The minty smell of cardamom pods floated up into the air, and underneath a plastic shade he had laid out blankets and was busy turning the tuner on his radio.

'She can go,' amma said. She looked down at the line of wire marking the earth. 'Even the circus must be better than this.'

'I promise, Sunita, it will all work out for the best.'

I'd never heard him use my mother's name before, and his hand shook as he offered her a cup of tea, but amma turned away and buried herself underneath one of the blankets on the ground.

It broke my heart that she would not take the tea and that she couldn't gather herself up just like all the other women, but dadi said nothing, only pulled another blanket up around her legs. He knew what he was asking of my mother, of the sacrifice that she was prepared to make.

'Don't worry, Dadi; I'll help you.' We began to gather up sticks of firewood, piling them up by the stove.

As night prayers drifted out towards us, my father reached into the pocket of his trousers and withdrew a handkerchief. He motioned for me to sit before him and then placed it between us, unwrapping it to reveal the white face of a Zenith pocket watch.

'Gandhi had one just like this,' he whispered, lifting it up in the palm of his hand.

The watch had belonged to my grandfather, and when he turned it over in his hand, I could see the scratch of his initials: *S. T. T.* Then he handed it to me, the weight pressing down in my hand. 'I want you to have it,' he said, curling my fingers around it.

'Dadi, it's yours.'

He placed his finger firmly against his lips to hush me. 'It will keep you safe.'

There was something in his voice that sent a small shiver down my spine, and the thought crossed my mind then that I might never see him again.

Lying on the ground by the dwindling fire, unable to sleep and running my thumb over the back of the watch, I imagined a faint ticking. In my sleep I saw my grandfather's arm, with the watch at the end, reach out and slash Mr. Parthiban across the throat. Mr. Parthiban had been the landlord of the duplex bungalow in Kallikuppam where we used to live. He owned all the good houses in Ambattur, and we were never allowed to mention his name. 'Why did he do it?' I whispered out to my dadi in the darkness, but in return only the sound of his snoring came back to me.

By morning time the watch had left an imprint on my hand, and using a piece of string, I hung it around my neck, tucking it in under the collar of my kameez so that amma wouldn't see.

'I dreamt that we were all back on the lake.' She removed the blanket from over her head and looked around her. 'Belli and Safa, too.' She rested her head back down on the ground for a moment. 'Where's your father?'

'They're all having a meeting with Mr. Mody; they're going to tell the government that we won't stand for it.'

'Those worms don't care.'

'When he comes back, he is taking me to the circus.'

She rose up suddenly and shook herself. 'Breakfast!' She began to re-light the stove and pull out jars of flour and spices from boxes onto the ground. 'How am I supposed to find anything? Nothing is where it's supposed to be.'

'You can come and see me perform; the train to Chennai goes straight from Avadi.'

'I'll make missi roti.' She didn't look at me. 'Just go and fetch me some water.'

When I returned with a pitcher of water, my father was there, amma had repacked a bag with my belongings. 'There are two new printed cotton cholis in there,' she said. 'Aunt Gounder sent them last time. I was saving them for something special.'

Neither of them spoke over breakfast, and amma concentrated on tearing her missi roti into pieces and then moving them around her plate. It made me uneasy, and I began to hum the tune to *Nahin samne tue*.

'Always such noise,' my mother snapped, raising a hand to her head. 'It's time you were making a move.'

'Yes, the circus waits for no one.' My father released an empty laugh. 'We must hurry to catch the train.'

Amma quickly made up a paste with turmeric and applied it to my forehead, and then she steeped a length of string in the paste and tied it around my wrist. 'By the grace of God, when all this is over, we will have a home to bring you back to.' She kissed me gently on the head, and then she turned away and set about clearing the breakfast dishes.

■ ■ ■

When my father and I were out on the path, the tears came, bringing with it a feeling that it was wrong to go. 'Amma needs me to help her.' I stopped in my tracks. 'She can't do it all on her own.'

'The circus is not work; it's an adventure. Don't you know what others would give to have such a chance?'

'Then let them go.' Turning, I made to start back up the lane, but my father caught me by the arm.

'Don't you want to *be* something? Like Belli and Safa?'

His words pinned me to the spot. 'Aren't we the same?'

'Yes, yes, but you can show them what you're made of, that you are more than just a roti wallah.'

My father understood that more than anything I wanted to be better than my sisters. 'I'll go for a while, until I've made a name for myself and enough money to build you a house in Morai.'

My father clapped his hands together. 'The Elastic Girl,' he announced out onto the empty road. 'Star of The Great Raman Circus of Chennai.'

By the time we boarded the train and took our seats, my spirits had been lifted by my father's bubbling praise of the circus and his excitement at what I could be. 'Once you're a star, you can do anything, go anywhere.'

'Grandma always said that I was unlucky, like a crack on the floor that should be stepped over.' I dipped my hand into the bag of salted alu wafers he had bought me at the station.

'Bad things can always change,' my father said.

7

The Great Raman Circus sprang up from behind a white picket fence in the SIAA grounds at Park Town, the red-and-white stripes of the big top piercing the clear blue sky. When it came into view, my breath stopped, and for a moment we just stood there, looking up at it.

'Isn't it something?' my father said. 'Like a big mutta puff.'

As we reached the gate, we could see two men underneath an awning. Their faces were painted white, and they were leaning back in plastic chairs, arms tucked in tight behind their heads, both dead to the world.

'Stand back, Muthu.' My father placed a hand firmly on my shoulder.

I followed his gaze to where it had settled on the wide back of a bear. The bear was stretched out like a rug across the ground, and as I moved backward, it poked his head out from between his paws and sniffed at the air.

'Don't move,' dadi told me, but it was too late.

The bear turned towards us and pulled on the chain that was trailing from his paw to one of the chairs. In one quick move, the chair overturned, and one of the white-faced men tumbled out onto the ground.

When he stood up and began to dust down his short little legs, we could see that the man was a dwarf. His green eyes stared out at us from the pale face. 'This good-for-nothing won't touch you.' He glanced down at the bear, who was now settling back into the shade. 'He prefers to eat handbags and umbrellas. The last handbag cost me over one hundred rupees.' The little man stepped forward, reached up to open the gate, and then motioned for us to come through. 'The gatekeeper has gone to visit his sick sister in Chittoor,' he said. 'The bastard's been gone now for over a week.'

'My name is Devesh Tikaram,' my father explained as we stepped into the grounds. 'We're here to see Mr. Prem.'

'And my name is Bose.' The other man slowly pulled himself up out of his seat, and stood towering over the dwarf. He had a large flat face and arms like hams. 'I'll take you to Mr. Prem.'

Bose led us through the dusty aisles between a maze of tents and caravans.

'Tulsi is my brother.' He nodded back towards the awning. 'When we were children, people used to laugh at us, so our parents brought us here. Twelve years we're here; can you believe it?'

As we walked, the smell of jasmine drifted from the tents, and behind the covers I glimpsed figures bent over tiny homemade shrines, and girls painting faces before handheld mirrors. My father kept tugging at my hand, hurrying me along past men carrying caged birds and snakes and top hats, girls with high heels and sequined dresses that scratched against my skin. It felt like the first time I had tasted a bowl of kesar kulfi, the cinnamon and cardamom dissolving into the ice cream as I held it on my tongue.

'Wait here.' Bose disappeared into a caravan, which shook with his weight.

When he returned, he was accompanied by Mr. Prem.

Mr. Prem stood in the doorway and looked down on us. 'You've an appointment?' he asked, smoothing out the ends of his mustache.

My father produced the circus card from his pocket and handed it to Mr. Prem. 'You told us to come on Tuesday,' he said. 'You remember? She's the Elastic Girl from Ambattur.' He nodded towards me.

Mr. Prem looked at me and then pressed his hands together. 'So you are; the girl in the box,' he said cheerfully.

He instructed Bose to stay by the caravan while he showed us around. Bose smiled, pulled out a packet of bidis from his pocket, and placed one between his yellow teeth.

As we made our way through the aisles, Mr. Prem waved his hands about him like a tour guide. 'I grew up in this circus,' he said over his shoulder at my father. 'Any kind of animal, any child I can train. It's my passion.' He paused at the entrance to the big top. 'Isn't she beautiful?'

We all stared right upwards until our necks began to ache. Then Mr. Prem whipped back the curtain on the tent and led us into a dark tunnel. It was flanked on either side by wooden stalls, and as we moved forward, the darkness scattered, and we could see the circus ring at the bottom of the aisle, circles of brilliant light swaying across it. Mr. Prem motioned for us to sit in the front row. 'They're training,' he said. 'There are no shows on a Tuesday.'

There were men walking on stilts, cyclists juggling clubs in the air, and girls walking across beds of glass, all of them calling to one another, their voices echoing across the floor. My eyes moved from one to the other and back again, afraid to miss one thing. Beside me my father's hands gripped the seat underneath him, as if he might fly away.

We watched as a huge hippo was coached to walk around the ring in a pink tutu, his mouth open wide. At the end, he was rewarded by the trainer with an enormous cotton-candy cone.

My father released his hands from the seat and clapped loudly. 'I've never seen anything like it in my life,' he said. 'Not since the dancing elephant in Pondicherry.'

'The hippo is a very clean soul, just like me,' Mr. Prem said.

Suddenly the lights flitted across to a web of metal posts and ropes that rose up high into the peak of the canvas roof. Performers spidered their way up along the sides, and one of the girls, who had reached the top, stretched her toes and sprang out, curving her back as she dived through the air. On the other side, a man swung forward, clipping onto a bar by his knees. He caught the girl by the ankles as she swooped to the floor.

My father sprang forward in his seat and held his hands out, as if to try to catch the girl.

'That's Gloria, Queen of the Air, and our finest acrobat,' said Mr. Prem.

From behind my hands, I opened my eyes to see the girl swinging back and forth.

'Couldn't someone fall?' my father asked.

'There are nets. None of our performers have ever come to any harm.'

We continued to watch as the trapeze swung like a pendulum to and fro, Gloria then flipping herself back up to catch the other bar. She curled her body around it until she was perched like a bird.

'Will I learn to do that?' I asked when Gloria and the other performers had finished and were making their way out of the ring.

'Your talent is different,' Mr. Prem said, 'but it will be just as dazzling.'

My father smiled, and at once I could see him, sitting there with amma, eating buttered popcorn as they watched me lower myself into a box. 'You will come, Dadi? You will have to come and see me; Amma too?'

'First things first, plenty of time for visitors once you are in the ring,' Mr. Prem said. 'But at the beginning you must focus on your training.' He clapped his hands and stood up. 'We must finish our tour.'

Outside we blinked against the sudden brightness of the day.

'What's that noise?' my father asked.

Someone was playing a harmonium, and there was also the beat of a tabla, but it was the sound of the animals that rose over everything: an elephant trumpeting, the whinny of horses, and the squawking and chattering of birds and monkeys.

'When the musicians practise, the animals join in, too.' Mr. Prem laughed, leading us to the rear of the big top. 'You'll get used to it after a while.'

We passed by a snake pit, where boas and pythons were wrapped around the fork of a branch and a cage with four ringneck parrots who whistled and plucked at their apple-green feathers, and when we arrived at an enclosure full of chimpanzees, they began to bang on the metal bars, releasing a series of high-pitched screams. 'Be careful not to look them in the eyes,' Mr. Prem said. 'They think it's feeding time.'

'They're just like us.'

'Except they can't talk,' Mr. Prem said. 'That's the very beauty of it.' He and my father laughed.

'Where's Raja?' I asked, peering through the bars.

'That one is very moody, so we keep him on his own.'

'Only dogs frighten me,' I said. 'When Maheesh was bitten in the leg by a combai, he had to have an injection.'

'Maheesh?' he asked.

'The boy who can dance—he's my friend.'

Mr. Prem laughed. 'Well, you and Raja will be the best of friends now.'

We moved on to a pen with four elephants. A man was standing on a chair, massaging oil into their crumpled scalps. The legs on his chair had sunk into the dung-covered earth, and he looked in danger of sliding off.

'Can they lift logs with their trunks?' I asked.

'Logs and barrels and little girls.' Mr. Prem winked at my father.

'Are they all a family?'

'They're all female—sisters,' Mr. Prem said. 'Laxmi is forty-five, the oldest.'

'Which is the youngest?' my father asked.

'Shanti, she's twenty-seven,' Mr. Prem said. 'Our baby.'

My father's face changed suddenly as Mr. Prem moved us on.

When we had seen the glum-looking camels and the horses, he took us back to the caravan, where Bose was still standing in the heat, the dust around him pelted by red mouthfuls of spittle. 'Fetch Mr. Kalpak,' Mr. Prem said, and Bose disappeared.

From outside, the van looked just the same as the one at the cinema hall, but when we stepped inside, the cleanliness was gone, and Mr. Prem's bed lay undone. Every inch of the floor was littered with heaps of unwashed clothing and banana chips, which crushed underneath our feet. The only thing that remained the same was the picture of the Shimla Mountains hanging from the wall.

'At the circus, we don't have wives to pick things up for us.' Mr. Prem lifted a cup off the floor. 'A man has to do everything for himself.'

'Without women to look after us, we are lost,' my father said.

I thought about the time he had burnt amma's best pot when he was heating milk.

'Come now, Mr. Tikaram, please take a seat.' He removed stacks of papers from the corner sofa and motioned for us to sit down. Then, from a fridge behind him, he produced a jug of orange sharbat and poured us both a glass. 'Something to ease the heat,' he said, handing them across the table.

My father and I cradled our glasses in our hands, waiting for him to take a seat, but Mr. Prem continued to stand, pouring himself a large glass of something from a blue bottle and then swallowing it in two large gulps.

When he finally lowered himself onto a stool, he was hidden by a mound of files on the table. Through the gaps I could see him adjust his stomach so that it was resting on his lap. Hairs sprouted from his chest and tangled with the jumble of amulets and gold chains hanging from around his neck, and when he inserted his little finger into his ear and wriggled it around, the chains jangled noisily.

My father and Mr. Prem chatted easily across the table. 'The whole government has gone to pot,' Mr. Prem said, and my father nodded. 'They want to make a foreigner prime minister; whoever heard of such nonsense?'

'If Sonia Gandhi wins, we will be a laughing-stock,' my father added.

They stopped their excited discussion when Bose returned. With him was a man who stood in the doorway and held on to the sides of the caravan, as though it were suddenly going to take off at speed. He reminded me of General Musharraf, with his round little glasses, downturned mouth, and hair that was greying at the roots.

'Ah, Mr. Kalpak, come in, come in,' Mr. Prem said.

Mr. Kalpak continued to stand there, watching us over the rim of his glasses.

'Mr. Kalpak is your acrobatic trainer, your guru,' Mr. Prem said. 'Everything you do will be guided by him—how you sleep, eat, and move; isn't that right, Mr. Kalpak?'

Mr. Kalpak continued to stand there looking at my father. He did not once look at me.

'Tell them how it all works,' Mr. Prem urged.

'First, I will speak to Devesh,' he said, stepping out of the van and inviting my father to join him. The fact that he knew my father's name seemed strange, but it only crossed my mind for a flicker of a second, and then it was gone.

'He's a peculiar little man,' Mr. Prem said, as my father rose from his seat.

We sat inside watching them through the open door. They had stepped away so that we couldn't hear what they were saying. 'He'll be preaching about God,' Mr. Prem said. 'He believes that prayer and discipline are the way to the top.' He pointed a finger in the air.

'He looks cross.'

'Don't worry; they are not all like Mr. Kalpak in the circus. That man has a special case of glumness that we have all managed to avoid.' He stopped then, as Mr. Kalpak and my father returned.

'She can start in the morning,' Mr. Kalpak said, and then he turned and was off.

'You're satisfied?' Mr. Prem asked my father. 'You've found our trainer agreeable?'

'I've every belief that he will look after Muthu; he's given me his word.'

Mr. Prem released a snort. 'Ah, we will *all* look after Muthu,' he said. 'That is our job.' He then reached across the table, lifted a file from amongst the pile, and rested it across the crest of his stomach. 'There are a few formalities before we can get going.' He removed a pen from the breast pocket of his shirt. 'Your occupation, Mr. Tikaram?'

My father shifted in his seat. 'Cleaner.'

Mr. Prem's pen hovered over the page. 'Not so good, heh?' he said bluntly. 'Oh, well, isn't it good you have found a way to make extra money.'

'Muthu is here to find some discipline, to make something of herself,' my father said, his voice now rigid. 'That's what we want.'

'No need to send you the money then?' The folder shook against Mr. Prem's belly as he laughed.

'We are setting up a new house,' my father told him. 'Everything makes a difference, I suppose.'

Mr. Prem scratched his pen across the page. 'Do you know Muthu's age?' he asked.

'She is eleven,' my father said. 'Just December past.'

'So small for eleven,' Mr. Prem said. My cheeks began to burn as he smiled at me and then returned to his file. 'It's quite rare to know their age; so many parents don't remember when their child was born.'

'I'll never forget how Muthu came into this world.'

'Of course, and now just like you, we will do everything for her: feed, train, instruct, and after that she will start to get two hundred rupees per month.' He removed the sheet of paper from the file and held it up in the air. 'It's a contract; sign this, and we send the money directly.'

'How long is it for?'

'After five years she's free to go.'

'Five years?' I asked. 'You said I could go whenever I wanted.'

'That's how long it takes to make a real star,' Mr. Prem said.

'But if I don't like it, I can leave?'

'If you leave, my heart will explode like dynamite,' he said. 'Let's not think so far ahead.' He handed my father the contract and told him to add his name across the dotted line.

My father stared at the page without moving, and Mr. Prem reached into a drawer and produced a pad of ink, offering it to my father. 'I can write.' My father scribbled his name across the page. 'I've not always been a cleaner.'

■ ■ ■

Outside the caravan the city had fallen into darkness, and as we walked back towards the white picket fence my father reached for my hand, my fingers cocooned inside his grasp.

'How can I be sure you will care for her?' His grip tightened. 'How will we know if anything is wrong?'

Mr. Prem placed a hand on my father's back. 'You know, my friend, sometimes I can't sleep thinking about them. What would they be doing? Are they ill? Have they eaten? It's like having children all of my own.'

My father nodded. 'Yes, it will all be fine; Mr. Kalpak said there was no need to worry.'

We stood there looking at the circus lights circling around the town, momentarily resting on the traders of Moore Market, on Kuavam River, on the gleaming white clock tower of the Ripon building.

'When I'm a star, I'll buy you a new radio, Dadi,' I said. 'And tell Amma that she can have a colour television.'

'I'll tell her that.' He squeezed my hand once more and then let go.

8

Mr. Prem placed his hand on my shoulder and urged me away from the gate and the disappearing figure of my father. 'At the beginning everyone is scared,' he said. 'But you'll soon get used to it.' He led me back towards the tents, which were now glowing like paper lanterns. 'This is yours,' he said. 'It's one of our best.' He stopped at the entrance to one of the tents. The canvas was the colour of lasuda pickle.

'I must sleep here on my own?'

'You're never alone in the circus.' He laughed. 'Your roommate will help settle you in.' He lit a cigarette into the curve of his hand, nodded at me, and walked away.

Out in the darkness of the circus, animals cried and screeched, like someone sawing at a piece of wood, and the flag above the big top whipped in the wind, but from beyond the circus the familiar hoot of traffic reached me, along with the crackle of the loudspeaker at the station as it announced messages to late-night passengers. Listening to those sounds, my breathing stilled, and my body stopped shaking.

'Don't stand out there like a ghost,' a voice called from inside the tent.

Stepping through the opening, I was greeted by Gloria—Queen of the Air. She was getting undressed, and her choli was caught halfway down her arms. 'Why are you staring at me like an owl?' Pulling the choli off she threw it onto a bed. She had a thick red scar down the curve of her neck.

Mumbling an apology, I turned away from her, my belongings clutched tight to my chest.

'You're a sensitive one,' she said. 'What's your name?'

'Muthu. Muthu Tikaram.'

'Ah, the Plastic Girl.'

'Elastic,' I said. 'Elastic girl.'

'Would you like a biscuit, Elastic girl?'

When I turned around, Gloria, who was now dressed in a bright-pink pajama suit, held out a packet of arrowroot biscuits. 'Have one,' she said. 'I don't bite.'

Setting my bags onto the floor, I reached for one, my stomach rumbling with sudden hunger.

'I'm Gloria, the trapeze artist,' she said. 'I've a good head for heights.' She pulled down the cover on a bed beside her and slid underneath, brushing away a scattering of crumbs.

'We saw you today on the swing.' I nibbled around the edge of my biscuit. 'You looked like a cockatoo.'

Gloria made a little laugh and then slipped her hand in beneath the thin mattress and withdrew a *Stardust* magazine. 'I'm going to be just like them.' She tapped the cover of the magazine.

'Me, too, like Kareena Kapoor.'

'We'll have apartments in Mumbai and villas in Goa,' she said. 'Isn't it exciting?'

'We will?'

'Maybe.' Gloria settled back against her pillow and began to flick through her magazine.

'Is that Hrithik Roshan from *Lakshya*?' I asked, pointing at the cover of the magazine.

'My Arjun looks just like him.' She held the magazine up for me to see. 'The same long face and strong chin.'

'Arjun?'

'He's a roller skater from Bombay,' she said. 'We're in love.'

Gloria was no older than Safa, who was fifteen but still needed amma to braid her hair.

'Doesn't your mother think you're too young?'

'You should go to bed,' she said suddenly. 'The circus rises early.'

'Is that mine?' I nodded towards a bed visible on the other side of a coral drape. The drape was hung the length of the tent, dividing it in two.

'No, you're here.' She pointed to a mattress on the floor.

'Then who sleeps there?'

'Mr. Kalpak of course.' She flicked a page in her magazine.

Turning my back on Gloria, I pulled on the long nightdress amma had packed for me, removing my clothes from underneath.

'There's no need to be shy,' Gloria said. 'We girls are all the same.'

But still I hurried below the covers. 'Mr. Kalpak might see.'

'He's like a father; he doesn't notice such things, not like some of them.'

Lying back against the mattress, my stomach growled again, and I thought about amma's missi roti, her hands pressing and stretching at the dough until they were shaped into perfect little discs.

'Chopra is thinking of quitting,' Gloria called down to me, not taking her eyes off the magazine. 'And hear this; Bipasha Basu was molested by a man in a public nightclub in Mumbai.' She laid down the magazine in her lap and leant over the bed so that she was hanging out over me. She reminded me of Aamna Sharif, with the same almond-shaped eyes and apple cheeks. 'What age are you?' she asked.

'Eleven.'

'Then too young to know about such things.'

'I'm almost twelve,' I told her. 'My sisters are older, and they tell me everything.'

Gloria smiled. 'You are too sweet,' she said, and my face burned.

'When you and Arjun marry, will you leave the circus?'

'He's going to meet me when we get to Mumbai,' she said in a whisper. 'We're going to start our own show with the money we have made, and then we will think about happy matrimonials.'

'You're going to Mumbai?'

'Of course; we are all going,' she said.

'What do you mean?'

'No one ever knows where we are going next: Bangalore, Mysore, Anantapur, Hyderabad, then one day soon it will be Mumbai.'

'There's been a mistake; my Dadi never said.'

'It's no mistake; that's what we are—a traveling circus.'

'I've never been outside of Chennai; I can't go just like that.'

'Then it will be an adventure.' She returned to leafing again through the pages. 'Salman Khan was in a hit-and-run case,' she said. 'The fool of a man had been drinking.' Gloria continued to talk as though she had just stepped out from a Bollywood party, but then a blast of air whipped at the drape behind us, and there was the sound of someone shuffling around the room as Gloria blew out the light and returned her magazine to its hiding place.

Stretching around on the mattress, I could see the figure of Mr. Kalpak moving back and forth, picking things up and then putting them down again. Then he folded into a corner and began to pray. The words of the gayatri mantra rose up into the air, crisp and clear, and when he was done, he settled himself on the bed just behind the drape. The springs creaked underneath him, and his shoes slapped against the floor, and then he began to breathe in heavily through his nose, the air whistling back out through his lips in a slow, steady stream.

Blood pumped noisily in my ears as I thought about what Gloria had said. It had to be a mistake; dadi would never have agreed to leave me here if he knew it was a travelling circus. I reached in underneath the neck of my nightdress and removed the watch belonging to my grandfather, placing it carefully below my pillow. Soon the sound of Mr. Kalpak was replaced by a gentle tick, as I plunged into sleep.

'You should not cheek him or answer back!' Gloria tugged at my bed clothes.

The tent was now filled with a soft yellow light, and Gloria was standing over me, dressed in a skintight red-and-orange suit, with a crystal motif in the centre of her chest. She looked much older than Safa now, and her eyes sparkled with a fan of silver and gold. 'Jaldi, Jaldi,' she said. 'You must hurry.'

'Is he still here?' I whispered, turning my head towards the drape.

'He's waiting in the big top; everyone is waiting on you now.'

Reaching into one of my plastic bags, I began to unwrap the lenghas amma had wrapped for me, but Gloria snatched them away. 'You must wear this.' She held out a silver leotard with a frill of a skirt.

I held it up against me, and my face grew hot. 'I can't wear this; Amma would kill me.'

'And Mr. Kalpak will kill you if you don't; it's what we all wear.' She pulled my nightdress up over my head and forced me into the leotard.

It was like paper against my skin, and the sequins scratched at my arms as I imagined my mother's downturned eyes.

'Such coarse hair.' Gloria scraped my hair back and fastened it with a band. 'We'll need to oil it later.'

She dragged me out of the tent and through the stir of The Great Raman Circus. Animals were being led wearily from their enclosures, and all around us tents had been opened up so that we could see women preparing their makeup and men shaving at cracked mirrors.

'Another monkey from the village?' one of the men called, chewing then on the end of a neem twig.

'Ha, such a smart fellow you are!' Gloria replied. 'A shame you forgot to tuck in your poolu when you were done.' The man's hands flew to his pants, and Gloria pulled at me again, guiding me underneath lines of morning washing that had been strung from tent to tent. 'Three performances a day, six days a week,' she called to me as we moved. 'We start at 6:00 a.m. It's simple.'

When we arrived at the big top, Gloria steadied herself and took a breath. 'He won't be happy.'

We made our way down towards the ring, to where a rainbow of girls stood neatly before Mr. Kalpak. 'Apologies, Mr. Kalpak,' Gloria said.

He swivelled around, drawing a cane up off the floor. 'Well, well,' he said. 'Another one who wants to be picked up, like a baby.'

Some of the girls bent forwards and sniggered, but when Mr. Kalpak held the cane out to his side, they fell quickly into silence once again. 'You are her minder,' he said to Gloria. 'You should have had her here on time.'

'She was trying to find your gift,' Gloria said. 'She'd placed it out of sight.'

'Come here.' He lowered the cane and indicated a spot on the wood-chip-covered floor.

Gloria motioned for me to follow, as she stepped up beside him. 'Muthu brought you something special,' she said. 'All the way from Ambattur.' Then she unclenched her fist and held out my grandfather's Zenith pocket watch.

It felt as though my body was sinking down into the ground, the sounds of the big top growing thin in my ears. Mr. Kalpak lifted the watch up between pinched fingers, and twirled it around in the air. 'S. T. T.,' he read. He placed it face down on his palm and ran a finger over the engraving.

'Samir Tushar Tikaram, my grandfather.'

He stood there holding the watch in his hand. 'It doesn't work,' he said at last. He deposited the watch back into Gloria's hand 'No wonder you are late.'

Mr. Kalpak turned to face the girls again, and Gloria quickly draped the watch around my neck. 'You owe me.' She nudged me forwards and then ran off towards her web, crawling upwards like a golden silk orb-weaver.

It was the first time Gloria would save me, but thinking nothing of it then, I joined the line of girls and followed the stretches demonstrated by Mr. Kalpak. Together we bent left and right, touched our toes, and turned circles with our arms, and all the time the eyes of the girls were fixed on me, taking in my frizzy ponytail, the scars on my knees, and the roundness of my face. When I looked at them, they turned away, all except one of the smallest girls, who smiled at me and wrinkled up her perfect little nose each time Mr. Kalpak spoke, as if he was releasing a horrible smell.

Just as we finished the warm-ups, a fight broke out on the other side of the ring, between a pair of dancing monkeys. The trainer was pulling on the ropes that were tied around their necks, trying to drag them apart.

'The new ones are always like that at the start,' one of the girls said.

Everyone laughed as the monkeys chased circles around the trainer, entangling the rope around his legs so that he could not move.

'Enough!' Mr. Kalpak shouted. 'Let's see if you can do any better than those monkeys.' He began to call on the girls one by one, bellowing instructions at them as they hand-walked, somersaulted and cartwheeled across the floor. 'Extend your toes,' he shouted. 'Arch your back.' When each girl had finished, they sat on the ground, their cheeks red, some of them lowering their head onto their knees.

'Rupa,' he called next, and the girl with the perfect little nose stepped forward. She reminded me of Belli, with her silky sweep of hair. Mr. Kalpak reached into a wooden chest beside him and pulled out a skipping rope, handing it to Rupa. She paced across the floor and positioned herself so that her feet were slightly apart, then she began to jump, the rope whipping dust into the air.

'Double-under,' he called, and Rupa jumped even higher, swinging the rope twice under her feet.

'Scissors.'

Rupa jumped again, this time putting one foot in front of the other, then switching back and forth before her feet touched the ground. On the second jump, her foot got tangled in the rope, and she collapsed in a heap.

'Hopeless,' Mr. Kalpak shouted. 'Worse than a monkey.'

Rupa pulled herself up off the ground. Her nose started to redden, and two tears rolled down her cheeks.

'You need to pray,' he said. 'You must take God's name to have focus.'

'Yes, sir,' Rupa said in a trembling voice, and she returned to stand beside me. 'Who wants to skip rope anyway?' she whispered. 'I'm supposed to be an acrobat; all this is just a waste of time.'

Mr. Kalpak tapped his cane off the wooden box. 'We'll resume after breakfast,' he called. 'I can't take any more on an empty stomach.'

The girls formed an orderly queue.

'Is he always like this?' I asked Rupa, as we made our way towards the breakfast tent.

'He's like a giant cobra.' She nodded towards the cage of snakes. 'He's poisonous.'

'What if he hates my act?'

'Then you're in trouble, just like me.'

When we reached the dining area, performers and groundsmen were gathered around tables, chatting noisily, and just inside the entrance, a cook was pouring batter onto a tava, spreading it out into a thin white layer. When it was my turn, he took a knife and carefully rolled a crisp golden dosa, placing it neatly onto my plate.

'Heh, you can sit with us,' one of the men called out as I made my way to one of the tables. 'We will look after you.' The others who were sitting with him began to laugh and my face burned as I looked down at my bare legs.

'They are harmless.' Rupa caught me by the elbow and lead me towards a bench.

'It's all so different.' I could feel myself about to cry. 'I'd hoped for something else.'

'It's not so bad.' She brought her dosa to her mouth. 'Those ones are just harmless drunks; it's Mr. Kalpak you need to worry about.'

'But I heard him pray last night; surely he is good underneath it all.'

'It's all a cover,' she whispered.

'A cover?' I looked over to where Mr. Kalpak stood in the entrance with his cane folded underneath his arm.

'Don't you know? He murdered his wife.' Rupa devoured the last piece of her dosa and then wiped away the oil with the back of her hand.

'People like that would be locked away; he would be in jail.'

'He's not well, you see.' She tapped at the side of her head.

'Why would Mr. Prem allow him to work here?'

'We have them all here: cranks, the deformed, homeless; the circus takes them all,' Rupa said. 'Besides, he can scare us into doing what he wants.'

'I won't stay.' A sick feeling rose up in my stomach. 'I'm going to tell Mr. Prem to fetch my father. This place isn't what he thought.'

'You can't just *leave*,' Rupa said. 'The contract is set in stone.'

'Dadi wouldn't have left me here if he'd known about Mr. Kalpak.'

'Don't worry,' Rupa said cheerfully. 'With Mr. Prem to look after us, we won't come to any harm.'

9

When we returned to the big top, Mr. Kalpak paraded before us, face tilted up in the air. He stopped then, like a soldier and turned towards me, his polished heels clicking together in the dust. 'Now, tell us what *you* can do.' He propped his glasses up onto his nose with the end of his cane.

My tongue seemed to be stuck to the roof of my mouth, and no matter how hard I tried, the words would not come out.

'We do not have all day,' Mr. Kalpak said. 'Do you have an act?'

'Tell him what you can do,' Rupa hissed, nudging me in the side.

'I can make myself disappear,' I mumbled, and the girls began to laugh.

'Is that so,' Mr. Kalpak said. 'You are a magician then?'

'No, I'm the Elastic Girl.'

'So, come on and show us what you can do, Elastic Girl.'

'There's no box.' I looked around me, waiting for Mr. Kalpak to bring the cane down on my back.

Mr. Kalpak snorted and began to make his way across the floor, towards Tulsi and Bose, who were encouraging a parrot to sing.

'Short short duck,' Tulsi sang through the bars. 'Quack, quack, quack.' The parrot plucked at his feathers and admired himself in the mirror fixed to the inside of his cage. 'You must hold his attention,' Bose barked, slapping Tulsi across the head.

Mr. Kalpak came to a stop before them and asked Tulsi to remove the parrot. Tulsi reached in and pulled out the bright-green bird, perching it on the crux of his short little arm.

'Don't let him unsettle you,' Rupa whispered. 'We can't let him win.'

We watched Mr. Kalpak lift the cage by its handle and carry it back across the floor. 'Go ahead,' he said, drawing back the cover at the top.

The bottom of the cage was littered with droppings and my arms and legs turned to rock. I thought about my father's face when he had watched Gloria soar through the air, and removing my sandals, I stepped into the cage. The droppings stuck like pomegranate seeds to my feet.

The line of girls glanced at one another and then at Mr. Kalpak.

'Is that it?' Mr. Kalpak called.

Closing my eyes and sucking at the air, I lowered myself into the cage and coiled up into a tight little ball. Through the bars, an upside-down Mr. Kalpak clicked his tongue, and Rupa, with her head cocked to the side, smiled in at me.

'That will do,' Mr. Kalpak said.

When I tried to come up, the cage had latched onto me like a tick. I struggled to release an arm up behind me, but it became trapped by the metal perch, and my toes caught fast in the bars. My breathing grew heavy, and the stench of parrot shit burned my lungs as I inhaled, making my stomach heave. In a final struggle to free myself, the cage suddenly toppled over sideways onto the floor; I was half-in, half-out.

Mr. Kalpak began to applaud. 'What a show,' he said.

Rupa rushed forwards to drag me from the cage, so that I was sprawled instead on the ground. It felt as though my elbow had been broken, because I couldn't push myself up.

Mr. Kalpak bent down over me. 'To be an acrobat, your mind and body must be strong,' he said. 'You have a weak mind, not like the ones from Nepal.'

Suddenly a siren sounded out across the big top in three high-pitched blasts, and everyone stopped what they were doing. Mr. Kalpak turned his back on me and began to deliver instructions. 'You two are with Hilesh, the fire-eater,' he said to two of the girls. 'And you are with Ratna on the cannonball.'

As each girl was assigned their act, they scurried out of the tent, none of them glancing back at me.

'You are with Raja,' he said, turning back to me. 'You will be the chimp's assistant. That is all you're capable of.'

Mr. Kalpak followed the girls outside, leaving only Rupa, who had been instructed to tidy up. She hurried over to me, along with Tulsi, who now had the parrot perched on his shoulder. Together they hoisted the cage back into position, and Tulsi returned the parrot to its bar.

'You're worse than me.' Rupa sat beside me on the ground. 'You really must be a godless soul.'

'He will kill me now for sure.' I began to cry. Great big waves rattled through me, streaming from my eyes and nose. Tulsi stood before us and produced a string of coloured handkerchiefs from his pocket. They streamed onto the floor, forming a puddle by his pointed yellow shoes, and with the last one, he wiped at my nose, his man-child hands circling my face. 'As soon as possible, I'm going home to my parents,' I said, once the sobbing had died down. 'It would be better selling roti than this.'

'I've already told you, its impossible,' Rupa said.

I thought about my father signing his name, the black ink sinking into the page, plumping out each letter. 'It can be undone; Dadi said he would come for me.'

'The circus is our fate,' Tulsi said. 'Even the bird's wings have been clipped.' He nodded towards the parrot, lifted the cage, and began to make his way out of the tent, the handkerchiefs trailing after him like a favourite blanket.

Bile rose up in my stomach again. 'Why would my Dadi have left me here?'

'I'm not sure,' she said. 'My parents used to beat me with that thing you lift up bowls with. It left three holes in my foot and that mark above my eye.' She rubbed a finger across her scarred brow. 'I ran away, and Mr. Prem saved me. He said that everything would be better in the circus.'

'This is better?'

'If my parents found me, they would kill me, but Mr. Prem keeps them away,' she said.

The siren broke out again across the tent, and Gloria appeared like a streak of silver lightning by our side. 'Look at the state of you.' She pulled me up off the floor and waved Rupa away.

'Mr. Kalpak hates me, and my elbow is broken,' I told her. 'He made me Raja's assistant because I messed up my routine.'

Gloria examined my arm, raising it up and down. 'That's nothing,' she said. 'Now hurry; the first performance is at twelve, and we need to get you cleaned up fast.'

'Raja and I haven't even practised.'

'You will need no practise for Raja's act,' Gloria replied, and I hurried after her towards our tent.

Gloria stripped me down to my underpants and had me stand in a basin. She took a bar of soap from the little arrangement on her dresser and began to wash me with the wet end of a cloth. Only amma had seen me naked before, but already I no longer cared, and closed my eyes as she poured jugs of cool water over my hair and my back.

'Is it true that Mr. Kalpak killed his wife?' I asked as Gloria helped me from the basin and patted me dry with a towel.

'Such nonsense; I suppose it was Rupa who told you that?' She handed me a fresh leotard. 'That girl is confused.'

'But he has such a temper, and he's always pointing his cane.'

'He's trying to teach you some discipline; if only Rupa would listen.' She turned towards the mirror and began to redraw the charcoal lines around her eyes.

'She said that Mr. Prem looks after her; maybe he could help me, too?'

Gloria snapped the palette of makeup shut and turned to me. 'Rupa wouldn't listen to me,' she said. 'You would do well not to follow in her footsteps.'

'But he told my father that he'd look after us like his own children.'

'Mr. Prem is like the demon Ravana, with ten heads,' she said. 'You never know which one you are looking at.'

'He said he would make me a star.'

'A star?' Gloria said. 'Only you can do that.' The siren blasted again, and Gloria rose from her stool. 'Time for you to start work.'

We made our way back towards the big top. The grounds had been transformed. 'Buttered popcorn, cold drinks, peanuts,' the stallholders called, leaning out through hatches on trailers. The air smelt of warm sugar, and groups of people stirred through the grounds, stopping here and there to watch men fashion dogs and swords out of twisted balloons, to clap to the music accompanying Bose and the dancing bear, and to stroke the skin of the giant snake, which was twisted around its handler's neck.

Gloria gripped my hand tightly, and for a moment, I was walking with amma during the Ugadi festival, the sound of firecrackers exploding in our ears.

'Your hands,' I said to Gloria. 'They're like lumps of coal.'

'It's from the ropes; they cause knots under my skin.'

'Why don't you do something else?'

'I'm Queen of the Air; this is the only thing I know.'

We passed by the ticket booth, where families and couples squeezed their way forward. 'Look, Amma.' A little girl pointed into the darkness of the big top. 'I can see it; I can see it.'

'Are they all coming to see us?'

'Some of them come more than once,' Gloria said. 'Several men have sent me flowers.'

A young man and woman came up and asked Gloria to pose for a photograph. She leant in between their faces as the man instructed me on how to work the camera. 'We love your act,' the man said. 'So terrifying, so brave.'

'See, some crazy fans,' Gloria said as we walked away. 'They think that we are like gods.'

■ ■ ■

Despite the dismal morning I'd had with Mr. Kalpak, the thrill in the air was catching. By the time we had reached the back of the big top, my head was buzzing with excitement and the thought came into my mind that I might stay afterall.

Performers and helpers raced back and forth carrying hoops and fire torches, some of them riding one-wheeled bicycles, and Mr. Prem walked up and down amongst everyone carrying a handheld loudspeaker. He was dressed in a red jacket with gold buttons, and he had a tall black hat on his head. 'Five minutes,' he shouted into the mouthpiece. 'Five minutes to start.'

'You'll find Raja over there with Sumi, his trainer.' Gloria pointed in the direction of a costume tent. 'I'll see you inside.'

My excitement turned to fear, and I reached for Gloria's hand.

'It will be OK. Just remember, this is only the beginning.' She ran off through the rush of costumed figures.

'Samson, the Strong Man,' Mr. Prem called out.

A hulk of a man appeared from one of the tents. He was dressed in a pair of tight red shorts, and his arms and legs bulged like plump mangoes. I watched as he made his way to the entrance of the big top, stopping at the front of a cart heaped with sacks of Gram Flour. Samson picked up a band that was attached to the cart and clipped it around his waist; then the curtains of the tent were pulled back and he moved on into the darkness, dragging behind him the heavy weight of the cart.

As the curtains dropped back into place, a light swooped down over him, and a cheer rang out from the shadows, sending a shiver through my body. The Great Raman Circus had begun, and my mind buzzed with a thousand thoughts and feelings so that it felt like my heart might explode.

When I turned around, Raja was standing close by, dressed almost as smartly as Mr. Prem in a tailored jacket and bow tie. He was walking upright, towards a scrawny little man with a pockmarked face.

'Come on, Raja, that's the boy.' The man offered Raja a fig.

When Raja reached him and plucked the fig from his fingers, he squealed and jumped up and down with delight.

'Are you Sumi?' I asked him.

'Who wants to know?' the man replied, patting Raja on the head until he sat down.

'I'm Muthu,' I told him. 'Elastic Girl.'

Sumi looked me up and down, and then he clapped his hands. 'Perfect! Here is your new baby,' he said to Raja, who was busy twisting his bow tie around and around. Then Sumi began to rattle through a rail of clothes that were hanging by his side. 'Here, you need to put this on.' He handed me some clothes. 'We will be going on soon.'

He made me go behind a trailer and put on a layered pink dress, frilled pants, and a baby's bonnet and boots. 'I can't wear this in the ring; I look like a baby.'

'You *are* a baby; didn't he tell you?' and he pulled out a pram from behind the clothes rail. 'You are Raja's baby girl; that's the act.'

My face burned as he made me climb up into the pram. 'Everyone will laugh.'

'That's the idea; the more laughing the better,' Sumi replied. 'Now hurry; we are up next.' He looked towards Mr. Prem, who had his loudspeaker raised in the air.

'Raja and baby girl,' he called.

Sumi handed me a pacifier with a pink ribbon attached. 'Put this in your mouth; then you are ready,' he said.

'I can't.' I held the pacifier back out to him, feeling the tears begin to form in my eyes. 'What if my parents are here? They will be ashamed of me.'

'Please don't cause a scene,' Sumi said. 'It will bring big trouble for me and the end of everything for you.'

'I'm supposed to be the Elastic Girl.'

'They are all supposed to be something.' Sumi waved around at the performers.

'Two minutes,' Mr. Prem shouted.

It was too late; Sumi was pushing me in through the entrance of the big top, Raja knuckle-walking behind him, his bow tie now tangled around his neck. The face of Samson the Strong Man loomed over me. 'What a big baby,' he laughed. 'One day you could be just like me.'

As I bit down hard on the rubber end of the pacifier, the bright lights shone down through the mesh on the pram, and in the ring, I could see the knife-thrower pitching blades at a rotating disc. Strapped to the middle of the disc with her arms outstretched was Rupa, her hair sweeping down across the floor. Her face was painted like a doll's and her mouth spread wide in a lipsticked smile.

When the last blade sliced past the side of Rupa's head and into the board, the audience erupted into cheers, and the knife-thrower took a bow. Helpers ran forwards and wheeled the disc away, Rupa still lain out like a butcher's quarry.

The shouts of the audience were hushed to a murmur by Mr. Prem, who had stepped out from the shadows and was holding a hand up in the air. His mustache had been greased upwards at the ends, like the horns on a bullock.

'Magnificent,' he boomed into a microphone. 'What a feat of nerves.' He paused for a moment until the crowd had completely settled down. 'Now, something to tickle and amuse you.'

The light trailed its way across the floor and beamed down upon the pram, forcing me to close my eyes. 'Please welcome Raja and his baby girl.'

The crowd clapped and cheered as Raja began to steer me into the ring. Beneath my dress, my skin grew sticky, and it felt as if someone was pushing a pillow in my face.

Round and round in circles we went, the sound of laughter ringing across the space, and amidst the noise, there it was: my father's voice. 'What about the Elastic Girl?' he called from the stalls, but then Raja popped the pacifier out of my mouth with his long wrinkled fingers, and the sound of a crying baby pierced through the tannoy. Everyone laughed, just as I knew they would.

'What a star,' Mr. Prem finally called into the microphone, and Raja stooped to the floor and took his bow.

'It's over now.' Sumi shook me by the arm. We were outside the big top, Raja clawing at Sumi's pocket, looking for a fig.

I spat the pacifier out of my mouth. 'My Dadi; he's come for me.' I jumped from the pram and raced across to the gates.

'You must be back here for the shows at three and six o'clock,' Sumi called after me.

They filed out: women with dimpled smiles and sullen husbands, children with red cheeks, and old aunties bent over walking sticks. I must have missed him.

'Did you see him?' I asked the gatekeeper when the last of the crowd had left.

'Who?'

'My Dadi; he came for me.'

The gatekeeper laughed and spat down on the ground. 'Best to forget about him now,' he said.

'What do you know?'

'Like the rest, he will never come, and you will get tired waiting.'

When Gloria had finished her act, she returned to find me lying face down on my mattress. 'You're feeling sorry for yourself,' she said. I heard her removing a magazine from its hiding place and lying back on the bed. 'Karan Johar has been given his own chat show on Star World channel,' she said. 'I can't see that pompous ass being a success.'

She continued for a while, and when I did not move, she put down her magazine and flung her legs over the edge of her bed, pressing a toe into the small of my back. 'Sit up,' she said. 'We will oil your hair.' She removed a bottle of Amla oil from a basket by her bed and poured a small yellow pool into the palm of her hand as I sat with my back to her, head resting against her knees. 'You're missing home?' Her palms pressed down on the top of my head.

'It was a mistake to send me here. I'll never be a star.'

'You give up so quickly?' Her fingers moved in circles. 'All the biggest stars started at the bottom, just like us; it's taken me four years to get this far.'

'Where did you come from?'

'From Cuddalore, a stinking landfill site for Pondicherry,' she said. I thought of how Gloria always smelt so good and her arrangement of little soaps on the dresser. 'When there were no more fish to be had, my father, like every other fisherman in the town, became a drunk.'

'What about your mother?'

'After she died, we had to sell everything just to survive, and my father beat me so much that I left.' I remembered the scar across Gloria's neck. 'I ended up in a tannery in Chennai; it stank worse than Cuddalore, but it was there that I met Arjun.'

'And how did you end up here?'

'Mr. Prem glided into the tannery one day and announced that he was looking for a star,' she said. 'Anything was better than staying where I was, and I took it as a sign that I was destined for better things.'

'But you left Arjun behind.'

'He said that when we had saved enough money, I could meet him in Mumbai, and then we would start our own show.'

'So, you *will* leave?'

'Not yet,' she said. 'Not until we reach Mumbai, and you will be a star by then.'

'Mr. Kalpak thinks I'm weak.'

'He tells that to all the best ones.' She returned the cap onto the oil and placed it back in the basket. 'Leave it until morning,' she said. 'Then it will shine like a polished table.'

Gloria turned to her magazine, tore a page from the middle, and handed it to me. It was a picture of a little girl perched on her mother's knee, the two of them holding the handle of a knife as it was pressed down into a birthday cake. 'Who is it?' she asked. 'Have a guess.'

The little girl wore a plain red dress, and her eyes were turned downwards at the cake, her lips tight in a shy little smile. 'It's just an ordinary little girl.'

'That 'ordinary little girl' is now Aishwarya Rai,' Gloria said. 'All of us come from nothing; you should remember that.'

We fell into silence, Gloria returning to her magazine while I continued to examine the picture of the child with the little bump in the middle of her nose and the short unruly hair. When I fell asleep, I was younger, standing at the side of my grandfather's bed, running a finger over his waxen face. He was dressed in white and decorated in sandalwood and white orchids.

'Do not touch him,' grandmother cried from the foot of the bed. 'Your bad blood will pollute him.'

When I awoke in the morning, my fist was wrapped tightly around my grandfather's watch, and every nerve in my body tingled with excitement. This was my chance to prove to my grandmother and to everyone else that I was not just an ordinary girl, that I, Muthu Tikaram was something.

10

For one whole month, it stayed that way. I was determined to put up with Mr. Kalpak's disapproval during training and the ongoing shame of being Raja's baby girl. 'You're not done yet,' Mr. Kalpak told me each time I asked if I was ready to move on. 'Your head is too rigid and your over-split too shaky,' he complained. 'Not enough concentration.'

It was exhausting—the training, the performances, the pitiful amount of food and rest—but Mr. Kalpak was not the pitying kind, and there were girls much younger than me who trained and performed under the tough circus schedule without ever once complaining, so I trained harder. It stopped me from thinking about home, but still after each performance I waited at the gates for my mother and father, and each time they did not come, my heart sank a little further, making the daily routine all the more difficult.

'There must be something wrong,' I told Gloria, as she read out more gossip from her latest magazine. 'They said they would be here.'

'People get tied up with other things,' she said quietly.

'The house!' Suddenly I'd settled on the reason. 'They must be busy building the house at Morai.'

'Yes, I'm sure that's it,' Gloria said, her voice not lifting. 'And when they come, they will not know you with such beautiful hair.' She leaned over to where I was sitting on her bed and scooped my soft hair up into her hands, letting it fall then against my shoulders like a curtain.

'It's the house,' I reminded myself each day and focused all my energy on The Great Raman Circus: always on time for training, perfecting the contortion moves that Mr. Kalpak had begun to teach me.

In the evenings, instead of waiting at the gate, I helped Sumi with looking after Raja. Together we cleaned out his cage, laid down fresh bedding, and prepared his meals of fruit, leaves and insects, hiding treats of raisins and seeds for him to find on the ground of his enclosure. All the while, Raja would sit grooming himself, carefully picking out pieces of soil and dried skin from his hair and reaching out a long arm every so often to pat me on the back.

'He likes you.' Sumi nodded towards Raja. 'Normally, he's a fussy kind.'

After three months, Raja and I were moved to the tandem act. 'One step at a time,' Mr. Kalpak said.

'Hold it steady,' Sumi called from the sidelines as Raja stood up on his seat and clapped. The audience made such a fuss, rising from the stalls, and soon my early embarrassment about performing with Raja in the ring was gone, and I was happy to bow and feel the applause rain down on us.

When we were finished, Sumi lifted Raja from the tandem and gave him a kiss. 'Well done, my baba,' he said. I could feel something tighten inside me. 'Why don't you take him for a walk?' Sumi said. 'He will be sore from the bicycle.'

Raja and I climbed up into the banyan tree at the edge of the circus and I taught him how to blast peas down on unsuspecting visitors through a bamboo pole. We performed backwards flips and swung upside down from the rope swing, just as Maheesh and I had done in the pump house, and leading Raja around the enclosure, his long fingers entwined around mine, I didn't feel alone anymore.

The monsoon rains had passed, leaving behind the dry October heat, and at the kitchen the cook handed us rare slices of juicy mango. I shared mine with Raja, and we lay on the sun chairs outside Mr. Prem's caravan, the juice dripping off our chins.

'You should stay under the shade, Elastic Girl,' Mr. Prem called from his caravan. He stood in the doorway and pointed to the parasols.

'Mr. Kalpak says I'm not ready to be the Elastic Girl.'

'Mr. Kalpak is like a potter. He can turn good pots out of poor clay,' he said, coming down from the caravan. 'But I'm the one who can turn dust into stars.' He perched a khussa slipper on the edge of my seat and raised his hands up towards the sky.

Raja began to screech and jump up and down on the sun seat, the mango juice matting together the hairs on his chest.

'I'll have to get him back to get washed before Sumi finds out.' I rose from my seat and took Raja's sticky hand in mine.

'That Raja is the luckiest guy around,' Mr. Prem laughed after us. 'He gets all the best girls.'

■ ■ ■

After the final show that night, Rupa asked if I wanted to come with her to a party. 'There will be music,' she said. 'Hilesh plays the sitar. Everyone says he sounds like Ravi Shankar.'

'Sumi wants me to help out with Raja.'

'You never leave that monkey's side,' Rupa said. 'It would do you good to be with real people.'

'What about Gloria? She'll wonder where I am.'

'Gloria will be there, too; everyone will be there,' Rupa said excitedly. 'Meet me at the canteen when you're finished your monkey chores, and wear something nice.' She disappeared out into the darkness, her long hair swishing behind her like a horse's mane.

■ ■ ■

Besides Diwali celebrations when amma would light a row of small clay lamps and dadi would let off a firecracker in the lane, this was the first real party I'd ever been invited to, so as soon as Raja was put to bed, I raced back to ready myself, dressing in the blue lengha amma had given me and borrowing a sweep of Gloria's powder for my cheeks. Making my way past cages of drowsy animals and towards the green cover of the canteen, my heart fluttered with expectation.

'You took your time.' Rupa appeared out of the shadows, and then she stopped and looked at me under the light. 'You look pretty,' she said. 'Almost as pretty as me.' She pulled me along behind her and up one of the dark aisles.

'Where is it?'

'It's over here.' She drew me in towards Mr. Prem's caravan. Outside, bunches of men were dealing out cards on tables, their faces clouded in a fog of smoke. Bose was among them, his face still caked in white. When they saw us approach, Bose and another man clinked their glasses together.

'Good, we have some nice young soothu,' Bose said.

'Where's Gloria?' I whispered to Rupa. 'You said she would be here.'

'She must have changed her mind.'

Looking around it was clear that we were the only females at the party, and suddenly my dress and red cheeks felt stupid and out of place. 'I'm going back.' I tugged on Rupa's arm, thinking of how Gloria had warned me against wandering around the circus late at night. 'Gloria will be cross.'

'Ah, you have come,' Mr. Prem called. He was standing in the doorway of the caravan, swaying slightly from side to side. 'I was just telling the men here about my Elastic Girl, a real star in the making.'

I pulled again on Rupa's arm, but she shrugged me away from me, lowered herself onto a chair, and began to repaint her lips, smearing them bright red. 'There is something that I forgot to do, so I'm going back now, and you should come, too.'

'Come inside first, and have something to eat.' Mr. Prem motioned behind him. 'Then you will make me happy.'

From inside the van came the smell of deep-fried vadas and lemon rice, and my mouth began to water as Rupa jumped up from her seat and nudged me forward. Inside, the table was no longer covered in files;

instead they were heaped around the floor, propping up empty beer bottles and overflowing ashtrays, and the table was covered in silver cartons full of all the foods I missed from home. 'Tuck in,' Mr. Prem said. 'No need to be shy.'

Rupa slipped in past me and settled herself next to Mr. Prem, who patted her hand and then reached out for a steaming carton of vegetable stew and offered it to me.

We ate together, Mr. Prem sucking on his fingers and then wiping his hands down the front of his shirt. He continued to top up his glass from a bottle of Imperial Blue. 'It's my birthday, you know,' he said, tipping his glass towards us. 'I've survived another year in this loathsome place.'

We stopped eating, and he began to laugh. 'Look at your faces,' he said. 'Don't you know that an old man can joke?' He pressed the glass against his lips and emptied the contents.

'An old *drunk* man,' came a voice from the corner of the caravan, and a man rose like a ghost from under a blanket. It was Hilesh, the fire-eater and sitar player. 'I must have fallen asleep.' He pressed his knuckles against his eyes.

'Too weak for your bottle,' Mr. Prem mocked, and Hilesh shook his head. 'The least you can do is to play our guests a tune.'

Hilesh reached down and withdrew the sitar from underneath his blanket. It was the colour of honey, and as he plucked at the strings one by one, a low mewing sound came at us, like a cat climbing upwards with all the time in the world. Then Hilesh's palms settled on the curved body of the guitar, and just when we thought it was over, his fingers began strumming again, the rhythm growing and growing, sputtering like rapid fire.

We clapped and cheered, and when Hilesh stood up and took a bow, Mr. Prem handed him a tumbler of Imperial Blue. 'You're wasted here,' he said. 'I'll call Kumar in the morning. Then you will be made.' Rupa looked at me and smiled.

Hilesh continued to play in the corner while Mr. Prem entertained us with stories about the great illusionist P. C. Sorcar and the other stars who had started out like us in the circus.

'Play your cards right, and I can do the same for you.' He reached over to run a finger under the curve of my chin. Then he pulled back suddenly and deflated into his seat, and Hilesh stopped playing the sitar.

'What is this?' We swung round to see Mr. Kalpak standing outside the door with his hands on his hips, staring wide-eyed at Mr. Prem.

'It's my birthday; why don't you join us for a drink?'

'They have no place here,' Mr. Kalpak said, looking at Rupa and me.

'*They* are my guests.'

Mr. Kalpak clicked his fingers. 'Come with me at once.' His voice rose at the end like the sitar. Quickly I made my way outside, but Rupa remained in her seat.

'Rupa, you must come, too,' Mr. Kalpak said. 'I won't ask again.'

'She doesn't want to leave the party,' Mr. Prem said. 'Some of us want to have fun.' He slammed the door shut on the caravan.

'God, shame you!' Mr. Kalpak shouted.

When we turned around, Gloria was waiting. She came forwards and slapped me hard across the face. 'Don't ever do this again,' she said, and began to cry.

'What about Rupa?' I asked, as Gloria pulled me back through the circus, my legs buckling underneath me.

'That girl would never listen; can't you see?'

Mr. Kalpak stormed ahead, his fists still clenched tight by his sides. 'I only wanted to hear the sitar,' I said.

Gloria stopped in her tracks, leant down, and pulled me towards her so that our faces were inches apart. 'Didn't I tell you that man is Ravana. If you listen to him, you will end up back where you came from, or worse.'

'What is it that I've done?' I asked. 'Is it because I borrowed your powder?'

Gloria didn't answer but continued to tug me along after her until we reached the tent. Mr. Kalpak was waiting under the night lamp at the entrance, a crown of white-bodied moths flitting around his head. He motioned for us to go in and then followed through.

'Come with me.' He pulled back the drape that led to his side of the room. His cane was propped up against the wall, but when I looked to Gloria, she simply nodded and turned her back on me.

My body began to shake, and my heart pounded hard against my chest as I followed him behind the drape. Mr. Kalpak made me squat on the floor before a picture of Rama, the god of virtue and self-control, while he lit an incense stick. 'I'm sorry.'

Ignoring me, Mr. Kalpak leant over and placed his hands on my head.

Closing my eyes and clenching my teeth together, I waited for the first thrash of the cane against my skin. Instead Mr. Kalpak began to pray, his voice flowing like a river, and underneath the weight of his fingers, the shaking stopped, and my body began to float upward, like a piece of paper in a breeze.

When he was done, he sat down beside me on the floor. 'You can open your eyes now.' When I looked up at him, he had removed his glasses, and his face had softened. 'Everything good begins with religion,' he said.

'You're not going to kill me?'

He pulled his shoulders back and rested his hands on his lap, palms turned up towards the roof. 'Muthu, it's not simply my job to make you a good artist,' he said. 'I've made a promise to protect you and teach you a new way of life.'

'What about all the other girls? What about Rupa?'

'It's impossible to help them all.'

I should have asked, 'Why me?' But I was too relieved to be alive, to be the one that he wanted to help. 'My grandmother always told me I was hopeless.'

'Not so; there is no such thing as hopeless,' Mr. Kalpak said. 'You will know this when you know the story of the great Giri Bala.'

As the crickets chirped time in the distance and Gloria's magazines rustled on the other side of the drape, Mr. Kalpak's voice began to flow again as he told me about the woman saint from Bengal.

'She has not eaten in over five decades.'

'She would starve without food.'

'Her nourishment comes from the finer energies, from within,' Mr. Kalpak said. He told me how the woman had received an apparition in the Ganges when she was only twelve, how from that day she learned to live without food.

'What does that tell us?' he asked me.

'That she's a saint.'

'That man is spirit. That the impossible is possible; you must always remember that.'

■ ■ ■

The Giri Bala would not leave me after that night. She came when I was sleeping, her long silver hair draped over one shoulder, a stroke of sandalwood paste between her grey eyes, and when I asked her if I would be a star, she nodded slowly and smiled. Each day I practised for hours with Mr. Kalpak until my body could fold neatly into a small glass box.

'You are nearly there,' he said.

But still Raja and I continued to perform our tandem act.

'How long until I can perform as Elastic Girl? The Giri Bala tells me I can do it.'

'Even the Giri Bala needs patience,' he said. 'Practise everything I teach you, and soon you will reach where you want to be.'

There was no time for playing with Raja in between acts, and each time Rupa invited me to join her for supper, I refused.

'It's rava idlis,' she told me one evening.

'They cause bloating, and Mr. Kalpak has told me to avoid wheat.'

'Then come and play; you can try my new cherry lip gloss,' she tried. 'It tastes of real cherries.'

'Only for ten minutes, then I must be back.'

We went through Rupa's box of lipsticks, blush powder, and hair oils.

'How do you have so many?' I asked as Rupa unscrewed the lid of a lip-gloss.

'Mr. Prem is very generous.' She instructed me to pout, and then dotted the gloss along my lips. 'Now press your lips together like this.' She pursed her lips tightly, as if they had been sewn together.

'Do you let him kiss you?' I asked.

'You watch too many romance films.' She returned the lip-gloss to her box and then rummaged around in it before triumphantly holding a plum-coloured powder up in the air.

'Gloria says he is like the demon Ravana.'

'Mr. Prem has taken me out of darkness,' Rupa said, sweeping powder along her cheekbones. 'He's going to bring me great things.'

When she was done, she popped the powder back into her box. 'You don't suit it as much as me.' She nodded towards my mouth. 'He says my lips are like a rising wave.' She ran off then, towards Mr. Prem's caravan, her hair flying loosely behind her.

11

By the time I'd been in the circus four months, my body moved like silk. 'It's strange, how I wanted to leave at the start,' I told Gloria.

'Shahrukh Khan said you *must* love your art,' she said, flicking a page in her latest magazine. 'Otherwise we would lose ourselves completely.'

'When I melt down into that box, it's like everything else disappears.'

'I've seen you practise,' she said. 'You're quite the genius, you know?'

'Then why can't Mr. Kalpak see?' I moaned. 'From tomorrow he's putting Raja and me on a Hula-Hoop act. He says that a chimp riding a bicycle is nothing special anymore.'

Gloria laughed. 'He's just afraid of letting you go,' she said. 'Once you become Elastic Girl, you will take off like a bird.'

'He says I need to work on my face, that my act requires *absolute serenity*.'

'He's your guru; you should listen.'

Sitting at Gloria's mirror, I examined my face: the same thin nose as my mother, the same round chin, and there was a stiffness in my face that amma always wore, as if she was waiting for something terrible to happen. As I breathed out suddenly through my nose, Gloria raised her head. 'I look nothing like my father,' I said.

'You're supposed to be practicing facial exercises to help you relax.'

Although I'd managed to put it to the back of my mind, my family had still not been to see me, and when I allowed thoughts of them to come, it was as if they were right there beside me: the clink of bangles on my mother's arm as she stirred the subji on our little gas stove, the heavy breathing exercises dadi performed each morning before breakfast, and the way amma massaged his feet each night, even when she was too mad to speak to him.

'Why don't you start with the eyes?' Gloria sat up on her bed. 'Try to lose that stare you have.'

'The house would be finished by now, don't you think? Safa and Belli are probably back living at home.'

'You could write,' Gloria said. 'Maybe that would set your mind at rest.'

'You could do it, write for me?'

'My writing's not so good, but I'll try,' she said. 'Anything to see that look disappear off your face.'

She fetched some paper and a pencil from the cook and set about writing a letter.

'Ask them why they have not come, and have they finished the house, and what does it look like and if Safa and Belli have their own room.'

'Not so fast.' Gloria raised her pencil in the air. 'First you must tell them that everything is fine and that you are becoming a great acrobat.'

'Why?'

'You must make them want to come.'

Gloria drafted a letter to my parents, asking when they would like to come to see me perform and telling them that they would get ringside seats.

'How long until we get a reply?'

Gloria wrote the plot number and address on the envelope. 'If it reaches them, then not too long. A week, maybe two.' She ran her tongue along the seal and then pressed it down with her fist.

'By the time they come, I will be ready; I'll be the Elastic Girl.'

The horn blew to signal the next performance. 'You can borrow my hand mirror,' Gloria said 'That way you can practise your facial exercises wherever you are.' She tucked it into the side of my leotard, where it could not slip.

At Raja's cage, Sumi was teaching Raja to roll through a hoop. 'This is your last night on the tandem,' he said to me. 'And soon you will be leaving us altogether.'

'Has Mr. Kalpak said so?'

'No, but I've a nose for these things,' he said. 'You are almost there.'

Throwing my arms around Sumi, I squeezed him tight, and Raja came and joined in.

'Off, off!' Sumi yelped. And then he showed me how to hold the hoop down low for Raja so that he could tumble right through. We moved like this, rolling our way across the ground, until we reached the end of the animal enclosure.

'I need to fetch a smaller hoop,' Sumi said. 'Stay where you are until I return.'

While he was gone, we looped our way back across the enclosure, and on his final dive through the hoop, Raja sprawled out flat on the ground and lay there looking up at Shanti, the baby elephant, who was being led towards the ring. He then jumped up suddenly and began flaying his arms about, drumming his fists down hard on his chest.

'Get the elephant away,' Sumi called, appearing now by our side.

'What is it?' I asked. 'What's wrong with him?' But Sumi was busy holding his arms out to Raja and hushing him like a baby.

Raja screamed and tore at the rail of costumes laid out for the show. He swung up off the metal frame on the camel hold and slammed himself down against the ground.

Shanti also got upset, flapping her ears wildly until a tar-like liquid began to flow from the lobes on the side of her head. 'She's getting ready to charge,' her keeper shouted as Shanti's trunk swiped him flat to the ground.

'Move her on!' Sumi shouted again. 'Or she'll bring down the bloody tent!' The keeper clasped Shanti's lead in his hand, and it took several helpers to haul her out of view, but Raja was still hysterical, his body convulsing wildly with fear. Sumi reached into his pocket and offered him a fig, then wrestled him down to the ground, but Raja wriggled underneath him, delivering a bite to Sumi's arm. 'Son of a bitch,' Sumi yelped, pressing Raja's head into the dirt.

Sumi continued to lie on top of him, until Raja began to calm down, his head lolling wearily to the side.

'What happened?' I asked.

'Stupid girl.' Sumi panted, gripping down on his bloody arm. 'Everyone knows Raja doesn't trust the elephants. He could have killed someone.'

'But nobody told me that Raja was afraid of elephants—only white people, Mr. Prem said.'

'Don't move,' Sumi warned as he disappeared off to have his arm dressed.

He had only just disappeared when a message came over the tannoy: *'Final call for the tandem act, final call.'*

'Come on, Raja; Sumi will be mad if we end up missing our performance, too.' Raja rose unsteadily to his feet. 'You scared me.' I dusted down his black jacket, and he shook his head.

When we took to the ring, Raja slumped miserably over the bars refusing to blow kisses to the crowd as he usually did. 'Come on, Raja,' I whispered as the crowd began to heckle, but he just sat there, staring glumly down at the floor.

Around in circles we went, the jeering growing louder in my ears, my hands sticking to the handlebars as I willed Raja to do something.

Mr. Prem appeared in the ring, accompanied by Samson, the Strong Man. 'Ladies and gentlemen, prepare to be amazed by this act of balance and power!' He boomed into his microphone. 'Never before has this been attempted!'

When he stepped back, Samson proceeded to lift the tandem up into the air with only one hand, Raja and me balancing up and down on either side. As soon as the bike touched down, the audience flared up, like an explosion of fireworks. Men and women rose up out of their seats and held children high in the air. It was a grand finale for the tandem act.

'Did you see them?' I squealed at Raja as we left the ring, but Raja slid from his seat, pulled his lips back tight, and trailed his way outside.

Pushing the bike out after him, I followed Raja as he made his way towards his cage. He climbed inside, lay down on the mossy bed and held his stomach. I stretched my fingers through the bars and tried to tickle his feet, but he just kicked me away.

'Please, Raja, what's wrong?'

When Sumi returned with a bandage on his arm, he took one look at Raja and pulled him out onto the ground. 'What have you done?'

'Mr. Prem called the tandem act.'

'Couldn't you see he was too weak after the fright he'd had?'

Raja was struggling to breathe, a rasping noise escaping from his throat.

'Help me, please!' Sumi called to passers-by. 'He can't breathe.' Sumi struggled to remove the bow tie from around Raja's neck.

Performers and circus hands rushed over, pushing me out of the way.

'It's his heart,' someone said. 'His tongue is blue.'

Through the gaps in the crowd, I could see them turning Raja onto his side. His face was twisted in pain.

'Somebody do something; he's leaving us,' Sumi called out again, but everyone fell silent.

Raja's arms fell limp by his sides, and his fingers uncurled one by one until his black coat stopped moving up and down, and everything was still.

Some of the women pulled chunnis down over their heads, and the men slapped their hands against their chests, but Sumi continued to kneel there massaging Raja's hands. 'My bachcha, my bachcha,' he wailed.

It was too much, but as I turned to go, Mr. Prem blocked my way. 'What's the commotion?' he asked.

'My only friend is gone,' Sumi said.

Mr. Prem pushed me aside and looked down over Raja. 'What happened?'

'She killed him,' Sumi whispered, looking up at me, his face wet with tears.

I tried to tell them that nobody had told me, that it wasn't my fault, but when I looked at Sumi, cupping Raja's grey face in his hands, my voice left me.

I ran away from them, racing away from them until I reached the base of the banyan tree. A screeching noise rose up from my throat, like the sound of Hilesh's sitar, and after it had settled, I climbed up wearily into the tree and clung on to the branches. Feeling an ache in my leg, I reached into my leotard and retrieved Gloria's mirror, the glass now shattered into tiny pieces.

When I closed my eyes I was back on the roof of our house in Ambattur. Down below I could see the toes of my grandfather turn up in the funeral pyre, puffs of thick black smoke drifting past my head. Grandmother spotted me, and pointed a finger in my direction. 'It's all her fault,' she said.

'You must get rid of it before the end of the show,' Mr. Prem told the men. 'It would be terrible for business.' They took turns digging a hole in the ground just outside the fence, their spades crunching again and again against the dry earth. When they were finished, they hauled Raja into a wheelbarrow and tipped him into his grave, laying a sheet of cardboard over his twisted body. They had filled in the hole by the time the audience streamed out, chattering and skipping past the mound of dirt.

Sumi came and sat beside the grave, Raja's bow tie coiled around his fingers. He did not hear me crying in the tree up above.

That night a vigil was held. A pundit was called from the city to read passages from the *Bhagavad Gita*.

'You should go and offer some flowers,' Gloria said. 'None of this was your fault.'

'Sumi said that I killed him.'

'He just needed someone to blame. Raja was only a baby when Sumi began to train him, so it's like losing his only family.'

'Then he will never forgive me.'

'Things will have settled down now. He will see that no one is to blame.' She threaded together a string of orchids and led me towards the animal enclosure.

The place was glowing with candles, and everyone sat on a white sheet beside Raja's cage, praying for his soul to have a peaceful crossover to the next level of his existence, their chants rising up like a song into the air.

Ribbons and cards were being pinned to Raja's cage, and women offered prasad on silver plates.

'See, it's all peaceful.' Gloria nudged me towards Raja's cage.

I reached up to hook the flowers over one of the bars.

'You have no respect,' one of the women said. She whipped the orchids off me and threw them down to the ground.

The pundit stopped reading, and the chants died away.

'No one wants you here anymore,' Sumi called from among the crowd. 'You're nothing but trouble.' Others began to stir, calling out for me to be punished, accusing me of killing Raja on purpose. 'She had bigger ideas,' one shouted.

'She wanted him dead so that she could become the Elastic Girl.'

Gloria pulled me away, tears streaming from my eyes as she led me back towards the tent.

'I told you that they wouldn't forgive me.'

'Fools! They will forget all this nonsense soon.' She held me in her arms until I fell asleep.

The following day the circus entered Teravih, a thirteen-day period of mourning. Everyone went about their business as usual, and the circus-goers came and went, but the cook served up only the plainest food, and there was no drinking or festivities. A hush had fallen over everything; even the animals seemed to fall into a trance.

Gloria had been wrong, for even after the thirteen days, they did not forget, and everyone except Gloria and Mr. Kalpak wanted to see me gone. Their loathing grew up like a bubble inside the circus ground, pressing down on me everywhere I went. At training the girls turned their backs, and when it was my turn to practise my act, some of them wrote 'khuuni' in the dust; murderer! The cook refused to serve me, and even Rupa and Tulsi had taken to turning away when they saw me approach.

It felt as though a heavy stone had been lodged deep in my chest. 'I think I'm dying,' I told Gloria. 'It must be my punishment from God.'

'You're not dying.' Gloria smoothed my hair. 'You're in mourning.'

'You must practise Niyama,' Mr. Kalpak said. 'It will bring you endurance in difficult times; it will help you find contentment.'

For a while I tried to listen, to meditate, but the peace I'd found in the circus had vanished, and it felt as though all my hard work had been a waste. 'It's no good,' I told Mr. Kalpak. 'How can I concentrate when everyone hates me?'

'Use your enemies to build your inner strength,' he said. 'It's only unpleasant experiences that teach us real patience and tolerance.'

In Raja's absence he put me on a new act with Samson, where I had to climb up a ladder and cling with one hand to the top as Samson raised it up into the air. Each time we finished our act, Samson would take the ladder away under his arm without looking at me. It felt that bit by bit I was disappearing, and soon there would be nothing left of me at all.

Gloria tried to reason with me. 'Keep your head down, and ignore them; it will all blow over soon enough.' But I began to shirk my exercises in the evenings, and now that Raja was gone, there was no longer any need to help out at the animal enclosure, so my time between performances was spent sitting in the tree studying them all. There was Rupa visiting Mr. Prem and coming back out with trinkets and sweets, and Gloria at the gates, sneaking in her film magazines from the Bayleaf Foods man. And I saw Bose slapping Tulsi around the head, girls turning dizzy to games of jalpari, and men playing kanchey with marbles on the ground. All of it filled me with gloom.

■ ■ ■

For three weeks I managed to stay out of Mr. Prem's way, fearful of receiving the punishment that everyone said I was due. 'You should be whipped,' one of the camel handlers had said to my face. 'When Mr. Prem gets his hands on you, he will beat you black and blue.'

But when I met Mr. Prem on the way to the wash pumps, he did not grab me or begin to shout. He stood very still, water dripping from beneath the towel that was draped around his waist.

'Have you been hiding?' he asked.

'I'm working hard, trying to improve.'

'You know you were so close, but now your contract is in great jeopardy,' he said. 'For something like that, you could lose everything.'

'Everything?'

'Your chance to be a star.'

'It won't happen anyway, not to me.'

'I can make it happen.' He rubbed a hand across his lower belly. 'Just come and see me anytime.' And he walked on.

When I returned from the pumps, Gloria was busy sewing a button onto one of her suits. I thought about telling her about Mr. Prem and about how I'd decided that I no longer wanted to be a star. But she would only tell me to wait, that it would all get better, so instead when Gloria went to fetch her weekly magazines, I snuck out behind her, carrying a plastic bag with the few belongings I had arrived with. As she chatted to the gatekeeper, I climbed up into the tree and waited.

Soon the Bayleaf man would arrive through the gate, carrying a box of supplies containing bags of lentils and tins of ghee and Gloria's *Stardust* magazines. 'Romesh never lets me down,' she had told me. 'All I have to do is smile.' When they were distracted, I would drop down off the branches and disappear, hitching a ride in the back of the Bayleaf van. But when the van arrived, it brought with it not Romesh but a different man.

'You are new.' Gloria's voice fell.

'That lazy so-and-so didn't show up,' the man complained, then quickly dropped the box down onto the ground and was gone, closing the gate behind him.

Gloria bent over the box and sifted through the contents, as I continued to watch the van moving off down the road and disappearing from Park Town.

My plan to escape had failed.

When Gloria had made her way back empty-handed across the circus grounds, the gatekeeper looked up at me, as if he had known I was there all along.

'You can go into the cage, but you are never sure that you will come out,' he said.

That was when I decided to visit Mr. Prem.

12

He was lying on one of the sun chairs in front of his caravan, one hand tucked underneath his head. His lips were pinched tightly around the end of a Gold Flake cigarette, and his eyes were closed as though he were sleeping.

'Hilesh is a big star now,' he said without opening his eyes. 'You can hear him on Radio Mirchi.' He nodded towards the radio crackling by his side.

Hilesh had left the circus shortly after that night in the caravan. He told Gloria that he was going to sign a contract with EMR records in Delhi and that he was going to make it big.

'I want you to make me a star, like Hopi and Socar and Hilesh,' I said.

Mr. Prem propped himself up on his elbow and squinted at me. 'I always knew you were something special,' he said. He spread his legs out so that he was straddling the lounger like a pedal boat. 'Come and sit down, and we can talk about it.' He flicked his cigarette down into the dust and patted the space before him on the seat.

Perching myself on the end, with my back turned towards him, I felt his knee slide down to brush against mine, making my skin prickle.

'Your hair is different.' He flicked the end of my ponytail with a finger. 'Glossy, like a movie star.'

Staring down at the pointed toes on his gold-and-silver khussa slippers, my hands gripped tightly onto the hard metal frame of the chair. 'If you can make me into a star, I'll do anything; I'll work really hard,' I said, my mouth now dry.

'Anything?' He sidled in behind me until I could smell his stale, smoky breath on the back of my neck. 'Why don't we go inside for some sharbat and talk about it,' he whispered.

Even though my heart was pumping inside my chest, and the feeling of his breath on my skin was making me shrink in fear, there was a moment when I almost followed him into the caravan, but then, across the yard, an animal roared, as though it was being poked with a spear, and my body jumped. Suddenly his knees came up, clamping me on either side.

'Not going to leave me just like that?' He hooked himself around me and turned my face up towards him, so that it was cupped in his hands. 'Just one kiss.'

When I tried to pull away, he pried my mouth open with his tongue, and the foul taste of onions and cigarette smoke made me retch as he moved his tongue from side to side. Then, holding me tight with one arm, he began to unfasten the hooks on my kameez.

I closed my eyes and I could see amma brushing flecks from my father's collar. Forcing the palms of my hands flat against Mr. Prem's knees, I broke his grip on my body. He jolted, then reached out to grab the end of my chunni, but I ran, spinning myself loose like a cotton reel.

'I'm not finished!' Mr. Prem called after me, the chunni now dangling from his hands. It was then that Mr. Prem started to chase me like a Bengal tiger. By my own mistake, I'd become his prey.

He was always there, seated in the back of the stalls while we practised our acts, reaching out to run a hand over my bare arms as I raced back from training, and every so often a small token would appear on my pillow as if by magic—lipsticks and nail polishes, similar to the ones Rupa had received. I threw them all over the fence at the back of the big tent and into the scrub, but at night I could swear that it was his figure creeping back and forth across the taut canvas of the tent, and my body itched, like sugar ants under my skin.

'Do you have worms?' Gloria asked. 'All this scratching is keeping me awake.'

'It must be something in this bed,' I said.

After all of her warnings about Mr. Prem, there was no way that I could tell Gloria what I had done; it was all my own fault, but I stuck to her like a tick, and when she had to leave me for any time, I hid inside the trunk beside my bed.

It felt as if I was going crazy. My mind wouldn't keep still, I wasn't sleeping and in my ragged thoughts, grandmother's voice rang stronger and stronger, as I remembered cowering underneath the table in Ambattur, listening to her cracked voice. 'That child is tainted,' she told my father. 'If you don't get rid of her, she will always bring trouble.'

Perhaps she had been right, for everywhere I went, bad luck followed me.

I went to Rupa's tent and begged her to help me. 'How can I stop him?' I asked. 'That man is everywhere I turn.'

She made a tight little laugh and flung back her hair. 'You're just imagining it,' she said. 'You have hips like a boy.'

'He'll listen to you,' I said. 'Can't you ask him to just leave me alone?'

'You think your little glass box will impress him?' Rupa began to pick at the flaking polish on her nails. 'Those things don't impress Mr. Prem.'

'I don't want him following me! I can't eat, Rupa. My stomach is sick every day.'

'You want to be a star like every other girl; I saw you sneaking off to see him, trying to worm your way in.' She lay back on her bed. 'They all try it, but Mr. Prem has made a promise to *me*.'

'Gloria was right – he *is* like Ravana.'

'He says I'm his flower.' She curled up on her side. 'Sundar Phool,' that's what he calls me.

'I don't care what he calls you! Just keep him away from me.'

What was I asking of Rupa back then? We were both children, innocent, stupid children who couldn't make sense of the world we were in.

And from that moment, Mr. Prem was gone from around me. Rupa had claimed him back I believed. She was his flower.

The itch disappeared from underneath my skin, my sleep returned and I was able to concentrate on my training once more. But good fortune wasn't my friend and my fate was conspiring against me again, this time in the shape of a letter from my sister Safa.

The letter had snaked its way on the postal train from Aunt Gounder's house in Tiruvallur, along the Chennai railway line. It had arrived at the circus and straight into the hands of Mr. Prem..

'Mr. Prem has a letter from your family,' Rupa sniffed. She had dyed her hair red and piled it high on her head, like Priyanka Chopra in the film *Micky Contractor*. 'He said you are to come and fetch it.'

It had been five months since dadi had left me at The Great Raman Circus, and I'd heard nothing from my family. A hunger rose in my stomach, like when I thought about my mother's missi roti. 'Tell him I don't want it,' I told Rupa.

'He won't be happy.' She hurried off in the direction of his caravan.

My neck and shoulder began to ache again, leaving me unable to practise my act.

'Like the Giri Bala, you need to strengthen your mind,' Mr. Kalpak told me, and each evening he had me stretch my way through a series of postures. 'Keep your breath steady,' he said. 'Through the Yama we will bring death to the lower self.'

While Mr. Kalpak instructed me on self-purification and control, I returned to creeping through the circus like a thief, afraid of Mr. Prem and still loathed by most of the circus performers for Raja's death.

'Another letter has arrived,' Rupa whispered during breakfast. 'He has them both locked away in the drawer underneath his bed, but will give them to you if you come tonight.'

'I won't go near that man,' I said. 'Why doesn't he send the letters with you?'

'He says he needs to see you, just to talk.' Rupa looked tired and was always messing up her routines. She didn't eat a morsel of the food on her plate. 'If you don't come he will blame me; he will say that I'm keeping you away.'

'Can't you fetch them from his drawer?'

'Don't you know anything?' She slammed her plate down onto the floor, the food splattering over her skinny little legs. 'He has no time for me anymore, he says I'm getting careless.'

The rest of the girls at the table were looking at Rupa now, muttering under their breath.

'You don't need him, Rupa,' I reached out to take her hand, but she pulled away.

'If he won't help me, I'm nothing. Nothing.' She walked out of the tent and didn't reappear at training after breakfast.

Mr. Kalpak was furious, threatening the rest of the girls that any behaviour like that would see them cut from the show.

In my selfishness all I thought of was the fact that Rupa was now out of favour with Mr. Prem, and I could no longer rely on her to fetch my letters. Day and night I tried to think of an answer, a way of getting my hands on those letters. Maybe the house was ready in Morai, and they wanted me home?

It was on my twelfth birthday that I received a gift from Shiva. Mr. Kalpak was teaching me about the concept of Dharana: the importance of focusing the mind on one single thing, and it was in Dharana that the answer came: I must fix my mind on retrieving the letters from Mr. Prem. He would not give them to me, so I must fetch them for myself.

In order to do this, I had to find out everything about him, including where he held the key to the drawer underneath his bed, so in my free time I hid in the branches of the banyan tree and watched him come and go. I saw him in drunken stupors and the lady from the brothel house visiting every Wednesday afternoon, and once, when I peered in through the window, she was sitting on top of him, her huge breasts shaking up and down like amber jellies. My skin began to feel cold and clammy, as the woman climbed off and Mr. Prem removed the jumble of gold chains and amulets from around his neck, using one of the keys attached to a gold-plated star to unlock the drawer underneath his bed. He removed from it a bottle of whiskey, but there at the back of the drawer, I was sure that I could see the sharp edge of an envelope.

The only other time he took off the key was when he slept, placing it securely underneath his pillow. Mr. Kalpak said that if I pictured what I wanted in my mind, then it would happen, so every day I practised Dharana, sure that soon the letters would be mine, and patiently I waited until Pongal, the festival of harvest. It was the only time the circus ever stopped. While girls decorated the entrances to their tents with vermilion and sandalwood paste and performed puja in the yard, the men feasted on bowls of sweet rice and gallons of moonshine. Outside the circus gates, brightly painted cattle were paraded down the streets; garlands of flowers swinging from their necks, and the city became dotted with fires as Chennaites burned rubbish to symbolize the destruction of evil.

On the final night of Pongal, I watched from my tree as men gathered outside Mr. Prem's caravan. Their voices were full of cheerfulness as they sang and whooped into the cool evening breeze, stopping every so often to pass around a bottle, but the more they drank, the louder their voices grew, and soon a heated argument and scuffle broke out over a game of Kachufool. 'You are nothing but a cocksucker!' Bose shouted at one of the men and then wrestled him down onto the ground.

Mr. Prem appeared in the doorway of his caravan. 'This is supposed to be a celebration,' he called out to them, and when he held up a bottle of his Imperial Blue, the men perked up suddenly. Bose held out a hand to his dazed opponent, and the party was resumed. The circus musicians arrived and set up their instruments: a dholak hand drum, a large wooden veena and tanpura, and a portable harmonium.

'Kattabomman Villupattu,' Mr. Prem called to them and a bony-looking man took his place behind the harmonium and began to pump the bellows with one hand and play the keys with the other, nodding at his companions to join in. As they played and sang the familiar Pongal ballad, all the men settled down to listen: it was then that I slipped from the branches and tucked myself in behind the tyres of Mr. Prem's caravan.

The chime of ankle bracelets broke through the slow rhythm of the voices and alerted the men to the arrival of women from brothel houses in Thiruvotriyur. 'At last some nice koodhi,' one of the men said.

Gloria had told me about the women: 'They come whenever there is a festival or celebration of any kind, all painted and polished like cattle.' The music struck up a pulsating rhythm, and the women formed a circle and began to perform the kummi dance, holding their hands in the air and clapping, some of them clinking together small brass cymbals.

While all across the city women were performing Arati to mark the end of Pongal, asking that the men of their house should prosper, the men inside the circus leant back in their chairs, ogling the women, hands reaching out from time to time to grab them around the waist.

'Old age is coming to that one,' said one of the men. 'She's no good anymore.'

'That one has nipples like raisins, a real nice Thevidiya.'

My legs shook underneath me as I watched Mr. Prem, who sat among them all, sucking on some tambaku paan. The chains around his neck jangled as he threw back his head and spat, lines of red juice crisscrossing on the ground. Every so often he would go inside the caravan, and through the window I could see him remove cigarettes and alcohol from underneath his bed.

As the night wore on the air became drunk, and men and women began to pair off. One of the couples made their way around the back, forcing me to quickly wriggle in underneath the bottom of the caravan. The frame wobbled as they thrust back and forth against the side, the man sighing heavily at the end.

Below me the earth scratched at my elbows, and the fumes of engine oil stung my eyes, but the closeness to my own breath was comforting as the drunken voices of the circus were stilled. 'When you were a baby, you were no bigger than a glove,' my mother had told me once. 'We used to keep you in a box beside our bed, and you'd never make a sound.'

'You dog,' the other men shouted as the man returned to the front of the caravan, and the woman resumed her dancing, skirt turning in circles around the ground. From where I lay I could see a smaller pair of feet appear among the women, the toenails painted candy pink. It was Rupa, and she was dancing her way towards Mr. Prem.

'Move, you mollamaari, you stupid girl,' he shouted, and then pushed her away.

'Won't you watch me dance? I can do the Bharatanatyam very well.'

'You don't have the coordination,' he snapped.

Rupa knelt down beside him and began to weep. 'You said I was a star.'

'You're nothing more than a dog.' Mr. Prem knocked Rupa to the ground and then grabbed one of the other women, leading her inside his caravan.

'Why don't you come and sit on my knee instead,' one of the men said to Rupa. 'We can play a little game.'

Rupa made to get up from the ground, and her gaze settled on me as I peered out from underneath the van. She blinked, rose to her feet, and was gone. It was as if she hadn't seen me there at all.

The air turned cold, and my legs began to cramp, but then as light broke in the sky and the last of the men staggered across the ground like lost lambs, the woman climbed from the van. I watched her slip away with the other women of Thiruvotriyur, out through the gates, and then I was alone with only the sound of my grandfather's watch, ticking against my chest. It was time.

The door of the caravan had been left slightly ajar, and I could hear Mr. Prem snoring. He was stretched face down on the bed, a cotton sheet draped loosely across his lower body, one arm dangling out onto the floor. When the door clicked behind me, he shifted slightly, and I dropped to the floor, edging my way to the side of the bed on all fours. Right that moment it all seemed so foolish, to think that I could just reach in under his pillow and fish out the key.

My thoughts were interrupted as Mr. Prem began to cough, great big hacking sounds raking through his body. He turned around in the bed, bringing his hand up to rest over the curve of his forehead. In that movement, the pillow was unsettled, and the clutter of chains fell with a clunk to the floor. I peered over the edge of the bed at his face; he was still sleeping.

My hands fumbled with the chains, trying to find the gold-plated star, and then with the small key, I turned the lock in the drawer. It was littered with papers and magazines, and feeling my way among them. My hand settled on a small bundle of letters tied with cotton thread, and in the crack of light, there was Safa's writing neatly penned on the front.

My heart soared as I tucked the letters into my skirt, but then Mr. Prem turned over onto his side, smacked his lips together, and opened his eyes wide, fixing them onto me like magnets. For an instant he smiled and then reached out to grab me.

The Bengal tiger had caught his prey.

13

When Mr. Prem reached out to grab me, he forgot about the trousers caught around his ankles and toppled over like an axed tree to the floor. There wasn't so much as a sound as his head hit the corner of the bedside table, and then he lay slumped between the bed and the wall of the caravan, his legs bent in underneath him, as if he was praying. Something trickled down the side of his face and behind his ear, like dark brown treacle.

My heart stopped beating as I stood there staring down at him, and even when I poked my toe into his side he did not move, his arms remaining limp, face turned into the floor. 'He's dead,' I whispered to myself. 'I've killed him, too.' With shaking hands, I knelt on the floor beside his body and began to fix things inside the drawer, closing it carefully and then setting the key beside Mr. Prem's open hand.

My head felt dizzy when I rose to my feet, and a wave of panic came over me as I clambered up onto a chair and hoisted myself through the back window of the caravan, desperate to escape. Dangling there, a light began flitting about my heels like a yellow-bodied dragonfly: the gatekeeper patrolling the grounds. Clinging to the van, I waited for his footsteps to disappear and then dropped to the ground.

Soon they would find me and take me away to be locked up, but time ticked by, and all I could hear was the hum of the circus generator, the rumble of traffic in the distance, and the noise of someone shoveling and scraping out on the street somewhere. Scurrying my way along the fence, I began to dig, clawing at the dry earth until my fingers were numb and the letters from Safa had been planted firmly into the earth, and then as morning light began to sift down across the circus, I crept back into the tent like a criminal.

Gloria did not stir as I removed the pillow from underneath my blanket, slipped below the covers, and wept. Finally I fell into an exhausted sleep that carried me back to Ambattur and underneath the little round table in my mother's kitchen. The lace cloth hung down low around me, brushing the toes of three pairs of chappals. Above me I could hear grandmother's voice as it rose up sternly. 'She's been touched by the evil eye,' she said. 'It was always in her stars.'

Then my father's face appeared underneath the tablecloth. 'Come,' he said, reaching out for me. 'It's time for you to go to Aashiana.'

Hands shook me as I struggled to get away. 'It's over.' It was Gloria, standing alone at my bedside and dressed in a shimmer of kingfisher blue. 'Muthu, it's over,' she said again.

'Over?' I asked, gulping at the air. 'They know?'

'You were dreaming.' She pulled back a band of hair that had stuck to the side of my face. 'Pongal is over, everyone is back to work, and you're going to be late.'

As we made our way towards the big top, I stole a glance towards Mr. Prem's caravan; the curtains were still drawn, the ground outside littered with empty bottles, and people moved about The Great Raman Circus, as though nothing was amiss. Men with swollen eyes dragged props behind them and into the ring, and inside the tent a band of women worked their way along the stalls with buckets of soapy water. 'Arre, look at those useless dogs,' tutted one of the women at the sight of the men. 'Their mothers' prayers gone to dust.'

For a moment I allowed myself to believe that it had all been a dream, but then Gloria reached down for my hand. 'Your fingers,' she said.

There was a layer of grit underneath my nails.

'Such dirt; what were you doing?'

'I needed to go during the night.'

'Why didn't you use the washroom?'

'It's too dark down there.'

'You should have awakened me,' Gloria said. 'You can't go around digging holes like some kind of animal.'

When we arrived at the ring, the girls were moving slowly into position, some of them stretching and yawning like cats. Mr. Kalpak tapped his cane impatiently off the ground, like the watchful gatekeeper. 'Too much time off has made you all idle,' he snapped at them. 'Hurry up and get in line.'

As the girls jostled into position before him, my attention settled on Rupa, who was standing at the end of the line. She had seen me underneath the caravan and would know that I was the one to blame, but she glanced at me only once and turned away.

'We are going to perform the human pyramid,' Mr. Kalpak said when we had finished warming up. 'It will be something new for the return show tomorrow.'

The girls perked up at once, and the ring filled with excited babble. 'This is our chance,' one of them said. 'I've seen the men during Janamashtami festival, climbing on top of one another, nine stories high to reach the pots filled with curd and butter.'

'I don't want to be covered in buttermilk,' said one of the others. 'So I will be the one to break the handi.'

An argument broke out over who should be the one at the top.

'There will be no buttermilk and no handi,' Mr. Kalpak interrupted. 'And there will be no pyramid if you do not stop this gabble.'

'So, who is to be at the top?' Rupa asked.

'Muthu will be the top mounter,' he said. 'She's the smallest.'

'She can't be trusted,' one of the girls said, but Mr. Kalpak moved forwards and began to measure the height of the girls against his cane, rearranging the line, biggest to smallest.

'You will be the under-standers,' he said to the sturdiest girls, directing me to the far end of the line, next to Rupa.

'Isn't it fortunate that you're so small,' she said, without looking at me. 'Now you get to stand on us all.'

'What do you want me to do?'

'Do nothing.' Rupa's face was full of despair.

Mr. Kalpak put us to work. The first three rows practised shoulder stacking, the faces of the bottom row stretched as they bowed underneath the weight. 'Balance your weight and look straight ahead,' he said to them.

Like a stack of cards, they kept folding one by one.

'It's useless,' they cried.

'Mind above matter,' Mr. Kalpak told them. 'It's been done before.' He had them rebuild it again and again, until they were four and then five rows high.

All the while Rupa and I stood there watching them. 'He's not always so mean to me,' she said quietly, her face flushed. 'Please don't tell anyone what you saw last night, how he spoke to me.' And then Mr. Kalpak whisked her off to join the pyramid.

When Rupa and the last of the other girls were in position at the top, Mr. Kalpak turned to me. 'Top mounter,' he called, and I carefully stepped my way up onto knees and into the crooks of elbows until I reached the top, settling my feet into the nooks of the shoulders below.

'Now hold it,' Mr. Kalpak called. 'Arms out by your sides.'

Just as the pyramid reached a point of completion, someone began moving down through the aisle, drifting like a ghost. As they moved closer, I could see that the person had a bandage bound around his head, pulling his face back tight so that he looked as if he was pushing against the wind. Only when he reached the ring did I see that it was Mr. Prem.

My legs buckled beneath me, and the pyramid began to rock. Squeals erupted, and one by one everyone toppled over onto the floor.

Mr. Kalpak rushed about pulling girls up. 'It is nothing more than a scrape,' he said as they sobbed and moaned about the pain.

'I knew she would ruin it,' one of the others sneered. 'Now we won't get our chance to shine.'

Gloria appeared over me as I tried to raise myself up, falling back in agony against the floor. 'Whatever happened?' she asked, looking out over the mayhem.

'It was a ghost.' I pointed towards the aisle, but Mr. Prem was gone.

∎∎∎

At Malar Hospital we waited for over two hours, fetid air falling around us in pools of sweat. By my side, magazines rustled in Gloria's lap, and Mr. Kalpak paced the corridor, his shoes making sucking noises against the sticky white lino. 'How's the pain?' they asked from time to time, and their voices echoed against the hospital walls. Every footstep and clank of a trolley rang out loud as people were wheeled back and forth through swinging doors.

'Try to sit still,' Gloria said.

Mr. Prem was just around the corner; I could sense him waiting for me. I bent down and crawled in underneath my chair. It took Mr. Kalpak and Gloria quite some time to coax me out, Mr. Kalpak warning me that I'd get gangrene.

My wrists had been broken in the fall, and behind a thin curtain, a puffy-cheeked doctor wrenched on each arm until I fainted. When I came to, a nurse was wrapping layers of cold dressings around my hands. She cast an accusing look over my nails. 'You've been up to no good,' she said. 'You can tell a lot by someone's hands.'

Once we were back at the circus, they confined me to my tent. 'You will stay here until you are better,' Mr. Kalpak said. 'I don't want to see you wandering about the circus.'

Most of my time was spent lying in bed, hands fixed heavy by my sides. Each time the drape dividing the tent flicked against the breeze, every time a shadow moved across the tent, my breath stopped.

'You've been talking about Mr. Prem in your sleep,' Gloria said softly. Her face was lined with worry. 'Did he do anything to harm you?'

'He's alive? It wasn't a ghost?'

'That man will never die; whoever knocked him on the head should have finished him off.' She bent down to feed me a spoon of rasam soup.

'They won't keep me in the circus now; I'm no use to anybody.'

'The body can mend.'

'It's my bad luck that nobody wants me, even my mother and father sent me away because I brought them nothing but trouble.'

'I'm sure that's not true.' She settled the bowl of soup aside on the dresser. 'They will write soon, and then you'll see.'

'They've already written.'

'You never said. When did the letter come?'

Lying there, staring up at the crease in the canvas roof, I told Gloria how Mr. Prem had tried to keep the letters from me and how I'd then stolen them back and almost killed him. 'When I saw him that time in the ring, I thought he was a ghost.'

Gloria began to laugh, one hand pressed across her belly. 'You're full of surprises,' she said in between her squeals. 'So small but a real fire inside of you.'

'You're not mad at me?'

'He's the only one who makes me mad.'

'What if he comes to take revenge?' I asked, jerking forward, and then suddenly feeling the pinch of pain soar along my arms.

'That coward would not dare to come here,' Gloria said. 'He will stay in his den, no doubt.'

'Will you fetch the letters for me? They are buried somewhere along the fence.'

'And ruin my fingers like you?'

When she returned that evening, she was carrying the bundle of soiled letters. 'What if there's bad news?' I said, as she propped me up against a pillow. 'Or if they've decided that they don't want me anymore?'

'Then they would not write at all.' She set the four envelopes out on the bed.

'OK, you can read one now.'

I watched as she slipped a pink fingernail in underneath the seal on the first, and then she settled beside me on the bed and spread out the letter on her lap.

'*Dearest Muthu,*' she began.

The tears slid down the sides of my face and onto the pillow as I pictured Safa bent over at a table in Aunt Gounder's house, the pen fixed between her fingers, her lips pursed together in concentration.

'*Your sacrifice has solved the trouble at Morai,*' Gloria read. '*Mummy and Dadiji have been able to find a home in Avadi.*' She wrote about the double-bedroomed house, with an attached bathroom and separate water source. '*Aunt Gounder knows the landlord and arranged a very good price.*' Page after page she went on: '*Dadi has got a job with Janaki Couriers, delivering parcels at night. Belli has passed her exams and decided on a diploma in beauty therapy at Molly An Institute,*' and, '*Next year I will stay home and do a coed course in English, while a suitable husband is found.*'

'See, they are all better off without me.'

'Better off *because* of you.' She folded away the first letter.

'Did they mention when they are coming?'

'Maybe in the next one.' She opened up the second envelope.

As Mr. Kalpak settled in for the night on the other side of the drape, Gloria worked her way through the remaining letters, her voice lowered to a whisper. We learnt about a dispute with the new neighbours over a boundary wall, about my father's boss, Mr. Begum, who had recently acquired a third wife, and about Belli's new stepped hairstyle. When Gloria reached the end of each letter, she looked at me. Safa had not asked about me or about the circus, and she had not said when they were coming to see me.

'Most girls in here never hear from home.' Gloria unfolded the final letter. 'You should be thankful that Safa took the time.'

The fourth letter was short and sharp but filled my heart like a balloon. 'Amma says you are too big now to be bothered to reply,' she wrote, 'that your head is full of wild ideas.'

'They think I have forgotten *them*.'

'And they *are* coming.' Gloria tapped a finger at the end of the line. 'They are coming to see you on February 8th.'

'How many days is that?'

Gloria counted it out on her fingers. 'Nine,' she said.

Straightaway I had her write to tell them that I was waiting, and then I made her burn the letters one by one. 'They mustn't find them now, or that would be the end.'

'You're lucky to have such family.' She pitched the letters into the little wood-fired stove we had been given for the winter.

'You have Arjun, and you'll meet him in Mumbai.'

'Yes, he calls it the City of Dreams.' Gloria perked up. She closed her eyes then, one hand resting flat against her chest. 'We are *both* lucky,' she said.

That night my mind was filled with thoughts about the new house in Avadi and about the taste of my mother's rotis. It was all so clear in my mind that I could almost reach out and touch the coloured beads on my mother's kameez.

■ ■ ■

For the next nine days, nothing could destroy my happiness, and as if my luck was finally turning, little gifts started appearing at my bedside each morning: plates of sticky jalebis, herbal concoctions wrapped in muslin cloth, and pots filled with white sprays of delicate neem flowers.

'They're all sorry now for treating you so bad,' Gloria said. 'Didn't I tell you that they would see sense?'

'Why now?'

'Your hands, I suppose.'

But something about the appearance of these gifts unsettled me; it was almost as if they had been set there during the night by a ghost.

'They are all from him, you know,' Rupa said. She had called by to deliver my evening meal from the kitchen and was casually stripping off the petals from one of the neem flowers.

'From who?'

'From Mr. Prem,' she said. 'He has sent them all.'

'Why?' My hands began to sweat underneath my casts.

'He said he needs you to get better, that you are no good to anybody while you are ill.' She shred the last petal from the stem in her hands. 'He's never given me flowers, you know. He's done with me now.'

Rupa continued to sit there, but I didn't ask her anything more. In two days my family would come for me, and then it would all be over.

14

Just as a ship rises on the crest of a wave, the following morning we were plunged back down into the depths of the sea, woken before dawn by the clank of hammers and the sound of hissing lorries as they reversed their way across the yard.

Above me Gloria pulled a pillow over her head and moaned.

'What's that racket?'

'We're moving,' she said, her voice muffled.

'Moving where?'

'The circus is moving on, that's how it is.'

For a moment I didn't speak but listened to the noises outside until I felt myself sliding down into the trough between two swells. 'We can't.' And when I tried to reach out to her, my arms pulled me back, like weights by my side. 'Go and tell them, Gloria, tell them my family are coming to Chennai.'

'It's already decided.' She removed the pillow from over her head. 'We're like sandpipers migrating for the winter.'

'They're to come tomorrow, February 8.'

'And we'll be gone, Muthu; there's nothing you can do.'

'No! I won't go; I'll stay here all on my own and wait for them.'

Gloria swung her legs over the bed and came to kneel beside me on the floor. 'We've got no choice,' she said, resting a hand on my shoulder.

'It's all written in our contracts, and if you don't go, your family will have to pay back all the money.'

'Mr. Prem tricked my father; he wouldn't allow it.'

Gloria pulled the cover down from over me. 'Come on now, you're being foolish. I'll help you get dressed.'

'Leave me alone. I'm staying.'

When Gloria began to pull me up off the floor, I bit into her arm.

'You little snake.' She tightened her grip on me as I wriggled and twisted against her efforts.

'Let me go!'

A cough announced Mr. Kalpak's presence in the tent, and when we looked up, he was looming over us with the cane in his hands. 'What's all this shouting about?' he asked. 'This is not a time for squabbles.'

'Muthu is upset about leaving Chennai,' Gloria told him.

'What's so special about Chennai? There are hundreds of cities just like it all over the place.'

'My family is coming tomorrow.'

'They can come to the next place,' he said.

'I won't go.'

Mr. Kalpak took a couple of steps forwards and lowered himself so that he was squatting beside me. 'Without the circus your family will be like rice paper in a monsoon,' he said.

'Dadi has a job now; he's a courier.'

'But it's the circus that is keeping them all afloat.' He stood up abruptly. 'All hands are needed in the move.' He ushered Gloria outside.

'Gloria, stay with me.'

'*You* will stay here and think about the teachings of Niyama,' Mr. Kalpak said. 'And when we are ready, Gloria will come and fetch you.'

The emptiness of the tent closed down on me until I was floating on a sway of the water, the current sweeping my lifeless body towards the open sea.

Outside, animals bellowed and roared as they were coaxed into boxes and trailers, and against the tent the shadows of the circus workers moved to and fro, fetching and carrying lengths of pole. And then through the gap in the bottom of the tent, I saw a pair of red-and-yellow khussa slippers. 'Jaldi!' Mr. Prem shouted as he hurried everyone along, and quickly I slid down onto the floor and underneath Gloria's bed. With my eyes closed, I could see grandmother's thick ankles as they rose up like tree trunks from soft black leather, straps hanging loose about her feet.

'Why did I have this misfortune?' she wailed. 'Why, why?'

It had been one month since my grandfather's funeral, and the house was still filled with gloom. Grandmother had instructed amma to remove all her coloured saris from the wardrobe, until there was nothing left but white, and Belli and Safa had stripped columns of coloured bangles from her arms, leaving only one thin bangle on each of her wrists. She tapped one against the top of the table as she spoke. 'If only that child had never been born at all,' she said. 'My Samir would still be here.' And my mother's silver chappals disappeared from under the hem of the tablecloth and slapped their way quickly across the floor.

'Bangalore,' Gloria moaned, returning to the tent. 'We're going to Bangalore.' I could hear her move about the room, packing up her little perfumed soaps and strings of jewellery. 'Hyderabad, Kattur, Vishakhapatnam, and still they don't move to Mumbai,' she said. 'It's almost as though they are keeping me away from him.'

When she was done, she came and knelt down at the side of the bed, dipping her head to look in at me. There were black smudged lines below her eyes. 'Come, Muthu, its time to go.' She reached in underneath the bed towards me.

'Wherever we go, I will run away,' I said, as she scooped me up into her arms and laid me on top of the bed.

'You know that's impossible; how would you survive out there? Where would you go?'

'I'll live in an ashram,' I told her. 'At least they will respect me there.'

'What about your parents, your sisters, huh? You talk as though you are an orphan.' Gloria selected one of the lenghas amma had given me and carefully lifted each of my heavy arms and passed them through the sleeves of the choli. 'Besides, you heard what Mr. Kalpak said; if you desert the circus, your family will be penniless again; do you think they will thank you for that?' Gloria smoothed down my skirt and returned to the job of collecting together everything we owned.

'We're worse than one of those caged animals.' I fell back onto the bed and began to sob. 'He might as well kill me now.'

'Who?'

'Mr. Prem,' I said. 'It's only a matter of time before he catches me.'

'Nonsense,' she said. 'That beetle will never do you any harm.'

'And what will happen when you leave? Who will take care of me then?'

Gloria stopped what she was doing and came to lean over the bed. 'You could come with me; when we reach Mumbai, you can come and work in the new show with me and Arjun, then we will both be free of the circus.'

'Promise?' I asked, my voice cracking.

Gloria placed a hand flat against my head. 'I promise,' she said. 'Together we will become real stars.' She helped me to gather up the rest of my belongings, and when we emerged into the midafternoon sun, The Great Raman Circus was gone.

Skeletons of tents were still being unpicked, but the big top had vanished, and the ground along the enclosure was marked here and there with the striped outline of absent cages. A red and yellow convoy curved its way around the perimeter of the circus fence: horseboxes, caged lorries, candyfloss vans, and long, narrow lorries with their hunched backs sheltered under thick canvas sheets.

At the front of the line sat a pickup truck with an advertising board pitched up on the back; it carried the name of The Great Raman Circus, written out in bold red letters underneath a picture of the Wheel of Death.

All around us performers and circus workers went about the business of repacking their belongings with ease, chatting and laughing amongst themselves while they tied together boxes of clothing and piled them into the underbelly of a battered-looking Falcon bus. When they were done, they joined the queue along the side of the bus, the air about them prickling with excitement as they inched their way towards Mr. Prem. I could see him standing at the front, one foot resting on the step of the bus, a clipboard in his hands and the bandage around his head now gone. The skin underneath my casts began to itch.

'What's he doing?' I asked Gloria.

'Head count.' Gloria tied together our bags of belongings and placed them snugly into the darkness of the bus. 'It's his way of making sure no one has escaped.'

We joined the back of the queue, my body shaking. 'What if he says something about the letters?'

'Just pretend that you don't know what he's talking about.'

As we grew closer to Mr. Prem, I could see a yellow gash across the middle of his forehead, turned up like a smile. My insides began to tighten.

'Name?' he asked without looking up from his clipboard.

'Mmhm, Muthu, Muthu Tikaram.'

Still he did not raise his head, but the corners of his mustache twitched as he marked his sheet with an X, and then Gloria pushed me forwards up onto the step, my skirt brushing against Mr. Prem's knee.

'No *Filmfare* awards for you,' Gloria tutted into my ear as she joined me beside the squat little driver, who was propped up on a cushion behind the wheel.

'We haven't got all day,' the driver said, directing his thumb down the aisle. 'Get a move on.'

The bus had been divided in two by a tattered grey sheet. The women and girls were crammed in at the front, some of the cooks balancing baskets of pakoras, puris, and spicy samosas like babies in their laps. The men stretched out across the back, some of them laid out on the double-decker sleepers.

'Always the same,' one of the women sniffed. 'They pack us in like chickens and give them all the space.'

'I've kept you a seat,' Rupa called out.

Slipping in past her, I tucked myself into the folds of a window seat. The covers smelt of dough balls that were beginning to sour in the heat.

'I'll be sitting with Shulisha if you need me.' Gloria nodded towards a seat on the far side of the bus.

'She's with me; I'll look after her.' Rupa smiled sweetly and dipped her hand into a bag of lime drops.

'Aren't you finished with him?'

'He's changed,' she said. 'It must have been the blow to his head.'

'How?'

'So sweet, so calm.' She held a lime drop up to my lips.

'That man won't change. Gloria was right about him all along.'

'You will see; it's like a different soul has entered his body.'

Suddenly Mr. Prem slapped a hand against the side of the bus. 'That's everyone,' he called to the driver, who promptly closed the door.

As the bus grated into life, he walked back across the yard and stepped up into a truck loaded with the rusty lump of a circus generator. He waved cheerfully out at the bus as it edged away.

'See,' Rupa said, nodding towards him. 'The old Mr. Prem has gone.'

The thought came into my head then that maybe it was possible for everyone to mend their ways, and as the circus wound its way out of Park Town, the itch on my hands began to fade away.

'Bangalore is the garden of India,' one of the women behind us announced. 'Full of greenery.'

'You are stupid, eh?' one of the men replied. 'It is high-tech—India's Silicon Valley.'

Arguments continued up and down the aisle as to what Bangalore would be like, and when my eyes closed, it was just like being on the bus with my parents, making our way to Morai, everyone full of excitement and hope.

'Look, look.' Rupa nudged me in the side. 'You're missing the river.'

As the bus made its way across the Kovum River, Sona, one of the ladies from Chennai, stood up and began to tell us all about the sights unfolding before us. Her hands moved about in front of her, coming up every so often to brush the side of her face where a birthmark streaked across her cheek like a slick of crude oil. Her parents had been unable to deal with the shame, so they sent her to the circus when she was ten. 'Her father didn't even ask for a contract,' Gloria had told me. 'They simply gave her away.'

'The high court and the post office,' she announced, directing us to the square archways and stained-glass windows. 'Anderson Street for paper, Govindappa Street for fancy foreign goods, and here at Parry's corner, it is fruit,' she said. 'Amma always took me here to buy the mangoes for her pickle.' Sona's hand came up then to touch her face, and she sat back down in her seat.

All along Parry's corner, butta and phalsa sellers handed over paper cones of purple and red fruits, sprinkled with salt and masala, and smiling children ran alongside the bus, holding up baskets full of sapotas, guavas, and papayas.

'They think we're famous.' Rupa blew them kisses, like a movie star.

As we travelled up past the lighthouse on the corner of North Beach Road, the salty air reached in to us, and everyone shoved their way towards the windows. Rupa leant over me, her arms reaching out towards the shimmering blue sea. Excited voices rose and fell as children tossed through the waves, the smell of crispy sundal and murukku making my mouth water.

'Look,' Rupa shouted. I followed the direction of her gaze up towards the flock of paper kites as they twirled and rolled in the breeze, but as the bus curved away from the beach and past the billboards showing Ravi Krishna and Sonia Agarwal, we reached the outskirts of the city.

Shelters with corrugated roofs and mud walls stretched out before us. Cows and dogs nosed through the garbage on the ground, and children with dirty faces appeared out of nowhere, bounding along the side of the bus shouting, 'Me, me!'

'What is it they want?' I said.

'They want us to save them,' one of the women behind me answered.

A silence settled over everyone as the Falcon moved on, winding its way dutifully behind the circus procession and out onto National Highway number four.

15

Leaving Chennai behind us, the driver began honking his horn as he trundled past the other lorries in the circus parade and past Mr. Prem with the generator.

'It's always a race with them to see who gets there first,' one of the women said, gripping the underside of her seat. 'They've no regard for our safety.'

'We will all be sick,' someone else cried.

But still the driver continued, banging a fist down on the steering wheel each time he succeeded in passing another circus truck. I could see him in the rear-view mirror as he threw back his head and exposed a mouth full of yellow teeth. Only when he was satisfied that he had reached the front did he begin to slow down, leaning back against his headrest and continuing to check his mirror every so often for any sign that somebody might catch him up.

'Now we are safe,' one of the women said. Heaving up a basket of food, she made her way unsteadily towards the back of the bus. 'You want some puri, some pakora?' she asked, peeping in behind the curtain.

'You got anything else on offer?' one of the men replied, laughter erupting out from behind him, the smell of beer already thick in the air.

'That will be fine.' Mr. Kalpak came forwards and took the basket from her. 'I will divide them out.'

When the woman returned to the front, she clicked her tongue. 'Their minds are like sewers.'

'Brains between their legs,' added someone else, and all of the ladies began to laugh.

The women carried on like this mile after mile, laughing and arguing amongst themselves about Indian men, and through the gap between the headrests, I could see Gloria as she leant forwards excitedly, laughing and slapping her hand against the seat in front of her each time a remark was made.

'That stupid olmaari spent so much time with the brothel women that he is not able to walk anymore,' one of the women said.

'Let's hope his poolu falls off,' Gloria scolded. 'That will put an end to his games.'

As the women began to laugh again, Rupa pulled me back down into my seat.

'*They're* the fools,' she sneered. 'You shouldn't listen.' She spread a hand flat against her knee and began painting her nails a deep shade of red, the bottle wedged between her legs, the brush working steadily despite the sway of the bus.

'They're only having a joke.'

'Have they forgotten that they are the ones who married the drunkards and the wife-beaters? They're no better than the women of Thiruvotriyur.'

'They've seen it all; that's why they say such things.'

'So, now they can look down on everyone else?' The brush slid from her nail and smeared the side of her finger.

'They're only passing the time.'

Rupa waved her finger about in the air, as if it had just been nicked. 'They have never liked me,' she said.

I knew that it was because of her comings and goings to Mr. Prem that the women disliked Rupa, but the mood on the bus was light hearted and I didn't want to spoil it. 'That makes two of us,' I said instead. 'Its their old age making them wicked.'

I nudged Rupa playfully in her side with my cast, causing the bottle of polish to slip from between her knees. It fell with a clank to the floor, the red polish spreading out like a pool of blood underneath our feet.

'See, your touch is cursed,' she teased, bringing her brush down to mark an X across my cast.

'Then I'm in good company.' The two of us fell back against the seat and laughed, our fits of giggles rising up every now and then as Rupa continued to mock the conversation of the ladies, picking holes in everything they said.

'Listen, they are disagreeing over the best way to make hari chutney,' she said. 'Some of them who have never even rolled a roti before.'

'A pinch of amchur; that is the secret,' one of them said.

'Nah, you are stupid; it is the lemon: one whole one, fresh.'

'Some warm water added to the paste.'

'You know nothing of cooking; no wonder your husband left you.'

Everyone fell silent, and Rupa and I turned together to peek through the gap. The two women who had been arguing were standing in the aisle, their hands reaching out either side to steady themselves against the seats, the one who had lost her husband staring down at the floor.

Shulisha, the plate-spinner who spoke only when she had something important to say, cocked her head. 'My parents were married for twenty years. She cooked, cleaned, and fetched after him like a housekeeper, and then he left her for my mother's cousin. It's nothing to do with chutney.'

They all slowly nodded in agreement as Shulisha curled her feet in underneath her and rested her head against the window. The two women in the aisle quietly returned to their seats.

'See, they are turning on each other,' Rupa said, twisting back to face the front. 'In all they have seen, they have learned nothing. I'll never be such a fool.'

Soon the scent of oranges filled the bus as a bag was passed out among the ladies, and while they peeled the skins and sucked on the juicy segments, a quiet camaraderie settled over them, so that by the time the driver pulled in at the town of Vellore, many of the ladies had drifted off to sleep. As the bus lurched its way into the car park, and the lights over the aisle fizzed into life, everyone began to shift and stretch in their seats.

'Thank Krishna,' one of the women breathed. 'We can finally get some air.' I could see wet patches at her armpits as she raised her hands above her head, and her light cotton clothes clung to her stomach and the gap between her thighs.

The few windows on the bus had served only to pipe more heat through so that the Falcon burned like a furnace, and many of the women looked as if they had been caught in the rain, some of them fixing back locks of damp hair and reaching down underneath their cholis to wipe pools of sweat from between their breasts.

'We must see the fort,' Sona announced excitedly, nudging her sleeping neighbour with the butt of her elbow. 'And the Golden Temple.'

'It's only for the latrines,' the driver shouted back at them. 'We have no time for sightseeing if we are to get there first.'

'We will bring you back some nice cold goli soda,' one of the women told him, pinching him on the cheek as she made her way down the steps.

The driver shook his head. 'Half an hour only,' he told them. 'Or I will leave without you.'

Rupa helped me into the chappals, which had slipped from my feet, but when I stood up, the floor almost gave way beneath me, so that she had to reach out and catch me from falling. 'Travel sickness,' she said. 'You'll feel like you're still moving.'

But there was lightness in my body, and my mind felt exhilarated, as if I had just run through a storm. 'It's the first time I've ever been this far, have ever left Chennai.'

'It's the start of a great adventure,' Rupa said. 'Just wait and see.'

'We will go quickly to the fort; it is the closest,' Mr. Kalpak announced as he joined us at the side of the bus. 'Everyone will follow me.'

In twos and threes, we wove our way after him, like a school of Ribbon fish. It was my first time outside of the circus since dadi had taken me to Chennai, and the feast of sounds and smells surged through me, bringing me to life: the smell of bidis drifting across from a group of construction workers who had congregated for their break on the edge of the car park, the swarms of black-and-yellow rickshaws whizzing past, the jasmine flowers, women haggling over prices of spices, and the aroma of fresh-roasted peanuts.

'Let's skip the fort,' Rupa whispered as our party came to a standstill at the side of the road. 'It will be nothing more than crumbling walls.'

Excitement surged through me as Mr. Kalpak led his followers across the road, and a truck rumbled its way over the crossing, allowing Rupa and I to break away.

'We've lost them,' she said brightly, tugging on my arm. 'Let's go.'

Mr. Kalpak was swallowed up into the flow of people on the other side of the street, his arms waving about over his head.

Rupa wove in and out between rickshaws and scooters, dragging me past stalls selling leather goods and carts piled high with coriander and spinach. It was as though she had been in Vellore many times before.

We arrived at a row of chaat restaurants.

'My mouth has been watering for some masala dosa,' Rupa said. 'I could smell them a mile away.'

Outside, ladies sat at tables covered in red-and-white cloths. They fanned themselves with coconut straw fans and sipped from steel tumblers of chai. We walked past them, continuing on down the street until Rupa stopped outside a crowded restaurant called Amiritha. 'This is the one,' she said.

A man seated at one of the tables, sprinkled his dosa with milagai powder and salt. Then he tore off a piece of the dosa, scooped up a mound of pickle, and popped it into his mouth. Rupa watched him closely, her teeth biting down on her bottom lip.

'We've no money,' I said.

'There's always a way.' Rupa pulled me on past the restaurant and in through a back alley. 'Just one thing; don't say anything,' she warned me, as we sidestepped bags overflowing with restaurant waste and a clutter of pots waiting to be scrubbed. A man was seated on the back step of the Amiritha, peeling a bucket of potatoes. 'We're the new girls,' Rupa announced to him.

The man looked up at us briefly. 'You're late.' He swung his legs to the side to let us through.

'How did you know?' I asked.

'My uncle ran a chatt house in Adyar; he was always losing staff. *Thieving bastards*, he called them.'

When we entered through the door, we found ourselves in a steaming kitchen filled with the noise of plates being scraped clean, cooks bellowing orders, and the sound of a bell ringing impatiently on top of a long stainless-steel counter. 'Where are the lazy dogs?' someone shouted, and then a face appeared over the top. 'Take these to table six,' he said, nodding down towards the row of dishes underneath the heat lights. 'Jaldi karo!'

'Just stay tight behind me,' Rupa whispered. 'Don't let anyone see your hands.' She reached forwards and lifted two plates containing masala dosas.

Just as we were about to make our way into the restaurant, the door swung open towards us. 'What do you think you're doing?' asked a waiter from behind a stack of empty plates.

'We're only new,' Rupa said.

The waiter deposited his plates into an overflowing sink, reached into a cupboard, and handed an apron out towards her. 'There are pots to be washed outside.' He nodded towards the door. 'Agency staff don't serve Amiritha customers.'

Rupa continued to stand there looking at him.

'Didn't you hear me?' He pushed the apron in her direction again. 'What's the name of your hire company? I'll ring them right now.'

'On the count of three we run,' Rupa whispered back at me, and all of a sudden, the plates she had been carrying crashed to the floor.

Customers looked up from their meals as we dived through the swinging doors and scrambled our way among the tables, some of the manicured ladies letting out pinched little screams. Out on the street, passers-by stopped to look towards the bawling waiter, who was waving his fists in the air.

'You bloody thieving dogs,' he shouted after us, continuing to chase us up the length of the street.

We ran until our chests burned and the shouting had been replaced by our laughter; it jumped out of me in thick, heavy bursts.

'Did you see his face?' Rupa gasped, coming to a standstill at the foot of some steps. 'Maybe we should take cover in here?'

She motioned up the steps to the front of the Ananda Cinema.

'They will be leaving soon.' I thought of Mr. Kalpak and his sightseeing tour.

'Just until that crazy man has given up.' Rupa pushed open the doors and led the way into the foyer. It was empty, except for some cleaners who were busy sweeping popcorn off the floor.

'They have all started,' Rupa whispered, and she drew open one of the doors along a corridor. In the darkness we made our way up into the stalls and found a seat at the back. On the screen Sunil Shetty was in the midst of saving Raveena Tandon from a gang of convicts inside a prison. 'It's *Mohra*,' I told Rupa. 'Gloria read about it in her *Stardust* magazine.'

Rupa shrugged, reached into the neck of her kameez, and pulled out two limp dosas. We began to giggle, and Rupa danced about in her seat until a man behind us pulled on her hair and threatened to call the usher if we didn't quiet down.

We were enjoying ourselves, and the spicy potato filling of our dosas so much that we forgot about everything, so when the lights suddenly came back up and the audience began to filter down the aisle, we both sat rigid in our seats for a moment. The bus was waiting to take us to Bangalore.

'They will kill us for sure,' I cried, as we pushed our way past the crowd trying to get to the door. 'We might as well not go back.'

'We will think of something.' Rupa wiped a line of masala sauce from her mouth.

By the time we arrived back, everyone was bunched up in groups around the near-empty car park, the men leaning over drunk in the dust playing a game of rummy, the women seated here and there on concrete benches, and the driver slumped on the steps, head in his hand. In the middle of them all was Mr. Kalpak, his back turned towards us, his head nodding as he spoke to two police officers.

'The waiter from Amiritha must have reported us,' I said. 'We'll be sent to a correctional centre, and no one will ever see us again.'

'Hush,' Rupa said. 'Say *nothing*.'

'They are here,' Gloria shouted. She came forwards and began to beat Rupa about the head. 'It was you, leading Muthu astray.'

'Let us deal with this.' One of the police officers drew a lathi out to his side. 'Empty your pockets,' he instructed.

Everyone crowded around us as Rupa turned her pockets inside out, and then mine. The officer examined the empty cotton lining. 'It's a criminal offence wasting police time,' he said, turning to Mr. Kalpak.

'My greatest apologies, but of course a good man like you would always treat a missing girl as a serious problem?'

The officer sniffed, nodded at his colleague, and walked away.

'What did you think you were doing, running off like that?' Mr. Kalpak asked me. 'You had me worried.'

'We got lost. We couldn't find our way back.'

'Not worried about me?' Rupa asked, a wicked smile on her face.

A thick wedge formed in Mr. Kalpak's brow. 'You are the one leading her astray,' he snapped. 'Now get onto the bus.'

'We were chased by two men,' Rupa said. All the women gasped. 'And they had knives.'

Mr. Kalpak steered me away from them. 'Don't ever do anything like that again.' He removed his glasses and pressed his fingers against his eyes. 'Anything could have happened.'

'You poor thing.' Sona came over to pat the cast on my arm. 'Such a shock for you to have.' She led me back towards the bus, where Mr. Kalpak was still standing with his glasses in his hand.

Back on the highway, the driver crawled along, having lost his place in the race, and for the remainder of the journey, Rupa and I continued to entertain the ladies with details about our close shave. 'They looked like crooks,' she said. 'Yes, they were wearing dark sunglasses and leather gloves.'

'Vellore is full of criminals,' one of the women said. 'Too many Muslims.'

'Thank God we are going to Bangalore,' another agreed. 'There are only Hindus there.'

In the distance, low, rocky hills spread out before us like welcoming arms, and I felt like Raveena Tandon—rescued, just when everything had looked so doomed.

16

Shopping centers stretching ten stories high and brand-new apartment blocks lined the dual carriageway leading us into Bangalore. When the bus stopped at traffic lights, we could see girls riding solo on their kinetic Hondas, hair blowing back in the wind, and clusters of stylish people eating and drinking outside a restaurant called Lemon Grass. It was like being on the set of a Bollywood film.

'Didn't I tell you? It's high-tech city; there is no greenery here,' someone said triumphantly.

Mile after mile we continued past walls of concrete and hotels called The Oberoi and Taj West. All eyes roamed longingly up the tree-lined paths and the polished marble steps.

'They have chocolates in the rooms and little bowls of figs,' Sona said. 'My niece used to work in the Taj Connemara.'

'For the fat foreigners,' one of the women spat.

'Amitabh Bachchan has probably stayed there,' Gloria said. 'He stays in all the best hotels when he is shooting a film.'

I was trying to imagine myself sitting inside the Taj West with Amitabh, sipping a glass of mango lassi, when suddenly the bus turned off at a roundabout and pulled up at a set of golden gates.

'We are here,' the driver said.

'It's a castle,' Rupa squealed. 'Why have you brought us here?'

'This is palace grounds, owned by the Mysore royal family,' the driver corrected her. 'This is your new home, for now.'

Rupa began to jump up and down on her seat. 'The maharani, we will see the maharani!' she yelped, and some of the other girls began to cheer.

A guard, who had stepped out from a wooden hut, began waving his arms in the air. The driver wound down his window and leant out to hear what he was saying.

'This is private access only,' the guard said. 'You're supposed to come around the back.'

'I missed the turning.' The driver looked into the Falcon's cracked wing mirror. 'The road is very busy, eh?' he said. 'You wouldn't want an accident.'

'Stupid man,' the guard tutted. 'You are all the same.' He directed the driver up towards the side of the building and through an archway. 'Follow it all the way around, and whatever you do, don't stop, or I'll have you arrested for trespass.'

The bus crunched its way up the driveway, winding past the freshly cut lawns, manicured hedges, and neat little beds of exotic flowering plants.

'Didn't I tell you—the garden of India?' one of the ladies returned to her friend.

Faces were pressed against the bus windows as we made our way past ivy-covered towers and along the west wing.

'Look, see the lamps hanging from the ceiling and the red velvet curtains,' someone cried.

'But where's the maharani?' Rupa asked.

The bus made its way underneath a stone arch at the side of the building and followed the path past a cluster of houses, where women sat in doorways washing pots and churning butter. Some of them pulled the end of their sari pallu up over their mouths to guard against the belch of fumes from the bus.

'We are the last ones here,' the driver said glumly, as we pulled into a car park. He reversed into a gap, beside Mr. Prem's generator truck and it felt as if I'd fallen to the ground out of a peaceful sleep.

'You are on foot from here.' The driver nodded towards the gardens beyond.

'We're not staying in the castle?' Rupa asked, and all of the ladies laughed.

'You're so full of foolish ideas,' one of them said. '*We* must return to our cage.'

A shudder ran through me as everyone began to unpack bags from the bus. 'This place gives me a bad feeling,' I said to Gloria.

'Don't be so silly; we've never performed anywhere as grand as this.' She began hunting through the upturned muddle of bags.

'The Rolling Stones played here,' one of the men announced, 'and Elton John.'

'We'll all be famous,' Sona said. 'Everyone will hear about us now.'

We made our way through a narrow tree-lined passageway, which was overhung with pink-and-yellow shala flowers. The men led the way, the air around them thick with the smell of stale beer, some of them staggering as they tried to balance belongings on their shoulders. 'Hurry up,' one of the women urged. 'You are slower than a leatherback turtle.'

All of a sudden, from amid the trees, the lush palace grounds spilled out before us, stopping us dead in our tracks. There were rockeries, vast ponds, and dense beds of hyacinths and amaryllis, and there amongst all of it were the red and white stripes of the big top, spread out across the ground.

Some of the girls, including Rupa, broke away from the group and began to run, bounding across the grass like newborn lambs, whooping and cheering into the open space. It was their last breath of freedom before the grind of the circus would begin again.

'Come on!' Rupa shouted back at me, but I wasn't in the mood to join in, for my eyes were fixed on Mr. Prem in the distance, standing with his hands on his hips.

'Look, he's waiting on me,' I whispered to Gloria. 'He hasn't forgotten what happened after all.'

'He's angry because we are late.'

By the time we arrived at the big top, Mr. Prem was hammering stakes into the ground around the perimeter of the canvas. 'Where have you been?' he barked. 'This circus cannot build itself.'

'There was an accident,' Mr. Kalpak piped up. 'A stray camel on the road.'

'We'll have to work through the night,' Mr. Prem snapped. 'No one will stop until everything is done.'

Everyone was assigned tasks—unpacking, attaching ropes, hauling materials, cleaning out cages and tending animals—but with my hands, there was nothing for me to do.

'You're lucky; because I'm a trapeze artist, I have to fasten the top to the stakes.' Gloria nodded towards the men who were positioning the canvas of the big top over its metal frame. 'Those loops are tricky, and if anyone lets go of a pole at the bottom, it would all come down.'

'I'll keep an eye on them for you,' I said. 'I'll shout if I see the slightest shake.' I settled down outside on a straw chappa and watched Gloria climb up nimbly onto the big top. It was a slow job, and soon my head grew heavy, and my gaze drifted to the castle on the embankment, the yellow light seeping out from majestic windows and up against the walls, making it twinkle like a brass lantern.

Amma's arms were wrapped around me, her voice singing softly into my ear. We were in Ambattur again, and since grandmother had returned to Pondicherry, amma had taken to sleeping with me each night, her body curved in against mine.

'Where is Aahnaji gone?' I asked her.

'Don't worry; you've done nothing wrong,' she said, and I could feel her begin to shake.

'Some good you are,' Gloria was shouting at me. 'I could have been left paralysed.'

'Did you fall?'

'No, but if I had, it would have been thanks to you.'

A fire had been lit across from me, and some of the ladies were sitting up around it, cradling mugs of tea, their weary bodies folded over their knees. Beyond them tents appeared to have mushroomed out of the earth overnight, and the animal handlers were leading the horses and camels out to get washed.

'I'm going to have some rest,' Gloria said. 'In a few hours we will have to perform.'

'Wait for me,' I said, rising up from the ground and rolling up the chappa.

'Mr. Prem has put me with Shulisha,' she said. 'You are with all the other girls in the big one over there.' She pointed towards a long, narrow tent at the edge of the circus.

'But you must stay with *me*,' I said, following her across the yard, my heart beating hard in my chest.

'There are new girls starting this week,' she said, sweeping open the covering on a tent. 'They will keep me busy.' She began to open her belongings, pulling clothes out onto the floor, arranging her soaps on top of her dressing table.

'What if he comes?'

'I've left your things in your tent; you're the first bed on the left.'

'Is it because I fell asleep?'

'I'm no longer responsible for you,' she said.

'You said you would look after me.'

'If I don't do as he says, he will take my job away, and I will never see Arjun again.'

'Why would he do that?'

'You need to be careful,' she said, bringing her hand down on my shoulder.

'Careful of him?'

'Promise me, Muthu, that you will stay away from him and never go anywhere alone.'

My body began to shake, and I sank down onto the floor. 'Why couldn't I have stayed in Chennai? My family would be taking me home by now.'

Gloria came and knelt beside me. 'There will always be Mumbai,' she said. 'That's still my promise.'

We walked back across the grounds until we reached the other tent, and then Gloria poked her head in through the opening. 'There are others here,' she said. 'You will be OK.' She turned and left me there, her head wilted towards the ground.

Inside, the tent was set out with a row of low beds on either side, each one accompanied by a Jali trunk and a small gas lamp. Some of the trunks had been decorated with garlands of flowers and photographs, and on the bed nearest to me lay my two bags of clothes. 'So, she has abandoned you, too?' Rupa called out. She was lying flat on the bed next to mine, her toenails freshly painted in a bright shade of pink.

'Gloria hasn't abandoned me.'

'You're too much for her,' Rupa said, raising one foot into the air and wriggling her toes. 'It was the same for me.'

Turning my back on her, I sat on the edge of the bed and began fumbling with the strings on my bags, unable to open them with my hands.

'Don't worry,' Rupa said, coming to sit behind me. 'You have me now.' She began to unpack my clothes, folding each item carefully and placing them into the Jali trunk. 'Just think of all the fun we can have!'

'Did Gloria tell you about Mumbai? Did she promise you that?'

'What about it?' Rupa sneered. 'She's probably hoping to get picked up by a big movie boss, just like everyone else!'

My breath steadied. Gloria had promised Mumbai only to me; she would not let me down.

■ ■ ■

Rupa was in the middle of painting my nails when Mr. Kalpak appeared at the opening of the tent. 'What's going on?' he asked. 'Don't you know there is a show to put on?' he said to Rupa. 'Mr. Prem has been looking all over for you.'

'He has?' she said cheerfully, and Mr. Kalpak tutted.

'Akshi has had an accident during training, so you are needed for the wheel,' he told her. 'I'll wait.' He stepped back outside. We could see him through the canvas as he began to pace.

'I'll tell him that you were with me, that I had to look after you,' Rupa said, as she slipped into her leotard.

'No, don't mention me. Tell him that you had fallen asleep; tell him something else.'

'He's a changed man,' she said, pulling back her hair into a comb. 'You will see.'

Outside, Mr. Kalpak scolded Rupa. 'You should have heard the siren,' he said. 'But you have never been one to listen—even to the loudest warnings.'

Rupa ran off then. 'I'm good with danger!' she shouted back at him. 'That is why you put me on the wheel.'

Mr. Kalpak stood there for a moment with one hand raised to his cheek.

'*You* must come, too,' he called back in to me. 'We have work to do.'

I followed Mr. Kalpak across the lawns, my legs struggling to keep up with his long strides, and when we reached the edge of the pond, he stopped. 'For all my teaching, you have learnt nothing,' he said. 'You need to be cleansed.'

The soft, moist grass curled between my toes; it reminded me of winter in Ambattur, the trees dense with leaves, grass sprouting everywhere, and the air filled with the sweet smell of jasmine and gundu mallis. It would be a good place to die.

'You two lied in Vellore,' he said. 'There were no crooks.'

When I looked up at him, my face burned with shame. 'How did you know?'

'Your face—it gives everything away,' he said.

'Then why were you so worried?'

'I will always worry.' He looked away. 'See that little myna?' He pointed at a brown-bodied bird that was perched on the end of a low-lying branch. Its black-hooded head bobbed up and down towards its reflection in the water. 'That bird belongs to the woodlands of India, but it has travelled all the way across the world, settling in places like Australia and Singapore.' He held his hand out before him. 'It's no bigger than my palm, but it has the resilience of any man.'

We stood there, watching the myna as it fluffed its feathers and continued to bob up and down, whistling and clicking in time.

'Do you think that everything that happens is set out for us, like Karma?' I asked. 'From before we are even born?'

'That is what we are all about,' Mr. Kalpak said. 'It is written in the *Gita*; for death is certain to one who is born; to one who is dead, birth is certain; therefore, thou shalt not grieve for what is unavoidable.'

'I am not a myna; I was not born to fly,' I said. 'My grandmother said I should never have been born at all.'

Mr. Kalpak turned suddenly and made his way up the bridge that was perched across the pond. 'Your fate has not been decided by her but by someone much greater,' he said. 'And if you want it bad enough, you can be the myna bird of Chennai.'

'But everything keeps coming back to me, reminding me of how useless I am.'

'You're plagued with hindrances,' he said briskly.

Up on the curve of the bridge, I leant over until I could see my thin reflection staring back at me. 'Sometimes it feels as though I *am* made of elastic,' I said. 'That I'm not a real girl at all.'

'You must practise Vinyasa,' Mr. Kalpak said. I could hear his feet shuffle against the bridge. 'If you practise every day, and stay away from trouble, then we will see who you are.

'How long?' I straightened myself and turning towards him. 'How long until I can become the Elastic Girl for real?'

'Strengthen your mind, and everything else will follow,' he said. 'Watch me.'

I stood opposite him, my face turned up towards his. He took a steady intake of breath and then spun it out like golden thread through his lips. 'Now you,' he said.

We practised together, breathing in and out with a mirrored rhythm until the circus, the palace, and the gardens around us disappeared, and I was Bhoodevi, the earth goddess, being raised up gently by the mighty Emusha from the ocean floor.

17

'You are ready now,' Mr. Kalpak said as we made our way back in a rickshaw from Manipal Hospital. 'Your apprenticeship is over.'

I looked down at my hands. The skin underneath my casts had grown dry and scaly. 'There isn't enough time; these arms feel like they don't belong to me anymore.'

'You have practised ashtanga for four weeks now; a strong mind means an able body.'

'I've forgotten everything; all the things from training—the positions, the moves.'

'You're panicking,' he said, turning to look out the little window.

With each bump on the road, my stomach rolled and lurched. 'Maybe we should wait a little longer; just until they have strengthened again.' I held my white hands out before me.

'In one week you will debut as the Elastic Girl,' he said. 'This is what you have wanted, and now there is no more waiting.' He poked the driver in the back of the shoulder. 'You are as slow as cold molasses,' he shouted at him. 'Don't you know that we have urgent things to do?'

I had to dig my nails down into my hands to stop myself from being sick, and by the time we arrived at the grounds, my legs had grown as weak as lemon whip so that I was barely able to make it to the tent.

'He says it's time for me to perform,' I told Rupa, collapsing onto the bed. 'I'll look like a fool.'

She came to sit on the side of the bed and wrapped her arms around me so that she was lying with her cheek pressed against the back of my head. 'Don't you see; we *can* become stars.' A lock of her hair fell down around my face.

The smell of Rupa's hair is with me even now: sandal rose shampoo.

'Has he asked you to perform as well?' I asked.

'*You* this time, but soon it will be me,' she said. 'Mr. Prem has always said that we would both be stars, and now it's starting to come true.'

There were only six days left until I had to perform, so the following day I returned to training.

'Mr. Kalpak said you must be there by seven,' Gloria said, running a comb through my hair.

'What if I let him down?' I asked. 'What if I let everyone down?'

'Mr. Kalpak wouldn't let you fail.'

'But it's what I always do: let people down.'

She turned me around in the chair so that I was facing her. 'It's not possible; Mr. Kalpak knows when everything is in place.'

When we reached the ring, Mr. Kalpak had not yet arrived, and a handful of girls sat in twos and threes on the ground, Rupa amongst them. 'Didn't I tell you?' she exclaimed as we arrived. 'Didn't I say she was coming back?'

The girls rose up from the ground and huddled around me.

'Good luck,' Gloria called, as she pushed her way out between them. 'Try not to break anything this time.'

'They look like eggplant,' one of the girls sniffed, pushing her finger into the rubbery flesh of my arm.

'How will they be able to move like before?' someone else asked.

'You will soon see.' Rupa pulled me away. 'These girls will never amount to anything; they have minds like empty leaves.'

Mr. Kalpak, whom I had only ever seen wearing plain-coloured dhotis and shirts, arrived at the ring wearing a deep-red kurta suit. He looked around at the girls, and when he spotted me, he raised his cane up slightly in the air. 'Ah, we are all here,' he said.

'He looks like a sadhu,' Rupa giggled. 'All his meditation has gone to his head.'

The girls began to gather before him. 'Is it true that Muthu is going to perform?' one of them asked.

'We were all here before her,' another complained.

'Deities never favour the lazy and indolent.' He pointed his cane for them to get in line. 'When you stop being idle and learn to focus your mind, then you might have success.'

The girls shuffled into position, their heads dipped like dogs to the floor, and then one by one Mr. Kalpak began to call on them to perform. Strain creased its way across their faces as they tried their hardest to jump and bend and turn, just as Mr. Kalpak instructed them, but still he managed to find fault in everything.

'*We* will never be good enough for him,' one of the girls grumbled to her friend. 'It's the colour of her skin.'

For a moment I looked down at my pale arms and wondered why it was that Mr. Kalpak had chosen *me*. They had all advanced, and some of them were only one step away from being faultless; even Rupa was no longer skipping rope but walking over one with her arms outstretched, yet Mr. Kalpak continued to criticise. 'Your head is still too low,' he told her. 'You must look straight ahead.'

'Whatever he tells me now, I will do,' she said, returning to my side. 'It has worked for you.'

'But why me? Why has he decided to pick me?'

Rupa did not have time to answer. 'The Elastic Girl,' Mr. Kalpak called out, the words blooming up into the air.

The girls nodded at one another, and suddenly it felt like that first day in the circus, when I had humiliated myself in front of everyone. Stepping forwards it was as though the entire big top was tilting away from me, and I began to sway.

Mr. Kalpak placed a glass case on the ground before me. 'Go ahead,' he said. 'You know what to do.'

Closing my eyes I began to breathe just as Mr. Kalpak had shown me, until there was only me, and the sound of the air whistling against my lips. I thought of the myna bird, which had since disappeared from the pond, and imagined it settling into the eaves of some high building on the other side of the world. My body melted down into the case, pouring into each corner like a pot of Kejriwal honey.

When Mr. Kalpak released the lid, I unfurled myself until I was standing upright again. The girls looked at me with wide eyes, the pinched look now gone from their faces.

'You disappeared,' someone said. 'One moment you were here, and then you were gone.'

Mr. Kalpak just stood there with his lips pulled tight, making me wait for his words of criticism to bite at the air. Instead he began to clap, and then others joined in until everyone was clapping, and the sound spun around my ears, like a thousand myna birds flapping in the air.

'You did it,' Rupa cheered. 'We are on our way.'

■ ■ ■

From that moment, Mr. Kalpak fussed over me like a father about to send his first-born son out into the world, and each day he had a new list of instructions for me:

'Even though you can't see them, remember to smile.'

'Drink only ginger tea.'

And 'rub this into your arms and legs every night.' He gave me a bottle of Brahmi oil. He guided me step by step on how to walk into the ring, which way to bow, how long to hold each move. His devotion to perfecting my performance was exhausting.

'You'd think no one had ever performed for the first time before,' Rupa said.

Everyone was talking about the Elastic Girl, and my head was filled with a new belief in myself, the notion that success was just around the corner. By the night of my performance, I couldn't sit still.

'You're making me dizzy,' Gloria said. She had come to help me prepare and had brought me a suit the colour of the Bay of Bengal, swirls of green and blue circling out from the bodice like a storm, the arms splashed with silver sparkles. 'I wore this for my first show; it will bring you luck.'

Everyone stood around in the tent and admired me. 'When it's my turn, I will wear red,' one of the girls said.

'Pink: it brings out my skin,' said another.

They reached out every so often to touch my arm or pat my head, as if I had become a Devi to be worshipped.

All the attention brought on a bout of nerves. 'I'm shaking,' I told Gloria as she braided my hair with a ribbon.

'Me too.' She squeezed my hand.

Beside us a ripple of laughter broke loose. Gloria had become guardian to two new girls from Nepal, who couldn't speak any Tamil or Hindi but followed Gloria around like silent shadows. The girls sat on the edge of the bed watching me closely. They didn't wear any chappals on their feet and their arms and legs were as pale and skinny as candlesticks. When the siren belted out across the yard, they jumped, and then began to laugh again.

'What do they find so funny?' I asked Gloria.

'Just like all of us at the start, they think they have been saved,' Gloria said. 'They think the circus is the answer to their prayers.'

Gloria led me across to the big top, her arm linked in around mine, and behind us the Nepalese girls bounded along like excited pups. When we reached the tent, they came and pressed their hands together before me. 'Good luck, Elastic Girl,' they chimed.

'Can't you make them go away?' I asked Gloria, but when Mr. Kalpak appeared through the opening in the tent, the girls scarpered.

'What took you so long?' he barked, pulling us through into the tent and bouncing from one foot to another. 'You are up after two more acts.'

Inside the big top, Sumi was performing the Hula-Hoop act with his new chimpanzee called Yashvir. He was a big brute of a thing with a glum-looking face, and when Sumi held the hoop to the floor, Yashvir just sat there scratching at his chest until a fig was held out before him. The chimp tumbled awkwardly through the hoop, sprawled out flat on the ground, and then reached up to snatch the treat from Sumi's hand. The audience in the stalls clapped indifferently, and Sumi just stood there looking down at Yashvir, as though he didn't know what to do.

'I can't look,' I said, turning my head away.

'It will be over soon,' Gloria said, misunderstanding what I meant. 'The first time is always the hardest.' She removed my arm from hers and took to the ring, replacing Sumi and Yashvir, who had disappeared into the darkness at the back.

Gloria moved like a cat, swaying her body into position in the middle of the ring, her head held up in the air so that when she turned around, she was looking straight out into the audience. As she waited for the trapeze bar to be lowered from the roof, the echo of 'shanti, shanti' sang out across the music system, and then, settled on the bar, she began to float up into the air. Suddenly she flicked herself around the seat and then dropped like a stone, until she was hanging from the bar by her toes.

The audience rose up like a wave, and a rod of terror pierced through me, pinning my feet against the floor.

'It wasn't your fault.'

It was Sumi, behind me, Yashvir now gone.

'Raja had a mind of his own, not like that other one, who has no mind at all.' He nodded towards the back of the tent and the animal enclosures.

'I shouldn't have made him perform.'

Sumi reached out and pressed Raja's black bow tie into my hand. '*Raja* means hope, you know,' he said, nodding towards the ring. 'Now it's your turn.'

Gloria was taking a bow, her fingers dipping down to the floor.

'Just breathe,' Mr. Kalpak whispered.

When I turned around, Sumi was gone.

'Prepare to be amazed,' Mr. Prem boomed through his microphone. 'In all of India, you will find nothing that compares to the skill of the Elastic Girl.'

A couple of circus hands began positioning the glass box on a raised wooden platform in the centre of the ring.

'They are waiting,' Mr. Kalpak said, nudging me forward. 'It is all yours.'

Somehow I found myself standing over the box, not knowing how I'd reached that far, and then all about me went black. Someone coughed, a baby screeched, and then a beam of light swooped down over me as I squeezed my fingers around Raja's bow tie.

With my eyes closed, I was in Palace Gardens again, stepping down into the glassy pond, water rattling in my ears as my body sank down beneath me, and everything was very still. Even though my body ached so much that it felt like I might snap in two, the air slipped through my lips, and my mind was calm. It was clear to me in that moment that once the box was opened, nothing would be the same again.

When I began to resurface, Mr. Kalpak's voice reached me. 'Don't forget to smile,' he said.

I smiled and bowed out into the terrifying darkness. They didn't like it, I thought, but then, in one thundering roar, all of Bangalore fell upon me, and my heart sprang up and away.

'They loved it!' Mr. Kalpak shouted, as I left the ring. He threw his arms around me so that I could feel the buttons on his kurta pressing against my face.

'You've stolen the show.' Gloria drew me away from him and hugged me close too. 'A real class act.'

'We will have the box raised up higher during the act,' Mr. Kalpak raced on, his face glowing with excitement. 'Maybe a drum roll or sparklers perhaps.'

My mind buzzed like a hive of honeybees, but then from over Gloria's shoulder there was Mr. Prem standing in the shadows, his eyes fixed firmly in my direction. I turned away. That moment was mine: Sumi had forgiven me, the audience loved my act, and I wasn't going to allow Mr. Prem to take it away from me.

Still, I was glad when Mr. Kalpak whisked me off. 'We need to have you measured for new costumes, and there are posters to get printed. *Elastic Girl—The Grand Finale*,' he said.

True to his word, the posters for the circus were reprinted. A picture of me, curled up inside the glass box, now replaced the circle of death.

New costumes were made in every possible colour, and before each performance I always pinned Raja's bow tie underneath my bodice. His hope was still with me, for after each new performance came standing ovations and bunches of flowers.

'The numbers are up,' Mr. Kalpak said. 'People are spreading word about the Elastic Girl.'

In one way it all felt separate from me, as though Maheesh and I were simply watching it all happen on a movie screen. But the praise and success began to make me feel much bigger than I really was; it began to take away my fear.

'Write and tell them they must come,' I told Gloria.

Two letters were sent to my family, but still they did not come to see me.

'It's a long journey from Avadi,' Gloria said.

'They won't let me down,' I said. I was sure of it then.

But as days turned into weeks, I buried myself in my training and in my practise of ashtanga until my head was filled with so many thoughts and ideas that I didn't have space to think about the reasons why my family had deserted me.

There was no time, either, to notice the changes in Rupa—the way that she had distanced herself from everyone, that she no longer bothered with lipsticks and rouge blusher, and that her long silken locks of hair sat untidily on her head.

'You will be going soon,' she said one evening. She was lying in the bed next to me with her shoulders bunched up, facing into the wall.

'Going where?'

'Why would you stay when you can go anywhere now?'

We had barely had time to talk since my first performance. 'You're doing really well; soon you'll be a sky-walker, and then we will *both* be stars.'

'Mr. Prem has no time for me,' she said into the wall. 'It's only you he's interested in now.'

'It's Mr. Kalpak who will decide; he'll see to it that you perform soon.'

'Mr. Prem told him to put me on the peacock dance; he says there's no hope for me after all this time.'

'I'll help you,' I told her, leaning up onto my elbow.

Rupa turned to face me. 'It's too late; my parents always said I would never amount to much.'

'At the start I used to think that good things could never happen to someone like me, but now, there has been a change in my stars, and it's possible for you, too.'

Rupa smiled across at me in the dim light of the tent. 'We'll see,' she said. 'Maybe you are right.'

■ ■ ■

The following afternoon, Rupa's fate was decided while she was performing the peacock dance with some of the other girls, their brightly coloured feathers rustling as they spun and wove in and out among one another. What nobody knew as they watched the dance was that the lion cage leading into the ring had not been properly fastened after the previous act. The lion escaped, and, thinking that Rupa was a real bird, he plucked her up by the back of her neck and tossed her around like a doll.

The audience erupted in panic, a pregnant lady in the front row fainted, and people began to scramble back over the stalls in a bid to escape. Like searchlights, the overhead beams swooped crazily back and forth across the ring, and the lion, frightened by the uproar, dropped Rupa's limp body and returned to his cage. The place where Rupa had been dropped quickly filled with people, and over their heads I saw her being raised up on the rungs of a ladder, one arm falling loose down by her side.

'Is she dead?' I reached up to touch her fingers. 'Is she gone?'

'Unconscious.' Mr. Kalpak pulled me away from the men as they carried her out of the ring. 'They will take her to the hospital; the doctors will know what to do.'

Mr. Prem entered the ring and waved his hands around until everyone had backed away. 'See how the peacock has frightened the poor lion,' he called into his microphone, gesturing towards the lion that was crouched in the corner of his cage, his nose pressed in against the bars.

Some of the audience laughed, others continued to stand there in a daze, unsure if this was all part of the act, and just behind where Mr. Prem stood, I could see a patch of Rupa's blood slowly soaking into the sawdust.

Mr. Prem made us continue with the show, and while I was receiving applause, poor Rupa was slipping away.

She made it no farther than the medical tent. 'Her neck was broken,' Gloria told me. 'They said it was quick.'

'But, she never got her chance.' I picked up one of the bottles of polish from Rupa's bedside and squeezed it between my fingers, tears beginning to blind me. 'She wanted to be a skywalker, that's all she wanted.'

The lion didn't eat for a week, and the drunken handler was sent back home until things were 'cleared up.' When Rupa's father came with her two brothers to take the body away, they were told she'd had a fall.

'The circus is a dangerous place,' Gloria said. 'None of us are ever really safe.'

18

Inspectors from the Bangalore City Police came to visit the circus. They cordoned off the ring and paraded around the grounds with their hands cupped behind their backs. Nobody was interviewed, the inspectors didn't venture near the lions' enclosure, and no one checked the latches on the cages or questioned the whereabouts of the man who had been responsible for controlling the animals.

'What will they do?'

'They'll do nothing,' Gloria said. 'They're just waiting to have their pockets lined, and then they will be off.'

The following day Inspector Deedayal submitted a report to conclude that it was an accidental death. 'The dogs said that she lost her grip and plunged thirty feet to her death,' Gloria read in the *Deccan Herald*. 'They say there was no clear reason for her fall.'

'Why would they say that?'

'Because that's what they were told,' she said.

Unlike when Raja died, there was no puja or offerings of flowers, and Rupa's name was never mentioned again. Everyone knew that the truth would ruin The Great Raman Circus and put an end to their jobs, so they all kept quiet, as if this terrible thing hadn't happened at all.

Rupa's family had not even bothered to clear away her belongings, so I took her little box filled with broken makeup, jewellery, and assorted buttons and, standing on the bridge, threw it all into the pond at the bottom of the palace gardens. There was a clap against the water, and then the box disappeared from view, clusters of bubbles frothing to the surface as I made a promise to Rupa. 'I will show them that it's possible,' I whispered down into the pond. 'That someone like us can reach the stars.'

■ ■ ■

Mr. Kalpak watched me practise my act again. 'You will wear yourself out,' he said. 'You must allow the body to rest.'

'There's something missing; we need to make it more daring.' I convinced Mr. Kalpak to hoist the box up into the air during the act.

The following evening the audience exploded as the music soared and the glass box was spun around from the end of a chain, my body wrapped around itself like a roosting fox bat. From up high I could see the spectators bent right back, staring open-mouthed into the air.

'The Maharani Pramoda is coming,' Gloria gasped at me that evening. 'Can you believe it?'

We knew that the Mysore royal family no longer lived at the palace but visited from time to time, keeping staff there throughout the year at their urgent disposal. 'Have you seen the line of luxury cars?' Gloria asked, nodding to beyond the palace gardens. 'They say she alone has four cars that are all chauffeur-driven.'

Mr. Prem gathered together all the performers. 'There has never been a royal visitor to The Great Raman Circus before,' he said. 'This is a great honour, a real momentous event.'

'Why now?' someone asked. 'How come they have decided to visit now?'

'Don't you know that everyone has heard about the Elastic Girl? Even the Mysore royal family,' someone else replied.

'She will come on Thursday,' Mr. Prem continued. 'You will *all* be expected to put in one hundred percent.' And he turned his back to us and returned to his caravan.

'Is it true?' I asked Gloria. 'That the maharani is coming to see *me*?'

'Of course; you're the talk of Bangalore.'

My mouth felt suddenly dry, and a flutter of butterflies rose up inside my stomach. 'It feels like only days since I was performing with Raja. How can it be real?'

Gloria pinched me on the arm until I squealed. 'See: it *is* real,' she said.

'Rupa wanted to see the maharani,' I said. 'She would have given anything.'

'I know.' Gloria wrapped her arm around me and led me back across the grounds. 'Rupa wanted to see it all, but it's not too late for you.'

∎∎∎

Right then it felt like my whole life had been leading up to this moment, and that maybe everything had happened for a reason. The Gods had washed us out of Ambattur on purpose, the disappointment in Morai was meant to be, all so that I would end up at the Great Raman Circus of Chennai. Perhaps my fate was not conspiring against me after all.

The place hummed with excitement. Men swept out the animal enclosures and hosed down the dust from the big top; women spent hours stringing together garlands of flowers, hanging them from the awning over the circus entrance until it looked like a wedding mandap.

And in my tent, Gloria trawled through stacks of new costumes, which had been brought in for the event. 'You need a regal colour.' She finally settled on a long-sleeved costume in crimson red with a cutaway back. 'Just the thing for our star attraction.'

'What about you? Don't you want the maharani to notice you, too?'

'Arjun's waiting on me: my very own prince,' she said. 'This is *your* chance, Muthu.'

Word had spread across Bangalore that the maharani was attending the circus, and on Thursday afternoon, the grounds became thronged with people jostling for tickets to the show.

'We're all sold out,' the ticket master shouted out at them, but they continued to tussle with one another, and several of the youngsters tried to climb up onto the canvas roof until Mr. Prem called on his friends at the Bangalore City Police, who beat the crowd away with their batons and then stood guard at the fence, green caps tilted on the sides of their heads.

'With all this going on, she might not come,' I fretted. 'It would be too dangerous.' And for the hundredth time, I peeped out through the opening in the tent again and scanned the grounds.

'She'll come,' Gloria said. 'These people are used to plenty of mayhem everywhere they go.'

■ ■ ■

At six o'clock the maharani made her way down the lawn, a following of staff forming barricades around her. Gloria and I hurriedly joined the rest of the performers and helpers who lined either side of the path. Some of them threw handfuls of petals in the maharani's direction, others reached out to try to touch her, and in the commotion Gloria and I were pushed and shoved out of the way.

Unable to see anything, I wormed my way in underneath their legs, crawling to the front, until I was standing only yards from the maharani of Bangalore.

She was dressed in a simple blue sari, a long red tilak in the centre of her forehead, and her hair was pulled back into a loose plait, exposing the slack skin around the sides of her face and the jut of her chin. As she made her way down the lawn, she played with the ring on her little finger, as if she was simply stepping out into the garden for a relaxing stroll. 'Maharani, maharani!' the crowd shouted, and she would look about her and nod, her face hardly changing at all.

She reminded me of amma, and for a moment I almost cried, but then Mr. Prem was there, bending down before her, a blue vein pumping in the side of his head. The maharani waved at him to stand up and then promptly disappeared with her staff under the gleaming cover of the big top, leaving Mr. Prem standing with a gold-plated Ganesh still resting in his hands.

When a booming cheer rose up from inside the tent, he jolted suddenly as though he had just been shot in the chest. 'Why are you all dawdling about, like there is nothing to do?' he shouted.

Everyone hurried past him, towards the back of the tent.

'Only two gold bangles,' someone said. 'And those diamond earrings were so small, like pinholes.'

'Her hair is all dried up and grey,' another added. 'You would think that she could afford to have it hennaed.'

Everyone seemed disappointed in the maharani's appearance, but it was her very ordinariness that had captivated me, for it seemed even more possible that someone like that could rescue me.

Mr. Kalpak made his way along the line of performers. 'Don't forget to smile,' he told them. When he reached me, he scratched at the back of his neck, as if he had forgotten what he needed to say.

'Smile and bow?' Gloria suggested, leaning over towards him.

Mr. Kalpak nodded and moved on, tapping his cane along the ground.

It was Gloria who opened the show, wowing everyone with her new finish, as she propped her chin over the bar and balanced the whole weight of her body below. 'You can see her in the front,' she said, as we waited for my turn to take to the floor, and a wave of panic rose up in me.

'But the audience are always in darkness.'

'Not her.'

And it was true, for when I took to the ring, I could see her floating in the corner of my eye, like a speck of dust in the light.

My arms and legs had grown stiff, and when I looked down into the case I could have sworn that it had shrunk to half its size. Either way, it seemed impossible that I'd ever be able to manoeuvre myself into position. My heart began to pound as the music filling the big top grew faster and louder, but I couldn't move.

It could have ended for me then, but when I closed my eyes, Rupa came to me.

She was standing just below me in the ring with her shoulders pushed back on her small body. 'Come on, Elastic Girl,' she said. 'Show them that you are something.'

I began to slip down farther and farther, until I was inside the case and it was swinging like a hammock in the air. When I finally opened my eyes and looked down, the maharani was staring right back at me. I don't remember being lowered to the ground or stepping from the box, but I remember her face. Her head was tilted to the side and she had a faint little smile across her lips, as if she had just heard something amusing.

'She wants to see you,' Mr. Kalpak told me after the show. 'Don't speak unless she asks you something, and don't stand too close or fiddle with your hair.'

'This is it.' Gloria escorted me to the tent reserved for her royal entourage. 'Next I will be reading about *you* in the *Filmfare* magazines.'

We stood in the opening and watched as she lifted a cup of chai to her lips.

'Lurki, come here,' she said, seeing me standing there and lowering her cup onto a saucer.

Mr. Prem, who was standing inside, urged me forward, and I moved towards her, pressing the palms of my hands together.

'What is your name?'

'She is our Elastic Girl,' Mr. Prem volunteered.

The maharani lifted her hand to silence him. 'Your real name?' she asked.

'I'm Muthu. Muthu Tikaram.'

'Ah, like a tiny pearl.' She reached out and pressed my chin gently between her fingers. 'Very interesting.' Her eyes, like shards of onyx, looked straight into mine, and in that very second, I was sure that she could see inside my head, that she could see all the thoughts about my parents and my grandmother and Mr. Prem. It felt as if someone had just cut a rope loose from about my feet.

'We have another engagement,' one of her staff whispered into her ear, and the maharani straightened herself and nodded.

As she rose from her chair, Mr. Prem rushed forwards holding out the statue of Ganesh. 'A small token of our gratitude.' He bowed once more as she took it from his hands. 'You're most welcome here at our humble circus anytime.'

The maharani handed the gift to one of her followers and then turned to look around her, as though she had just remembered something that she had left behind. She was looking at me.

'You should come visit me,' she said. 'I'll send for you.'

Someone lifted back the cover on the tent, and just like, that the maharani was gone.

■ ■ ■

After that evening the circus was sold out weeks in advance. Mr. Prem raised the ticket prices to one hundred rupees apiece; most of us were earning only two hundred a month, and when there was no change in our wages, the men began to complain that The Great Raman Circus was ripping us off. They threatened to stage a strike, but Mr. Prem was quick to come to an arrangement with the ringleaders.

'See that line at the gate?' he told the women when they dared to add their complaint. 'Performers from cities all over India in search of work at this circus; I could replace any one of you just like that.' He snapped his fingers and then handed over a pair of his slippers to one of the girls. 'Shine them for me; you might need the practise if you are going to end up on the street.'

My face burned as I thought about my father's shoeshine box.

'I pray that in the next life my soul will be clothed as a man,' Sona said.

Most of us had never seen a paise of our wages anyway; it was forwarded in envelopes to parents and family who were more than happy to spend it, and when I received my next letter from home, it was clear where *my* money was going.

Safa wrote to tell me how dadi had found her a nice boy from his hometown of Pondicherry. *'His name is Keshav, and he is a railway guard,'* she told me. *'Amma has already set to work on collecting my dowry and has purchased a new colour television and video player, a Godrej front-loading washing machine, and a twenty-two-carat gold wedding necklace.'* She had not yet met Keshav, and I imagined amma telling her, 'All in good time.' *'The family feels that education is not a bad thing in a wife,'* Safa continued. *'I will be able to finish my BA after I am wed.'*

Gloria read the letter right through, and when she reached the end she shook her head.

'What is it?'

'We did not make it to Chennai, but we will come to Bangalore. Amma says that in Bangalore there are shops selling the best Banarasi wedding sarees.'

'They did not come?'

'Isn't it a good thing that you did not stay behind after all?' Gloria said. 'You would have been left there all alone.'

'They said that they would come.'

'We will write back and tell her about the visit from the maharani and about the reviews in the paper; that will certainly make them come.'

■ ■ ■

There had been no word from the maharani since her visit to the circus, and now this letter from home plunged me further into a black mood. It seemed that nothing had changed after all.

'Your concentration is wandering,' Mr. Kalpak complained at training. 'You look like a rhino struggling in the mud.'

'The maharani has forgotten me.'

'She has too many things to do,' he said. 'It doesn't mean that she's forgotten you.'

Gloria tried to entertain me by teaching the Nepalese girls to sing 'Hai Na Bolo Bolo,' in their broken Hindi, but even that failed to brighten my spirits.

It was nobody other than Mr. Prem who drew me out of despair. He appeared in the opening of my tent the following afternoon, and as he stepped inside, I pulled myself up on the bed and drew my knees in towards my chest. The other girls had not yet returned from performing.

'This came for you this morning.' He held out a letter up in the air. 'It's from the palace.'

'What does it say?'

'The maharani has requested that you attend the palace for dinner on Wednesday evening,' he told me. 'You must be there at seven o'clock.'

'She's invited only me?'

'It appears that you're the lucky one.' He turned to go. 'Oh, and she has asked that you do not tell anyone—a *private meeting*, she called it.'

By the time Gloria came to fetch me for the evening performance, I was fit to burst. 'The maharani wants to see me,' I blurted out, kneeling up on the bed and clapping my hands together. 'She's called me to dinner at the palace.' The Nepalese girls, who were following behind Gloria, looked at each other and began to clap their hands, as though they had understood, and my hand flew across my mouth. 'I wasn't supposed to tell.'

'They're just excited to see you happy for a change,' Gloria reassured me. 'They still know nothing more than "Hai Na Bolo Bolo."' She sat beside me on the bed and took my hands in hers. 'This will be your making,' she said. 'The maharani knows people in all the right places.'

Gloria provided her best salwar kameez for the occasion. 'It belonged to my mother,' she said. It was a light-pink colour, embellished with sparkling sequins and silver embroidery on the neckline and came with a matching dupatta. She pinned it around my narrow hips and turned it up at the ankles.

'Perfect,' she said. 'Fit for a queen.'

'I won't be able to eat a mouthful, and how will I ever find anything to say?'

'Just wait for her to ask the questions. It's she who wants to meet you.'

For two whole days, we talked about nothing else, and then on Wednesday evening, Gloria walked partway with me across the lawn. 'Are you sure you don't want me to walk as far as the palace?' she asked.

'No. The maharani might be watching from one of the windows, and I wasn't supposed to tell anyone, remember?'

Gloria hugged me tightly so that it felt as though I was leaving the circus for good. 'Good luck.' She let go of me, and set off back across the gardens. When she had made it halfway, I carried on up the embankment.

It was already dark, and shadows from the giant tamarind trees loomed across the grass, so I hurried my way along the narrow pathway leading out of the gardens. Just as I made it to the opening beyond the Shala trees, a crunching sound reached out at me, like someone stepping on a dry branch. My body froze, and in an instant a man's hand came from behind, and clamped down on my mouth.

His skin smelt of tobacco, and in those couple of seconds, I thought that it was just a guardsman, mistaking me for an intruder and that he would let me go, but then he began to drag me backwards into the thicket of trees. As my sandals came loose, I tried to reach down to fetch them and caught sight of a pair of khussa slippers: it wasn't a guardsman; it was Mr. Prem. Fear gripped me, and I tried to break away.

'You better not scream,' he said. He released his grip on my mouth.

'The maharani will come.' I looked up towards the palace. 'She's waiting on me.'

'Haven't you worked it out?' he laughed. 'The maharani never called for you.' He pressed his hands down against my shoulders and forced me onto my knees.

I made to crawl away, but he pulled my legs out from underneath me, so that I was lying flat against the moist grass. For a moment he just stood there looking down at me and it crossed my mind that this was my chance, that I should take off and run, but my body shook so much that escape seemed impossible.

Trying to sit up, he pushed me back down easily, and then he was straddling me, his thighs spreading out on either side. He was over me, like the great wide back of a bullock and my spine pressed painfully against the ground as he rocked back and forth, the hard lump in his trousers pressing against my skirt.

'No! Please don't!' I cried.

'I'm warning you, shut up.' He started to work at my clothes, loosening the drawstring of the pink salwar and fumbling with the hooks on the kameez, and in the tustle my grandfather's watch fell away to the ground.

'I'll tell Mr. Kalpak,' I said. 'I'll tell Gloria.'

He pinned my arms down by my sides so hard that I thought they might snap. 'You'll tell noone.' His spit fell on my face. 'If you do, you will end up like that little other little telltale who couldn't keep her dirty mouth shut.'

He was talking about Rupa, poor Rupa.

'I've made you a star, Elastic Girl,' he said. 'Now it's time to show me how grateful you are.'

My muscles tightened as he leant down closer, pressing his wet mouth against my neck, his hands grabbing at my small breasts, squeezing and pinching. His heavy breath smelt of whiskey, but no matter how hard I tried, his body loomed like a great heavy tank over me.

He forced my legs apart and lowered his hand into my pants. 'Relax; stop shaking.' His fingers worked their way inside, hurting me. I counted in my head, but the fear overcame me and I wet myself.

'Dirty girl,' he said. 'Doing chi chi.'

The words of 'Hai Na Bolo Bolo' ran through my head over and over. 'Paapa ko mammi se, mammi ko paapa se,' I sang in my head, as Mr. Prem gripped my hand and clasped it onto his hot penis, forcing it up and down. Tears slid out from the corners of my eyes and down my cheeks as his deep, uneven breath burned against my cheek, and then he moaned, and my hand grew sticky.

'If you say anything to anybody you'll be sorry,' he hissed.' He leant over, wiped my hand with the end of the dupatta and then bent down to kiss the strands of hair on the side of my face. I didn't turn to look at him as he stood up and slowly walked away, leaving me there.

It was then that I should have rushed up to the palace and called for the maharani, should have wept and stormed in and let her see what he had done, but she hadn't sent the invitation, so instead I buttoned up my clothes and scrambled for my sandals among the leaves.

When I'd reached a small patch of earth where new seedlings had been planted, I sank down onto my knees and began to dig, smearing the clay across my face and down my arms and legs, until I was nothing like a pearl at all. It was only when the circus had fallen into complete darkness that I made my way to the washhouse and bathed. I scrubbed at my body until it was raw, but still I could feel nothing.

19

Gloria perched herself on the edge of my bed. 'Tell me everything,' she insisted.

Fear paralysed me. How could I tell her what had happened? It was too awful, too big for me to speak of, and besides Mr. Prem had warned me not to say anything. That man was capable of murder, I knew that then.

'Come on, don't keep us waiting,' Gloria prompted again.

Words came out of my mouth, descriptions of chandeliers and silver dining ware. 'There was a piano in the corner of the dining room and a sweep of stairs with thick red carpet.'

'What about the maharani herself; what was she wearing?'

'Blue, I think.'

'Oh come on, Muthu; you promised to tell me every detail.'

'My stomach hurts,' I turned over in the bed.

'What was it you ate?'

'Fish, some kind of fish.' With my face turned away from her, I bit down on my lip to stop myself from crying.

'You can rest now,' she said. 'But I will come back later to hear it all.'

Underneath the bedclothes my body was bruised and sore, and not wanting anyone to see, I stayed in bed for three days, until Mr. Kalpak threatened to call a doctor. 'If you're sick then we need to get it seen to,' he said. 'Mr. Prem is losing his patience with your absence from the shows.'

I couldn't risk being taken to the doctor, so there was no choice but to continue to perform as the Elastic Girl, even though it felt like my insides had been scooped right out. When I heard Mr. Prem call me into the ring, my mouth filled with bile, and I had to stand there with my eyes closed until he had disappeared off into the shadows. It was only when I was up in the air, swinging above the ring in my little glass box, that I felt safe; nobody could touch me there.

On the ground it was different. Mr. Prem waited only one week, and then he started to pay me visits in the middle of the night, when everyone was fast asleep. 'You better not make a sound, or they will all know what kind of girl you are,' he said, as he slid in underneath my covers.

The bed beside me, where Rupa used to sleep, was still empty, and the rest of the girls slept soundly whilst Mr. Prem undid the buckle on his trousers and forced my hand down into his pants. Underneath my fingers he throbbed, and then he would place his hand over mine like before and make me pull up and down on it, up and down, until he came on me. Then he would shift to the side of the bed, pull his trousers back up, and reach into his pocket for something to place underneath my pillow; a bottle of nail varnish, a hair clasp, a silk scarf—all of it went into the palace pond along with Rupa's things.

It continued that way for two weeks, but then one night when he came to me, he was wildly drunk and rough, pulling my hair and biting on me so hard that tears rolled down my face. Without raising his head, he clamped a hand over my mouth, pulled down my pants, and rammed his penis inside me. His great hulk of a body humped over me, sending pain searing through me like a burning rod. When he was done, he grunted and collapsed down onto me like a sack of gram flour.

After a few moments, his hand slipped from my mouth. 'Good girl,' he slurred, as he rolled out of the bed and dragged his trousers up over his legs. He didn't bother to leave a gift.

I hadn't even known about sex back then. Amma hadn't warned me of the things men were capable of, and he shock of it overwhelmed me. I turned my head to one side and retched, vomit splattering down onto the floor.

Somewhere I fell asleep and dreamt of ants crawling all over me, and of my grandfather slitting the throat of Mr. Prem. Before anyone else rose for the day I limped my way to the pumps, but no matter how hard I scrubbed, the smell of him stayed on my skin—like burnt rubber.

'Your arms are raw,' Gloria said. 'Have you got an itch?'

'It's the heat; inside the box it's like a pyre.'

'Lemon juice and coconut oil: that will soothe them.'

She couldn't see the purple bruises I was carrying underneath my costume.

I was unable to eat or sleep, my face grew thin and pale, my hair lost all of its shine, and after two weeks of his visits, I fainted during my act, toppling over on top of the box. It felt as though the ground had collapsed below me, and that I was hurtling down deep into the centre of the earth.

'What's wrong with you?' Gloria asked as she draped a cloth across my forehead. 'Have you started your menses?'

'I'm just tired; I need to rest.'

'It's Rupa; her death is only hitting you now,' she said. 'That kind of thing can happen: a delayed reaction.'

'You should eat almonds,' Mr. Kalpak insisted. He instructed Gloria to massage mustard oil onto my neck.

There was no way of telling them what was wrong. There was no way for me to explain, so I took the only action I could. In the middle of the night I clambered up the ropes in the centre of the ring and out onto the platform at the top. With my arms spread wide, I moved towards the edge. Everything looked so small, the contents of the big top reduced to nothing more than a scattering of children's toys. One swoop out into the air, and it would all be over. I felt calm for the first time in weeks.

'You are going to be a tightrope walker?'

It was Mr. Kalpak, standing down below. When I saw his tiny body looking up at me, my legs began to shake. 'Leave me; it's all over now,' I called down to him, but Mr. Kalpak made for the rope ladder, as if he had not heard me.

When he reached the top, he stretched his arms towards me. 'There is no need for this, Muthu. Please, take my hand.'

My body folded beneath me, like the bellows on a harmonium. I couldn't even do this one thing.

He carried me down the ladder in his arms and did not speak until we reached Gloria's tent. 'She's feverish,' he said.

Gloria sent the Nepalese girls to fetch some water, and she began to pull clothes and magazines from the covers of her bed. 'Set her there.' She began to loosen my clothes.

'Please, no,' I screamed at them. I wrapped my arms tightly around my chest, but already the marks were visible.

Mr. Kalpak and Gloria stood there, looking down at me, their faces changing like the sea, and then Gloria sat down gently on the edge of the bed and scooped me up into her arms. 'My poor chotee bahen.' Her hands moved around my face in slow, steady movements. 'We failed you.'

'That man is a beast.' Mr. Kalpak kicked the grille on the gas stove. 'A filthy animal.'

'Why did you not tell us?' Gloria asked.

'It was all my own fault; you told me to keep away.' The tears fell down onto the pillow behind my head.

Gloria tucked me up into her bed, and then she and Mr. Kalpak stepped outside the tent.

'We will report him to the police; the bastard can't get away with this,' Mr. Kalpak said.

'And what will they do?' Gloria said. 'He will only buy their silence again.'

'Then the owners should be told.'

'Mr. Prem has tripled the income of the circus and created a name for The Great Raman Circus across all of India; they would cast Muthu out into the street—us, too, if we speak,' Gloria told him. 'He has everyone eating out of the palm of his hand.'

They were silent, lost for something to say or do.

'We won't leave your side,' Gloria said when they returned. 'Not for a moment.'

'There were other girls? Just like Rupa and me?'

'We can't be sure,' she said, looking away to the floor. 'These things happen Muthu—in circuses and in all types of places.'

'And it can't be stopped?'

'We will try.' She lay down beside me, sleeping by my side, her soft voice soothing me out of my nightmares as she told me stories about what we would do in Mumbai. 'Arjun is searching for premises in the right part of Mumbai, where people will hear of us,' she said. 'Then, when we are big enough, we will perform at the famous Tata Theatre in Nariman Point.'

'What will we be called?'

'We will call ourselves Daksha or Damini,' she said. 'What do you think?'

'Damini, like the film with Meenakshi Seshadri.'

'Damini it is,' she said, and she smoothed my hair until I fell back to sleep.

During the day she brought me bowls of coconut rice, and Mr. Kalpak continued to coax me through the practise of ashtanga. 'It will help you to heal,' he said.

Sure enough, slowly my physical self returned. But it felt as though my body was a waterpot, my insides carved out like lumps of clay.

'He's sent you this,' Gloria said. 'It's a letter from your family.'

'He's trying to get at me again.'

I had stayed with Gloria since the evening I had fainted, and there had been no sign of Mr. Prem. 'He knows that there is something wrong,' she said. 'He'll be worried about what you might tell us.'

The letter from Safa sat unopened for four days; I wouldn't even touch it.

'You never know, but something could be wrong,' Gloria said. 'If you let me read it, I will tell you if everything is OK.'

'Just read it and tell me if they are coming to see me.'

Her lips moved as she read each line to herself, and when she reached the end, she shook her head. 'They are going to Delhi for wedding saris; your Aunt Gounder knows a tailor there who can get them a very good price. There is no more money for trips to Bangalore.'

Snatching the letter from her and tearing it into tiny little shreds. I cursed dadi for taking me to the cinema hall that day and for leaving me in Chennai. 'Write and tell them that I've drowned in Hesaraghatta Lake and that my body has been found bloated and washed up onshore. That is what they want to hear.'

'This is not their doing,' Gloria said.

'Then there is nobody else to blame but myself.'

'Hush now.' Gloria reached for my hand. 'Just think about Mumbai.'

So, Mumbai filled my head as I returned to performing three times a day, as Mr. Prem's voice boomed out across the microphone. I thought about Mumbai in the dead of the night when I could not sleep and my body stiffened every time there was a noise outside. Mumbai was my last hope.

Then suddenly Mr. Prem left for Nepal. 'He's looking for new talent,' Gloria said. 'He'll be gone for a while.'

Sleep returned, and able to eat and rest, my body began to strengthen. See, you are back to your old self,' Mr. Kalpak said. 'It's all about the power of the mind.' He placed me on the star act once more.

At night, I prayed that Mr. Prem would meet with some terrible accident along the dangerous hillside roads of Nepal, and I allowed myself to think of the circus van lying at the bottom of a rocky fall with his mangled body twisted inside the wreckage. Four months later, it was the middle of July, and he had still not returned. 'Do you think he's gone for good?' I asked Gloria one afternoon.

'When he has found what he wants he will be back,' she said.

My heart plunged back down into the depths of me. 'Then I will be gone.'

Like a magic trick conjured up by Upendra Thakur, it happened. The pre-monsoon showers began that afternoon, and as the rain drummed down on the canvas roof, Gloria came shouting across the yard, her words chopped off by the noise of the rain. When she stepped inside, her clothes dripped a wet puddle onto the floor. 'Didn't you hear me? The circus is going to *Mumbai*.'

She pulled me up from the bed and dragged me outside onto the muddy lawns. 'We're saved,' Gloria sang. 'Arjun will be waiting, and we are saved.' And as the thunder boomed up over us, we danced in the rain and Gloria punched at the air, swallowing up mouthfuls of rainwater.

Everyone else grumbled about the timing.

'Why move just as the monsoon starts?' they said. 'The rain and mud gets into everything.'

'We want to be set up in Mumbai for the start of Janmashthami festival,' said Mr. Kalpak. 'It brings big crowds to the city.'

At the Janmashthami festival in Ambattur we would tie mango leaves to the doorway of the house and draw kolams in the front yard to celebrate the birthday of Lord Krishna. Amma always remained inside, her head bowed before a small wooden mandapam decorated with flowers and containing a statue of a crawling Krishna. The soothing sound of her hymns and holy mantras reached out to us, and everything seemed at ease.

'You are daydreaming.' Gloria shook me by the arm. 'These things won't pack themselves.'

The Nepalese girls sat quietly on the floor, folding their clothes into neat little piles by the side of the bed. 'They are gone to me now,' I said.

'Who?' Gloria asked, bending to pick a kameez from the floor.

'My family.'

'Arjun and I—we will be your family now.'

'What about them?' I asked, nodding towards the girls at the foot of the bed. 'Who will look after them when you're gone?'

'Shulisha or Sona,' she said. 'It's not possible for me to mind them all.' She hurried the remainder of her belongings into a bag, and then clapped her hands at the girls, who promptly stood up, their clothes now folded inside crisp white cloth.

Outside, everything had become covered in a thin layer of grey mud, including the circus workers, who were battling to bring down the big top before the rains started again.

'We can help in the kitchen.' Gloria waved us along. 'At least in there it's dry.'

We set to work wrapping all the plates in paper and setting them into boxes, Gloria humming the tune to 'Maahi Ve.' As we wrapped and stacked, I found myself humming along, the Nepalese girls giggling by our sides.

'If you break anything, I'll have your life,' the cook snapped at us.

By the time the circus was all packed up it was starting to grow dark. The headlights of the Falcon beamed their way across from the car park beyond, leading us across the palace lawns, the light flitting across our faces as we moved. It was the first time for me to walk through the covering of trees since that night with Mr. Prem, and as we moved along the narrow path, I caught sight of him standing on the other side of the clearing, a cigarette balanced between his lips. The air was sucked from my lungs, and the ground rushed up towards me.

'Stand back,' Gloria shouted. 'Give her some air.'

'What's wrong with her?' they asked. 'Is she unwell?'

A light mist of rain was floating down towards us, dancing in the light from the bus.

'Mr. Prem, he was waiting on me.' But when I looked up, I could see that he was gone.

'You were imagining it; he's on his way back from Tulsipur,' she said. 'It will take several days for him to reach Mumbai, and by then we will be gone.'

Shutting my eyes, I rested my head against her shoulder, and then it came to me: the gentle ticking sound of my grandfather's pocket watch. 'We have to find it,' I said, pulling myself out from Gloria's arms and crawling into the thicket of trees.

'Find what? Gloria asked.

'My grandfather's watch.'

Gloria and Mr. Kalpak came after me, their arms flaying at branches, but they didn't try to pull me away and instead crouched down and began to feel their way along the damp earth, among sprouting mushrooms and clusters of fresh peonies.

'Listen.' I held up my hand to them. 'It's here.'

'There is nothing, Muthu.' Gloria shook her head.

As I was swivelling around on my knees, my fingers dragged their way along the ground. 'It's here. I know it is.'

The horn on the Falcon began to blow.

'We need to get on our way,' Mr. Kalpak said. 'It's getting heavy.' Overhead the rain began beating against the shelter of leaves.

'Let's go, Muthu.' Gloria took my hand and led me away. 'It could be anywhere.'

As we made our way out, my toe stubbed against the base of a rock, and when I bent to soothe it, there it was, shining like a newly polished coin in the half-light—the silver back of my grandfather's pocket watch.

I emerged from the trees with the broken chain held out between my fingers. Gloria and Mr. Kalpak stood there on the path looking at me in wonderment, their eyes blinking wildly. 'It's the only thing my father ever gave me,' I said.

20

It was a different driver this time, a tall man with a crisp navy handkerchief tied neatly around his neck. He stood at the front of the bus with his hand outstretched. 'You'll get them back when we reach Mumbai.' He confiscated bottles of toddy from the men and then placed them carefully underneath his seat. Like schoolchildren, the men scuttled down to the back of the bus, unearthing bottles hidden inside packages and up their sleeves.

'Will you take us past Victoria Gardens?' one of the ladies asked. 'Or the Gateway of India?'

'I'm not a tour guide,' he said, taking his place behind the wheel. 'We will stop at Belgaum for the night, and that will be all.'

Unlike the drive from Chennai to Bangalore, this one took on a slow, steady pace. 'We will never get there at this rate,' Gloria complained.

Gloria had written ahead to Arjun, telling him to meet us the following morning at Candies coffee house in Bandra. 'What if Arjun doesn't wait?' I asked.

'Three whole years he has waited; what are a few more days?'

By the time we reached Belgaum, various implements had been distributed up and down the aisle to catch the heavy rainwater, which was seeping in through the cracked roof, and the bus had suffered a flat tyre in the potholes of Karnataka. The driver pulled the bus into a lay-by and stood before us, beads of perspiration dripping from his upper lip and onto his handkerchief, causing it to wilt. 'You'll all have to go to a relief centre while the tyre is changed,' he announced. 'There is a gruel centre at Military Mahadev Temple on Congress Road.'

We trudged along the road, just as I had done at Morai. The women carried their sandals in their hands and hoisted up the ends of their skirts, but by the time we arrived at the Mahadev centre, our clothes were clinging to our skin, and some of the women and children had begun to whimper and shake. 'That careless driver could have taken us this far,' one of them said. 'Now we will all be sick.'

Inside the hall, children chased one another up and down, sliding their way across the wooden floor, and smiling ladies with red tilaks smeared on the centre of their foreheads rushed up towards us, some of them wrapping grey flannel blankets around our shoulders, others holding out trays laden with cups of chai and bread rolls filled with chutney and tomato sauce.

'It's only for a few hours,' Mr. Kalpak explained to them. 'We will sit very quietly.'

'You will stay as long as you need,' one of the ladies told him.

'They'll never be moved from here,' Gloria complained.

The ladies settled down in the corner of the room to enjoy their little picnic, and the men made for the station, which had been set up in the centre of the room.

From behind a row of desks, uniformed men handed out rations of flour, palm oil, and milk powder, but it was the tubes of toothpaste and soap bars that the men from the circus squabbled over.

'You have as many teeth as a chicken,' one of them complained to another as they pulled tug of war over a toothbrush.

One of the uniformed men settled the dispute by producing another box of brushes from underneath his table. When he held them up into the air, everyone clapped, as if he had just produced a magic trick.

Gloria returned from one of the other desks and held out a pen. 'A present for Arjun.' It had a picture printed down the side of Kapileshwar Temple in Chennai. 'My Arjun doesn't need a toothbrush; he already has such a perfect smile.'

By the time the driver returned to pick us up, everyone had been fed, the men had befriended a supplier of whiskey, and some of the women had managed to exchange items of their clothing with the women of Belgaum.

'Look, that woman has given me her chunni for my old hairpin,' one of them boasted.

Another had exchanged her gold loop earrings for a handbag studded with pearls and sequins.

'What need have you for such a thing?' someone teased her. 'Are you planning a stay in the Taj?'

The visit to the Mahadev Temple had put everyone in a cheerful mood, except for the driver, who had removed his sodden necktie and remained in a foul mood for the remainder of our journey. He did not bother to wake up the women, as they had requested, when we reached Mumbai.

Unable to sleep, I watched out my window as the bus made its way silently past the bright night lights of Marine Drive and the crescent sweep of the city's long, foam-flecked Chowpatty Beach. He stopped temporarily at the foot of Malabar Hill to take a drink from one of the bottles underneath his seat, and up in the distance, there was the outline of the hanging gardens and plush bungalows. Imagining what they looked like inside and the glamorous lives of their film star owners, my mind fell still.

■ ■ ■

'You're here,' the driver shouted, leaning heavily on the horn. 'You are in Mumbai.'

Pushing the sleep from my eyes and looking out the window, the richness of Malabar Hills had gone, and a yellow dawn light fell over everything, like a death shroud.

'What's happened?' someone asked, for it felt as though we had arrived at the end of some terrible catastrophe, with everything about us reduced to rubble.

'This is Dharavi,' someone else said.

It was an unending stretch of narrow lanes, open sewers, and huts not much bigger than those we had built at the railway station, and just beyond us a group of grubby-looking children clambered up over a wire fence to get to the road.

'This is Mumbai, the land of dreams?' A lump rose up in my throat.

Gloria reached over and held my hand. 'It's not all like this,' she said. 'Arjun has told me all about Colaba and the plush bazaars. Where we are going is nowhere near here.'

When the driver had stayed long enough to fill us with disappointment, he carried on his way, and by the time we reached the reclamation grounds at Bandra the wreckage had subsided, replaced by exhibition stalls set inside gleaming white marquees. Artists from across the country were gathering for the festival of Janmashthami, wanting to show their handicrafts, and inside the bus we pressed up against the windows to admire the rainbow of brightly coloured sarees spread out across rows of tables, the terracotta pots from Haryana, Rajasthani paintings, and gilded mirrors from Gujarati. Dharavi was quickly forgotten.

'It's like a film set: Film City.'

Gloria laughed. 'That's in Goregaon,' she said.

'Can we go there? Can we see where all the Masala films were made?'

'All in good time, but first we have to make it out of here,' she said, as the bus moved in through a set of high gates, to where The Great Raman Circus was beginning to take shape.

When everything had been unpacked, Gloria sent the Nepalese girls to help set up the beds. They were reluctant to leave her side, one of them pulling on her hand. 'Please, come, come,' she pleaded.

Gloria shook her off like a bug. 'Go now!' she shouted at them, and the girls scurried off like frightened little mice across the grounds.

Gloria's hands shook as she began to unwrap cutlery, setting it into plastic trays. 'It's not possible to save everyone,' she said flatly.

For a while we did not speak, the click of forks and spoons the only sound between us, the grounds outside growing dark.

'You haven't said how we will make it out,' I said.

'The bus is on hire; it will be heading back to Bangalore,' she nodded over to where the driver was squatting on the ground, enjoying a bowl of dahl and rice. 'When he isn't looking, we will sneak out into the trunk.'

'What if someone sees us?'

'Everyone's too busy. We won't be noticed until the morning.'

Gloria had stowed two bags of our belongings in among the crates of kitchen utensils, and every so often she reached her hand into them, like a mother tending her baby. 'He's finishing the last of his dahl,' she said at last. She reached in again to where the bags lay hidden and drew them out. 'We must go.'

We crouched down low like crooks, and as Gloria led me across the grounds and towards the bus, my heart thumped loudly in my ears. We were at the rear of the truck when someone reached out and placed a hand on Gloria's shoulder, making both of us jump. 'I knew you two were up to something.' It was Shulisha, the plate spinner. 'Kamala said that you'd given her all of your *Stardust* magazines.'

'We're leaving to set up our own show,' Gloria said. She looked over to where the driver was talking to Kani, one of the new Hula-Hoop girls. 'This is our only chance.'

'You won't survive out there; don't you know what the streets of Mumbai are like?' Shulisha said.

'No worse than here.' Gloria prised open the trunk.

'And what about the girls: Priya, Kamala, and the others? They'll think you've abandoned them.'

'They have you.' Gloria urged me to get in. 'You must look after them now; promise me you won't let them come to any harm.' She grasped Shulisha's hand.

'My father always said that I wasn't fit to look after the untouchables of Koothirambakkam, but I promise to take care of them as best I can.'

'Like all fathers, he was a liar.' Gloria hoisted me into the trunk. 'You will do it; I know you will.'

The inside of the trunk smelt of oil and damp clothes.

'Will you come back?'

'Not if there is any life left in us.' Gloria pulled herself up and over the edge of the trunk.

Suddenly we could hear Kani shout, and when we looked over, she was slapping the driver across the face. 'God shame you,' she shouted at him. 'You're nothing more than a baddu.'

The driver spat at her feet and turned to walk away.

'You must go now,' Gloria whispered. I could hear her voice begin to break. 'Go and look after the girls, and say nothing more about us.'

Shulisha turned to leave. 'We'll be nothing without you two,' she said. 'The circus will turn to dust.' And she was gone, disappearing into the shadows.

'We need to see where we are going,' Gloria said, removing a shoe and wedging it into the gap in the trunk.

Suddenly the Falcon belched into life, a puff of smoke escaping from the undercarriage and seeping into the trunk, where we began to choke.

'Cover your mouth,' Gloria said, pulling her dupatta up over her face.

We continued to wheeze as the bus trundled its way out of the reclamation grounds and away from The Great Raman Circus of Chennai. Through the fumes from the bus, the big top looked like nothing more than a haze.

'Look out for Lilavati Hospital.' Gloria coughed. 'Candies is close to there.'

Suddenly the road grew wider, and the bus turned its back on the city.

'We're on the highway; is this the right way?'

Gloria's breath grew fast and thick as she looked out at the stretch of traffic behind us and at the lights of the city as they rolled farther and farther away. Then suddenly the traffic began to slow, filing into a number of yellow lanes until we had come to a standstill.

'A toll bridge,' Gloria said. 'We must get out here.'

We wrapped our bags around our wrists, hoisted up the door, and clambered out onto the road. The driver of a Tata truck behind us leant out his window. 'Bangladeshi immigrants,' he began to shout, flashing his headlights over us so that we could barely see.

'Hurry.' Gloria pulled me up off the ground, and we began to weave in and out among the tooting lorries and cars.

We followed the highway back up towards the city, cars sweeping past us and blowing dust into our parched eyes, the air around us growing colder. 'It's still a million miles away.' I stopped to catch my breath. 'We will never make it.'

'Arjun will be waiting,' she said. Gloria picked up the pace, forcing me to run to keep up with her.

We passed by roadside fires, where men huddled together for heat, and a group of women balancing bucketloads of stones on their heads. None of them looked our way, and when at last we reached Bandra Fire Station, it was well into the middle of the night. 'It is along this road,' Gloria said, a smile creeping across her face. We followed the road all the way up until we came to Candies. A single light shone inside, down onto the display of cakes and cookies in a refrigeration case. Gloria rattled at the door, which had been bolted shut, and then she pressed her face against the window to peer inside. 'It's closed,' she said. 'There's nobody there.' She turned around and slid down against the wall, tiredness finally taking over.

'We will come again tomorrow; he'll be here.'

'Yes, of course.' She raised her head. 'He will come back for us.'

The night guards for Bandra Road came tapping their sticks along the ground. 'Move along,' they said. 'You don't belong here.'

We spent the night under the archway of Bandra station, alongside drunks and beggars. 'Hold on to your things,' Gloria said. 'And whatever you do, don't sleep.' All night long black-and-yellow taxis and rickshaws beetled their way along in the rain, and beyond that everything was dark. It was only when morning came that we could see across to the other side of the road, to row after row of houses covered with plastic sheets. They rose up high into the air, stacked one on top of the other. It was not much different from Dharavi, and it filled me with dread.

'We must wash.' Gloria pulled me away from the steps. 'There's no time to lose.'

We found a wash pump at the side of the station, and Gloria reached into her bag for a bar of soap and began to wash her feet and arms with delicate, frothy strokes. Little children watched from a distance as she fixed her hair up into a silver comb, pulling strands loose about her face, and then she drew dark lines about her eyes. 'Banno,' they called to her. 'She's going to meet her groom.'

'Hurry, hurry,' Gloria said, forcing me towards the pump, where she splashed the cold water onto my face and along my arms. 'We are free; we can go anywhere, do anything.'

I looked about me: at the stretch of huts and the little children with curved bellies and bare feet. It didn't feel like freedom.

'Come,' Gloria said. 'Let's go.'

A deep-red canopy had been drawn out over the front of Candies with 'Cake and Coffee Emporium' printed in slanted white lettering, and underneath it customers sat at tables drinking coffee and eating syrupy pastries. Inside, the place was humming with chatter and the clank of plates, as waiters in striped red-and-white aprons rushed back and forth.

Gloria stood inside the doorway for a moment looking around her. 'Can I help you?' one of the waiters asked. Gloria shook her head and then smiled at him. 'We will have a chutney sandwich and two chai,' she said brightly. We settled ourselves at a window seat. 'It's still early,' she said. 'He might not come for a while.'

Gloria talked excitedly about the new show, the importance of the right costumes and backdrops, jumping every time she heard the bell chime over the door. And then when we had finished our food she grew quiet and began to pick at the skin around her nails. When the waiter came to clear away our breakfast things, she ordered two more cups of chai.

'Where did you get the money?' I asked.

'It's all I have left from the time I worked in the tannery,' she said. 'So drink slowly.'

'What about your money from the circus?'

'I've been sending it on to Arjun,' she said. 'He's been keeping it safe for when we start the show. He calls it a nest-egg.'

■ ■ ■

We watched the people coming and going at Candies' Cake and Coffee Emporium: the students who ordered milkshakes 'to go' and talked loudly into mobile phones, the ladies with oversize sunglasses propped on top of their heads, and men in suits who stood at the counter clicking their fingers and shouting at the waiters to hurry up. Soon the place began to empty.

'Excuse,' one of the waiters said, running a floor brush underneath our table. When I raised my chai to my lips, it had grown as cold and tasteless as dishwater.

The last of the customers made their way outside and the waiters began setting chairs up on top of the tables. 'He didn't come,' Gloria said. 'It was all a mistake.'

There was nothing else to do but to return to Candies each day until we ran out of money and the manager asked us to leave. 'This is not a library.' He whipped the menu out of Gloria's hands. 'You have been here three days in a row and have not ordered a thing, so eat or leave.'

Gloria set the menu down on the table and stood up. 'We should never have come.' She made her way outside and began racing down the street.

'Where are we going?' I called after her.

'Back to the circus; there's nowhere else to go.'

I caught up with her and pulled on her arm. 'We can set up our own show, just like we had planned,' I pleaded. Despite the fact that Arjun hadn't shown, I couldn't bear the thought of returning to the circus and to Mr. Prem.

'Look at us.' She turned me in towards a shop window. Our clothes were already tattered and soiled from lying in doorways, and our hair was unoiled and hung limply about our faces. 'We would never be able to make it on our own.'

'Something terrible may have happened to delay him,' I said. 'What if he comes and we are not here?'

Gloria began to cry. 'You're right; he wouldn't just forget, not after all the things he promised.' She returned to sit at the corner of Candies so that she could watch for Arjun coming or going, and while she waited, it was decided that I would try to make some money, for we had nothing left.

Phoenix Mall was a concrete giant, its boulevards flanked with restaurants. It was there that all the tourists came to buy their Indian souvenirs: miniature Taj Mahals, statues of Ganesh, and silk scarves. As they moved about the mall, they would stop every now and then to watch the street performers, leaning over at the end to deposit crisp rupee notes into the tin cans. Just outside the Big Bazaar was the largest flow of people, and in the centre a boy was balancing a ball on a string. 'Ladies and gentlemen,' he called. 'Never will you have seen such a trick.' He whipped the ball up into the air higher and higher as the crowd roared and cheered. For a moment I thought it was Maheesh with his mop of hair, and my heart soared, but when I reached him he was much thinner, and his face was flat like a roti. When he had finished his act, he swept along the row of spectators with an outstretched hand, collecting note after note.

It was the only place for my act, so I secured an empty orange crate from the juice bar on the ground floor and placed it just outside the bazaar. As I folded into the box, it crossed my mind to stay there in the darkness all day, but when I emerged, there was only a sprinkling of silver paise on the ground, and the crowd had already moved.

'You should give up; this patch is only for *real* performers,' the ball boy called out to me. '*You* will drive them all to the Galleria.' He pointed up towards the top of the mall.

'I *am* a real performer.'

He bounced his ball up into the air. 'You look like a bird to me.'

Anger surged through me, like when our house was knocked down. I stood on top of the crate, my body puffed out like a myna bird. 'Roll up, roll up to see an incredible act,' I called. 'The magnificent Elastic Girl.'

The crowd began to turn towards me, and I bent right back, clasped my ankles with my hands, and walked like a crab. They began to laugh and clap, and then with their attention on me, I stepped down from the crate, opened the lid, and slipped inside.

They littered the bottom of the box with notes and coins. 'You will do me out of business,' the ball boy shouted out. By the end of the day, he had decided to move on, setting himself up outside Provogue, a shop selling sunhats and mini electric fans. Maheesh wouldn't have given up so easily.

Each day I returned, but the money I made was still not enough to put a roof over our heads or to provide more than one meal a day. 'If you join me, we could make so much more.' I tried to convince her away from Candies. 'It's the double acts that everyone wants.' But she continued to sit listlessly, dark circles forming underneath her eyes.

'Arjun will come,' she continued to say. 'He will rescue us soon.'

But it was Baba who saved us.

Just as we turned up at Candies each morning, he would arrive, taking away with him an iced tea and a slice of New York cheesecake. He had a hint of stubble along his jaw, thick dark eyebrows, and he always wore a black shirt and shiny patent shoes. When he passed us on the corner, he smiled. 'Namaste.' He nodded politely and did not step around us, or tut like all the other customers.

'You rest, sir; I'll fetch for you,' I offered one morning, motioning for him to take a seat outside and hoping to make a tip.

When I emerged with his cheesecake, I found him bent over, speaking to Gloria, who had the beginnings of a smile on her lips.

21

Baba owned an apartment in a seven-story complex on Mira Road.

'It's one thousand square foot.' He guided us around the rooms. 'It has air-con and Internet connection.' He stopped then, looked at our faces, and shook his head. 'You should have a bath,' he said. 'You'll feel much better after that.'

The bathroom was lined with an assortment of tubes and bottles: lime and black-pepper bath salts, herbal creams, Bhringraj hair oil, and Chandrika soap. Gloria went along unscrewing lids and breathing in the smells.

'I'm glad Arjun didn't come,' she said.

We lay in the bath together, taking it in turns to soap each other's back. I could feel Gloria's bones, like the wooden bars on a marimba.

'Why did Baba bring us here?'

'I think he's fallen in love with me.' Gloria rested her head dreamily against the rim of the tub.

'He's old enough to be your father.' I flicked water up into her face.

'A little chubby and grey.' She laughed. 'But he wears nice clothes, and he has eyes like Shiney Ahuja.'

'But what does he want?'

'He's just like Lord Rama.' She stood up in the bath and reached for a towel. 'He wants to save us.'

■ ■ ■

It was true; Baba seemed like the saving kind. In the mornings he would tear up our leftover parathas and sprinkle them out the back window for the pigeons and sparrows stalking the gardens below, and when he watched the news on NMTV, he became unsettled in his chair and began to preach about the divide between north and south Mumbai.

'They talk about equal rights for all, but that's all it is—talk,' he said. 'The truth is something completely different.'

'What is the truth?' Gloria asked.

'This country—it needs a complete overhaul,' he said. 'And it's up to people like me to do it.'

'Yes, Baba, you are the one who can change it all,' she said.

Baba reached out for her hand and pressed it against his cheek.

While she massaged his feet in the evenings and fetched him cups of tea, my job was to help Mary, Baba's housekeeper from Kerala. Mary's eyes were as black as her face, and she moved about the apartment like a shadow, speaking only in Malayalam, so that we could not understand a word she was saying. Every so often she came to stand behind me as I washed clothes or scoured pots, muttering at me with hard-edged words.

'She never takes her eyes off me.'

'The woman is old,' Gloria said. 'What harm can she do?'

'She tells Baba when I do something wrong; she even makes things up.'

'He doesn't have time to worry about such things; he is much too busy.'

Baba was a very busy man, often leaving early in the mornings before we stirred. He said he was into real estate and spent his days collecting the rent. When he returned each evening, I would watch him through the crack in his bedroom door, counting the money out onto his bed. He would roll the notes into neat little bundles, tie them with bands, and tuck them into the lining of a coat that hung inside his wardrobe. It unsettled me, the short yellowish fur of the coat like that of a wild dhole dog.

We knew what Baba did for a living and that he was from the city of Palghar, north of Mumbai, but Baba knew nothing about us, only that we had come from the circus.

'You never ask any questions,' Gloria teased him one evening. 'Don't you want to know about these strays you have taken in?'

'Think of it as a fresh beginning,' he said. 'You're starting life all over again.'

But, like cats, we could not help ourselves from meandering back to where we had come from. 'Mr. Kalpak always called them pancakes,' Gloria said, as we tucked into a plate of dosas for breakfast one morning.

Baba leant over and took her plate away. 'Our food does not compare to the circus?' he asked.

We sat in silence for a moment, Mary coming to clear the plates away, her tongue clicking loudly.

'Sorry, Babaji,' Gloria said. 'We're grateful for what you have done.' She stood up to help Mary with clearing away the dishes.

'Don't worry about such things,' he said, his tone lightening. 'All I ask is that you listen to me.'

'We do, Baba,' I said.

'From now on there is no more Elastic Girl, or Queen of the Air. To me you are Bishakha and Chandra: the Star and the Moon.'

■ ■ ■

The room we shared at the front of the house had a balcony that looked out over Mira Road Station and the western express highway beyond. One night I woke up to find Gloria leaning over the railings, her arms out at her sides. As I sat up suddenly, the blood rushed to my head. 'Gloria?'

When she turned around, there were tears on her face.

'What is it?'

'I'm thinking of the circus: the sounds, the smells, the feeling of soaring through the air.'

'You miss it?'

'It's as though something in me is missing.' She wiped her eyes. 'But, this is where we belong now. Baba is right; there is no time for looking back.'

'We could still perform. Maybe Baba knows someone in the entertainment business?'

'Have you forgotten what he said? We are the moon and the star now; he does not want us to perform.'

'We can't just stay in here forever.'

'And leave all this?' She waved her hand around at the cream curtains, the clean bedsheets and the polished wooden floors. 'Here we have everything we ever wished for.'

He made sure that we never went without, spoiling us with gifts from Elco market, and then day by day the circus became something imagined, as though it had never really happened at all. I continued to help with the chores, and Gloria dedicated herself to keeping Baba happy.

'Only the best for my Chandra,' he said to Gloria as she held up a new blue-and-orange salwar kameez, a sequined churidar.

'You shouldn't spend so much of your money,' she scolded him.

'Everything I have I want to share with you.' He sat back on the large velvet armchair and waiting for Gloria to go and put on the new clothes. When she returned he asked her to dance for him, and she performed some of the moves from the Bharata Natyam, the sound of her silver anklets tinkling as she moved.

'Viddy,' Mary scolded, returning to her work.

Watching Gloria dance around the room in her new Kameez and Baba lying back in his lounger, something made me shiver. More than anything I wanted to be away from Mira Road and that apartment, but the farthest we seemed to ever make it to was the small compound at the back of the apartment.

'Let's go to the Hanuman Temple or to Bhakti Park?' I suggested to Gloria as we strolled around the concrete garden.

'Baba says that the smell from the Bharat refinery would choke you,' she said. 'Better to stay here where we are comfortable.'

'So you do everything he tells you? You've no mind of your own?'

'My mind tells me that we are very blessed, that the two of us have been saved.'

'How is this being saved? We're trapped here like animals, just like in the circus.'

'Baba is trying to protect us.'

'You always said that we could be stars, that anything was possible once we reached Mumbai.'

'It was foolish talk.'

'Is that what *he* told you?'

'Baba knows best.'

'He reminds me too much of Mr. Prem,' I said. 'Its like he's playing some game.'

'You ungrateful child! He's nothing like that man.' Gloria left me there, making her way back up the steps to the apartment.

■ ■ ■

It was not long before Gloria and Baba were sharing a bed.

'Are you in love with him?'

'When he kisses me, it's like I'm the only thing left in the whole wide world,' she breathed. In the evening she would lay her head down in his lap, and he would stroke her like a prized pet.

In her eyes Baba could do no wrong, so I didn't tell her about him taking money from a young boy in the yard and then slapping him about the face until he cried, or about the knife that he kept wrapped up in the dhole coat, along with all the money.

There had to be something that would make it all clear, that would make Gloria see. So while she began to spend more time locked away in their bedroom, my time was spent watching Baba from the balcony as he came and went, and following Mary when she went out to do the grocery shopping.

Mary had locked the gate, but I pushed my way out through a gap in the fencing and followed her all the way to Asmita supermarket. She stopped off in the temple to offer fruit for her puja, and when she paused to talk to an amber-haired lady outside Vedanta Hospital, I tucked myself in behind the wheel of the flower seller's cart, so that I could hear what they were saying.

'Another one of the girls has been soiled.' The amber-haired lady nodded towards the pink hospital walls. 'Doctor Singh will see to it that all is taken care of.'

Mary spat out into the road and said something in Malayalam that sounded like a warning, and then she hooked her grocery bags over her arms and moved on.

'Plenty men, but not enough girls; that's what is wrong in this city,' the lady shouted after her. She reached into her handbag for a lipstick, and redrew the thick lines around her mouth.

Baba was more difficult to track, always leaving at different times in the morning and returning late at night, but on Diwali there was a chance. Mary had been given the day off to go and join in the celebrations, and Gloria, who insisted that she had a headache, did not wish to leave her room.

Baba made his way out of the apartment, and I popped my head in around the corner of her bedroom door. There was a crack of yellow light seeping in through the curtains, and the room smelt of burnt wood.

'I'm going to offer some prayers to Lakshmi.' I said. The blankets on the bed moved slightly. 'Then to see the Diwali fireworks at Maxus Mall.'

'It's Diwali already?' she asked in a throaty voice. 'I haven't heard any crackers.' Gloria had been spending more and more time in her room, like a sick old woman.

Outside the gates of the apartment, Baba hailed a rickshaw for Grant Road, and as he haggled with the driver over the price, I propped myself onto the bumper at the back and hooked my hands in behind the metal frame.

The rickshaw took us along a road lined with restaurants and bars. Girls stood in the doorways, passing their fingers through their hair and laughing among themselves, and every so often, the rickshaw would make a diversion down one of the narrow lanes, and Baba would enter a house. At one such house there was the woman with the amber hair. She came to the door dressed in a silk nightgown, and her face was ruddy, as if she had only just woken up. She disappeared for a few moments, and when she returned, she handed Baba a bundle of money.

The niggling pain in the pit of my stomach would not go away, as each night I listened to Gloria and Baba's moans in the next room. I was back in the Palace Grounds, Mr. Prem's breath thick against my face.

■ ■ ■

It continued that way for some time, until the monsoons had passed and the cool December evenings arrived, bringing with them my thirteenth birthday.

Baba bought a cake in the shape of a star.

'Open it,' he said, pushing a present wrapped in shiny red paper across the table.

Inside was a pendant, set with shimmering pink stones.

'It's to replace that old thing you wear.' He nodded towards my grandfather's pocket watch. 'Here let me.' Standing behind me he unclasped the watch, and hooked the new necklace around my neck, setting the pendant just right.

Gloria's face hardened as she watched his fingers.

'I've no need for this,' I said.

'Thirteen is not so young. Soon you will be a woman.'

While Mary served up stuffed capsicum and aloo palak, Gloria and Baba began to argue.

'You didn't get *me* a cake,' she said.

'Heh? You do not know your own birthday; what am I to do?'

'My sign is Kumbha,' Gloria replied.

'Ah, the water pitcher—emotional and petty,' Baba replied.

Gloria speared her capsicum with a fork, and behind them I could see Mary smile.

■ ■ ■

Their arguments continued, with Baba coming home later each evening. There were no more gifts from Elco market, and at night the only sounds I heard from their room were raised voices and then the sound of Gloria sobbing.

'That woman is a witch,' she complained about Mary. 'She's using black magic to turn him against me.'

The untidiness of the house, the way the food was cooked, how Mary spoke, all of it irritated Gloria, until one day she lunged at Mary, accusing her of trying to poison her food. Mary only stared at her through hard eyes, as though she had heard such things many times before.

'It's too bright,' she said when I tried to open her curtains or to coax her to get some fresh air, but when Baba returned in the evenings she would appear obediently at the bedroom door.

Like a malati vine, he had wrapped his woody stems around Gloria. I watched, as she grew increasingly tired and drawn, as life was squeezed from her body.

When it felt so wrong, I should have done something, but I was only a child who knew very little about the world, and before I had time to act Baba made the first move.

'I'm moving you to a new home,' he said. 'This place has been rented out.'

Gloria clung to him as if he had just saved her soul. 'I knew you would take me away from here and away from that woman.'

22

He took us to Falkland Road, to a three-story house up a narrow lane. It was a place that I'd been before.

'This is Chandra and Bishakha,' Baba told the lady who propped herself up in the doorway. Her amber hair was loose, reaching down to her waist. 'Bubbles will look after you,' he said. Her long face was familiar—the eyes and mouth painted on in a way that meant you could not tell her age.

'Pretty, pretty,' she said, placing a fingernail underneath my chin, and when I heard her voice, it came back to me; she was the lady I had seen Mary speaking to outside Vedanta Hospital.

'She's only thirteen,' Baba said. 'She can be a runner; that's all.'

Bubbles held the door open and led us inside. The corridor was dimly lit by a single bulb, which hung off a low-slung wire, and there was cracked blue paint on the walls, with streaks of damp running down towards the floor. In a hole in the centre of the wall, there was a picture of Krishna playing his flute and a candle burning weakly in the centre of a brass diya.

'What is this place?' Gloria looked about her as though she had only just woken up.

'This is your new home,' Baba said. 'You will stay here now.'

'This is not a home! I know what this is,' she screamed.

Baba stepped back towards the door, and Bubbles placed a hand under the crook of Gloria's arm. 'Come, come.' She drew her away from him, but Gloria broke Bubbles' hold on her and reached for Baba's hand.

'What are you doing, hey?' she whispered to him, pressing her lips against his fingers. 'Have I done something to make you angry?'

'It's only for a little while.' Baba removed her hand like a glove and turned towards the door.

'Tell me what you want, Babaji,' Gloria continued to plead. 'Just don't leave us here.'

Bubbles came up from behind and placed her arms around Gloria's waist, holding her firmly in place while Baba unlocked the door.

'You can't do this,' Gloria cried, struggling against Bubbles' hold.

'I will be back for you before you know it.' We could hear him on the other side of the door, turning the lock.

Gloria began to scream and yell at the top of her voice, and escaping from Bubbles, she hammered her fists against the door. 'Come back,' she called after him. 'Please, don't do this to us!'

'You are here to stay now,' Bubbles said to her. 'All this wailing will make no difference.' But still Gloria continued to pound on the door and shout for Baba to return. 'He said he loved me and that he'd never leave me.'

None of it made sense to me then: what this place was, why Baba had left us here, and why Gloria was so frantic to escape. But something made me turn and run, fleeing down the dark corridor and up the wooden stairs. When I reached a caged window, I pulled hopelessly on the metal bars, my body shaking with fear.

'Come back down here,' Bubbles called out to me. She was standing on the bottom stair with one hand resting on the handrail, the other on her hip. Behind her, Gloria was still crumpled on the hallway floor.

'Stay away from me.' I began making my way around the landing, banging on the bedroom doors. 'I'll go to the police.'

Bubbles threw her head back and snorted, but suddenly one of the doors behind me opened up, and a plump little girl appeared. Her face was caked in white powder, and she had big green eyes and knotted hair. 'Come,' she called softly. 'I'm Nisha; I'll look after you.'

When I looked back down over the railings, Bubbles was hauling Gloria up off the floor. 'I can't have you making a scene all evening, driving customers away,' she said.

'She will get her settled; don't worry,' Nisha said. 'Bubbles is used to this sort of thing.'

Inside, Nisha's room was no bigger than the washroom on Mira Road, with crumbling walls, one single bed, and a fan on the ceiling that did not work. It looked directly across at a row of old wooden houses. On the bottom floor of each house were cage-like structures, and inside sat girls, combing their hair and sometimes reaching through the bars towards the men who walked up and down the street. Looking down at them, one of the girls raised her skirt in the air, and it was clear, even from a distance, that she was wearing nothing underneath.

'Why's she doing that?'

'They're cage workers.' Nisha settled herself on the bed. 'They charge only two rupees a go, but they're treated very badly.'

'By who?'

'Their madam, the customers,' Nisha said. 'They do the sex things, you know?'

The narrow street was busy, a stream of lorries and taxis moving slowly around the procession of vendors selling medicines, magazines, and snacks. A flow of men snaked their way along each side of the traffic, their heads turned towards the cages. Some of the men stood with their arms folded, heads tilted to the side, as though they were deep in thought, and then a plump woman hauled herself up from the front step of one of the houses and beckoned to one of the men. He came forwards and pressed some money into her hand before disappearing into the house with one of the girls from the cage.

When I turned back into the bedroom, Nisha was lying on the bed, her hands cupped underneath her chin. 'Why are *you* here?' I asked, my heart now thumping inside my chest.

'My mother took me to a village in Karnataka and dedicated me to the goddess Yellamma,' she said. 'Then they took me here to be a handmaiden.'

'*This* is a brothel, too?'

'One of the best in Falkland Road,' Nisha smiled. 'Bubbles only takes the prettiest girls.'

'Baba?'

'You will meet Shirin and Renuka; he rescued them, too.' She rolled off the bed and reached down to the floor for a makeup box. 'The girls are all resting, but I like to be ready on time.' She began adding more powder to her face, drawing red lips.

'We'll leave; Bubbles can't make us stay.'

'There *is* no leaving—unless for trips to the doctor's or special messages for Bubbles.' Nisha pressed her lips together. 'And if you try to leave, you'll be caught and beaten, so it's foolish really.'

'Where has she taken Gloria?' I asked, crossing Nisha's room and opening the door.

'She will be in Asha's old room, at the far end of the corridor. They'll be busy getting her ready.'

Gloria was alone and laid out flat on a bed. She was dressed in a deep-red choli that had been pinned in tight under her breasts; her hair had been braided and her face painted white, like Nisha. When she looked at me, her eyes were unable to focus.

'What did she give you?'

'Some powders.' She looked up towards the ceiling. 'They're making me float.'

'We have to get out of this place; they're going to make you sell yourself, just like all the other girls.'

'Baba will be back soon; we have to wait for him,' her words fell away at the end.

'It was Baba who brought us here.' Sitting down beside her on the bed, I began to shake her. 'This was his plan all along; can't you see?'

Suddenly a chorus of voices rumbled along the corridor, girls making their way from room to room, laughing and singing, as though they were preparing for a party. Gloria rolled over to one side and propped herself up on her elbow. 'What's that noise?

'They're getting ready for the men. Bubbles has prepared you, too.'

Gloria looked down at the dress she was wearing. 'No, Baba is coming for us. You will see.' And she lay back down on the bed.

Out on the corridor, the girls began to make their way downstairs. Nisha rapped gently on the door and then opened it up into the room. 'You must come down,' she said cheerily. 'Muskan will have dinner ready.'

'Gloria's not feeling well.'

'Bubbles doesn't like to be kept waiting.' Nisha disappeared down the stairs.

Gloria slid her way over to the other side of the bed and sat up so that her back was turned towards me.

'What are you doing?'

'I'm hungry.' When she stood up, she swayed unsteadily so that she had to reach out and hold on to the window ledge.

'You're out of your mind; they will make you do dirty things, like those women from the brothel houses in Thiruvotriyur.'

'Don't worry, Muthu. I'd never do anything like that.' She reached out her hand towards my face.

'If you make any trouble, Baba will never take you back,' Bubbles said; she had entered the room without us noticing. She was now dressed in a bright-red-and-yellow sari, and her hair had been pulled back onto the top of her head, into a smooth ball.

'Tell Muthu that I'm not here to work. Put her mind at rest,' Gloria said.

'While you are here, you will do as I ask,' Bubbles said bluntly.

'Baba would not let them touch me.' Gloria reached out again for the dresser. 'I'm his.'

Bubbles' face turned to stone, and she thundered across the room, pulling Gloria roughly by the arm. 'You will come now; I'm tired of all this nonsense.'

Gloria pulled away and then staggered backwards until she was pressed against the wall. 'I won't do it,' she shouted as Bubbles caught her by the hair and began to pound her with a fist. Someone grabbed me from behind and pulled me away.

'She'll beat you, too,' Nisha said. She dragged me along the corridor and down the stairs. 'You must leave them alone, or you'll both suffer.'

'She will kill her,' I cried, and I tried to scramble back up the stairs.

'A new girl is worth a lot of money, so she won't kill her,' she said. 'Bubbles will only give her a lesson; that's all.' Nisha placed an arm gently around my shoulder. 'It will be over soon, then things will be back to normal.'

'Normal?'

'Come, you will feel better after you have eaten.' She took me with her down the remainder of the stairs.

In the kitchen, Muskan, the cook, was setting out plates of navratan korma and parathas before a group of women and girls. They all stopped talking and turned to look at us, their eyelids drooping heavily. 'So this is the one who's been keeping Habib awake,' one of the girls said. She had a baby nuzzled against her breast, wrapped in a soft yellow blanket. It looked at me with eyes as wide as saucers.

'She's new to all this,' Nisha said. She nodded at the space beside her on the bench for me to sit down. 'The other one is refusing to come down.'

Some of them shook their heads and clicked their tongues before resuming their conversation. The girl with the baby was telling them a tale about a customer who had asked for a price reduction. 'He said it was not the same with a condom,' she told them, pausing briefly to feed her baby a small ball of rice and raita. 'He said that he could do it like that anytime with his wife.'

As they laughed, one of the older women leant across the table and offered me a bottle of rum. 'It will help with the crying,' she said.

Raising my hand to my cheek, I found it came away wet with tears.

'She always buys nice food.' Nisha reached for a paratha.

'Yes, we all eat well here,' Bubbles said, coming into the kitchen. 'No one can work on an empty stomach.'

Her hair was still perfectly smooth and her face unruffled.

'Gloria?'

'She's resting,' Bubbles said. She clapped her hands in the air. 'Hurry along, girls; it's almost six o'clock.'

They began to clear off their plates and make their way out across the hallway. Bubbles offered each of them a blessing as they passed her at the door, before they disappeared behind a brightly coloured curtain on the other side of the hallway.

'Where are they going?' I asked Nisha.

'That's the waiting room,' Nisha whispered. 'The police will arrest us if we stand in the hall.'

'You too,' Bubbles called to Nisha.

Nisha paused in the doorway, and Bubbles laid the palms of her hands down gently on top of her head. 'Try not to talk so much,' she said to Nisha. 'Mr. Lathigra says you are like a radio in his ear.'

Nisha giggled and disappeared behind the curtain.

As I made for the stairs, Bubbles held out her arm to block me. 'You can look after Habib.' She nodded towards the girl behind me who was holding the baby. The girl planted a kiss on the baby's forehead, handed him over to me, and left the room.

'But Gloria will need me.' I tried to cradle the baby in my arms as it wriggled in its sleep.

'*This* is your job now,' she said. 'This and anything else I ask you to do.'

We sat in the kitchen, Habib sleeping in my arms as Muskan cleared away dishes and brushed the floor. Fresh tears came as I listened to the voices of men coming and going and the sound of their footsteps pounding on the stairs.

'You're worse than that baby,' Muskan tutted. 'Don't you know how lucky you are? You don't have those horrible men sticking their filthy thing in you night after night.'

When the house emptied of men and Habib's mother returned, I hurried upstairs to find Gloria coiled up on her side facing into the wall. The space beside her was still warm as I lay and smoothed her hair.

'Baba will come soon,' she whispered. 'He won't leave us here.'

23

Nisha showed me the white mouse she kept inside her wardrobe. 'I call her Alpa, because she's so little.' She allowed me to hold it and feed it some salt crackers.

'How old are you?'

'I've never known.' Nisha laughed. 'But I've started my menses, so I'm old enough.'

We had been in Falkland Road four months, and I had taken to sharing a room with Nisha. Gloria had started to murmur in her sleep, twisting and turning until her body was covered in a film of sweat.

'It's the drugs,' Nisha said. 'She's hooked.'

'It started with Baba. He was working on her all that time, and I never knew.'

'Some girls won't come any other way.'

'What can we do to make her stop?'

'There's nothing you can do,' Nisha told me. 'But if she's not careful, she will end up like Asha; in the end, Bubbles sent her out onto the street.'

■ ■ ■

It was up to me to do something.

'You need to go without.' I held a glass of ginger punch to Gloria's lips. 'With all these drugs, you just can't see sense.'

'You're going to poison me now?' She tossed the glass out of my hand.

'You need to stop; those powders are making you crazy.'

'*He's* the one making me crazy.' She lifted her arms to show me the purple bruises left by Mr. Iyer.

Mr. Iyer was a regular at the house on Falkland Road and had taken a liking to Gloria. He was an ugly brute of a man, who wore thick, rotting bands of pink thread around his wrists. He had a habit of urinating outside the doorway before he entered the house and then adjusting himself with his hand. The first time he had come to visit Gloria, she had been left with bruises all over her arms and legs.

'We have to get out of here, away from these monsters.'

'But they're everywhere,' Gloria said. 'Only Baba can save us.'

'He will never take us away,' I said. 'Don't you see that this was his plan all along? The gifts, the apartment! That's why Mary behaved as she did; she had seen it all before.'

'He said it's only for a while longer, until he gets somewhere fixed up for us to stay.'

'He's trying to trick you.'

Gloria screamed at me and pushed me towards the door. 'Stop saying those things, and just leave me alone.' She forced me out onto the landing and closed her door.

Baba still had her under his control, and each time he came to collect his money, he visited Gloria in her room in order to keep it that way. I caught him placing a white pill on her tongue before kissing her full on the mouth. 'Just be patient,' he whispered, as he worked his way down her neck. 'Soon I'll take you away with me.'

Nisha was right; there was nothing I could do. As Gloria continued to slide further away from me, Mumbai turned dry and dusty in the soaring June heat. There was something about the sticky air that attracted men to the streets off Grant Road. They swarmed about the place, like bees collecting nectar, and everything dripped with sweat: men with wet patches under their arms, shiny foreheads peeping out from rooms, walls damp from the moisture tripping off the fans that clacked their way hopelessly through the heat.

It seemed as though the girls never left their rooms, and Nisha was always too tired for games. 'Alpa needs to sleep.' She tucked the mouse down in under her covers. 'You're lucky that you have so little to do.'

'I run errands all day, fetching things for Bubbles all the way up and down Grant Road: stockings for Padmal, medicines for Lajita, milk for Habib, and cigarettes for Mr. Belwal.'

'Yes, but it's a busy time now; Bubbles will see to it that everyone is made to work the rooms,' Nisha said.

'*She* doesn't work.'

Nisha laughed. 'Bubbles is a Hijra: a man living as a woman,' she said. 'She doesn't have a koodhi for the men.'

Watching Bubbles more carefully, I noticed that she never left her room without her makeup on, and just like every other man, she had a lump in her throat that bobbed up and down when she talked. 'You have a stare like a tree frog,' she said, when she caught me watching her from across the kitchen.

'Do you want me to fetch your magazines?'

Every two weeks I collected her *Bombay Dost* magazines from Mr. Davesh at Chor Bazaar. Mr. Davesh always wrapped them in cellophane and then placed them in a paper bag.

'Why don't I come with you?' Bubbles said. 'There are some other things that we need to get.' She had a way of walking with her shoulders pushed back and her pelvis jutting out. It was a walk that made people look.

Mr. Davesh kissed Bubbles on both her cheeks and told her she was looking divine, and once the magazines had been tucked into her carrier bag, she pulled me on through the bazaar. 'Pinks and yellows are best for your complexion.' She held up lengths of material against my face.

My mouth grew dry as she made me try on choli dresses, columns of matching bangles, and silver anklets that tinkled when I walked, and when we returned to the house, Padmal was waiting for us behind the coloured curtain. Bubbles had her braid my hair and paint my face.

'Why get dressed when I'm looking after Habib all evening?' My hands twisted the end of a new dupatta. 'He is always making such a mess.'

'You're too good to keep for Habib,' Bubbles said.

'Muskan: she needs me to help with dinner; it's too much for her alone.'

'She will fetch a very good price, maybe three thousand rupees?' she said to Padmal.

Rising from the chair, I pushed Padmal away from me. 'Baba said I'm a runner; that's what he said,' I cried at Bubbles.

'This is not an ashram,' she said. 'It's time you paid your way; in two days you will start.' She turned then and left the room.

'They want new blood, and men will pay a lot of money for a virgin,' Padmal said. 'Bubbles has been saving you up.'

They didn't know what Mr. Prem had done to me, that I wasn't pure any more. 'I won't do it,' I said.

'That's what we all say at the start,' Padmal said. 'My uncle took me here when I was ten, and now look at me; I'm an old woman.'

With the back of my hand, I wiped the paint from my lips and then tore at my hair until the braid was hanging loose. 'No!' I screamed, running out into the hallway. 'They won't come near me.'

In the bedroom Nisha was sitting on the bed patting the soft curve of Alpa's back as he rested in her lap. 'She's going to make me work,' I cried, falling down onto the bed.

'The customers are getting bored.' Nisha placed a hand on my shoulder. 'Without new girls we'll lose them all, and then we will all end up in cages on the other side of the street.'

She returned to rubbing Alpa's back, while my mind swam back to the circus, and to the inside of the little glass box. The faces of the audience were turned up towards me: my father, my mother, my grandmother, Mr. Prem—all of them watching as I struggled to break free, gasping for air.

Nisha was gone when I awoke, and Bhavani and Seema were standing on either side of the bed looking down on me. 'We don't want a scene,'

Bhavani said, looking towards a man who was standing at the foot of the bed.

He was dressed in a blue shirt and carried a leather bag in his hand. 'I'm Dr. Singh.' He unzipped the bag and removed a plastic wrapper containing a small metal coil.

'What's he doing here?' I asked, sitting up in the bed.

Bhavani and Seema pushed me back down and removed my skirt and pants. 'It's to stop any more trips to Vendanta Hospital,' Bhavani said.

Struggling helplessly against their grasp, I watched as the doctor came forwards and removed a metal tool from his bag. 'Bend your legs.' He leant down over me. 'This will only hurt for a second.'

'You need to keep still, or it will sting even more,' Seema whispered to me as I whimpered and cried. 'Its for your own good.'

Dr. Singh nodded at Seema and Bhavani, and they strengthened their hold on me. He began to work the metal tool between my legs, prying me open like a can of Jyoti, just as Mr. Prem had done.

'Just breathe,' Seema said.

He removed the coil from its package, and when he pushed it inside me, my screams bounded through the house.

Gloria appeared in the doorway. She was wearing only a loose white choli, and there were purple marks around her bare ankles. 'What have you done to her?' She looked down at the stained sheet beneath me.

'Bubbles introduced a new rule,' Bhavani said. 'She will thank us in the end.'

Gloria came and rested her head beside me as the doctor laid out some pills by my bedside and a roll of cotton pads. 'The pain will ease, and then you will no longer know it is there,' he said.

As Seema and Bhavani accompanied him out of the room, I could hear the doctor telling them to keep an eye out for any hot flushes or blood clots. 'Otherwise she should be OK for work in twenty-four hours,' he said.

'It's all my fault,' Gloria said. 'Oh, Shiva, Shiva.' When she looked up at me, something in her face had changed. 'We will leave.'

'There's no escape; this place is just like the circus.'

'I will find a way,' she said. 'Leave it with me.'

All night cramps pressed down on my stomach as I clasped on tightly to my grandfather's watch.

'At least you won't have to worry if they won't use a condom,' Nisha whispered. 'That is what happened to Suli, and she ended up with Habib. No other house would have her now.'

'Will they know that I'm not a virgin?'

Nisha pulled herself up in the bed and leaned down to examine my face in the grey light of the room. 'You've been with someone before?'

'Someone attacked me.' The words sprang out at Nisha like a black leopard, causing her to jolt back suddenly.

'Who?'

'It was a man in the circus.'

'You can't tell anyone,' she said. 'Bubbles thinks that you are her prize calf; she's expecting you to make her rich.'

'It hurt, like this kind of pain.' I crossed my arms over my stomach. 'He made me feel like an animal, like my mind was someone else's.'

'It always hurts a little, but you'll get used to it,' she said cheerfully. 'Hopefully you'll still have some bleeding from the coil, and then they'll never know the difference.' Nisha settled down and went back to sleep.

My grandfather's watch ticked loudly in my ear, taking me back to Ambattur. Dadi was taking me on the train to Anna Nagar, and we were watching the man sitting opposite as he shelled a boiled egg onto a piece of torn newspaper and then ate it in three swift bites. And then we were there, standing outside the high walls of Aashiana. 'You can't tell anyone you have been here,' dadi warned me before we went inside.

My grandfather, the great Samir Tushar was sitting on a high-back chair beside a window, an electric fan blowing at his wisps of grey hair. 'Come here,' he said, in a voice that was raspy and deep. Clinging to my father's leg, I was dragged towards his chair. He had hairs growing out from the ends of his nose, and his bottom lip was the colour of a Jambul Fruit. 'There is something I want you to know.' He draped a huge hand across my shoulder. 'None of it was ever your fault.'

'Look, Dadi,' I shouted as I pointed out through the window at a red-and-purple kite as it sliced through the sky. 'Look, look.'

Both of them turned towards the window as the kite plummeted to the ground.

■ ■ ■

The following morning everyone knew about my visit from Dr. Singh.

'She's still sore,' Nisha told them.

'You need to do plenty of walking,' Lajita said. 'It helps to move it into place.'

'Hot baths to stop infection,' Suli added.

A buzz of excitement rose up over breakfast as they debated the best colour of choli for me to wear. 'White for innocence,' one of them said. Beside me Nisha dug me in the ribs.

'Red always makes them hot,' Padmal laughed. 'Then it is all over and done with quicker.'

Bubbles fluttered about between the girls. 'Now, now, it is already decided,' she said. 'It will be purple and yellow: mystical and pure.'

My stomach turned, and as I helped Muskan to clear up the dishes, I dropped one of the copper handis on the stone floor so that it rang like a bell. Muskan clicked her tongue but did not look up from the sink. 'You are to go and see Chandra,' she whispered to me. 'That fool of a girl has a plan.'

Gloria was waiting for me in her room. 'It's done,' she said. She told me how Mr. Iyer had paid her a visit the previous evening, and she had stolen his wallet, giving everything she found to Muskan as a bribe. 'She's going to leave the door open this afternoon, while she is preparing dinner; we must go then.'

Nisha did not leave the room all afternoon, making it impossible for me to pack any belongings. 'Do you want to play puppets?' she asked, holding out a sock dotted with eyes and a nose.

'The pain is too bad,' I moaned, lying on the bed and watching as Nisha moved the puppets about on the edge of the bed, pretending that one was a tea-estate owner, the other a poor tea-picker girl. 'You should get out of here,' I said.

'Leave? This is my home,' she said. 'And one day one of the men will propose, maybe Mr. Lathigra.'

As I began to cry, Gloria came through to fetch me. 'I need to oil Bishakha's hair; Bubbles said she needs to be looking her best.'

Nisha laid her socks on the bed. 'When you come back, they will be married,' she giggled.

'It's not fair on the girl,' Muskan whispered to Gloria as we slipped out past her. 'Someone like *you* can't survive on the street.'

We made our way through the passageways at the back of Falkland Road and all the way to Durga Devi Park. We lay down on the grass and watched the clouds up above us drifting by, and then Gloria reached out and placed her hand in mine; it felt sticky and frail, the calluses caused by the trapeze bar protruding out against her skin.

Even in the heat, my body shook.

'Mr. Iyer will kill me if he ever sees me again,' Gloria said.

'Or Bubbles; she's probably looking for us now.'

'We have to get away from here.' Gloria rose up unsteadily from the ground.

'We can get on a train to Avadi. My parents will have mercy on us now.'

'We've no money; everything from Mr. Iyer I gave to Muskan.'

'What about this?' I reached into my skirt and pulled out the pendant from Baba. 'The money would pay for our tickets.'

We found a pawnshop on Lamington road.

'It was my grandmother's,' I told the man behind the counter. 'She has passed on now.'

He examined it under a lens. 'A Meenakari Jadtar,' he said. 'They are worth two thousand rupees.'

'You are taking us for fools,' Gloria snapped at him, beads of sweat forming on her forehead. 'These are precious stones.'

He looked at her over the rim of his glasses. 'Four thousand and not a paise more.'

We went to the Geeta Bhavan restaurant. Gloria picked at her food, her leg bouncing up and down underneath the table, her eyes darting wildly about the room.

'Do you think they will find us here?'

'Who?' Gloria said.

'Mr. Iyer, Bubbles?'

'No, not here.' She fanned herself with a menu. 'They would never come here.'

We made our way to Victoria Terminus, where we enquired about tickets for Avadi. 'Eleven o'clock tomorrow morning, platform twenty-two,' the girl in the ticket booth told us. 'Sleepers will be three hundred rupees each.'

Settling down for the night in the doorway of the *Times of India* building, across the road we could see Victoria Terminus rising up into the air, with its stone dome and pointed arches. The clock above the entrance woke me with a start as it struck two o'clock, and without looking around me, I knew that Gloria was gone.

24

Troops of children came and went through the left-hand side of the station, carrying bags of plastic bottles and tin cans that they had collected from the lines. As I tried not to think about Gloria and where she might be, I examined the stained-glass windows of the terminus, the stone pillars carved with plants and misshapen animals, and the statue of a lady perched on top of the central dome—torch held high in her hand. Still Gloria did not come. Although it was still not light, it felt as though she had been missing for a very long time and that I was never going to see her again.

With shaking hands I checked the money we had received from the pawnbroker's; fifty rupees was missing.

All night I wandered up and down Naoroji Road, the eyes of Mumbai following me: hawkers pitched up at the traffic lights, taxi drivers pulled in along pavements, and vendors setting up their tea corners. 'Gloria, it's me, Muthu,' I whispered into every crowded doorway and in amongst the mass of sleeping bodies stretched out on embankments in the middle of the road. Finally I stopped to ask a chaat seller if he had maybe seen a girl in a yellow suit.

'You might as well try and fit a camel through the eye of a needle as find someone who is lost in Mumbai,' he laughed.

But he was wrong, because just as the sky brightened, I found her, slumped against the wall of the Manama Hotel.

She lay like a bag of rubbish as people stepped over her on their way to work. Her yellow kameez was filthy and twisted awkwardly about her legs, and her grey skin stuck like paper against her sunken face. Standing at a distance, I thought of my father's hand pressing down on mine when we had first watched Gloria swoop through the air. Now, as I looked at her, it was as though nothing of that girl remained.

'I've been looking for you all night.'

'Mr. Jaykar is a very good man,' she said, her head tilted to one side.

'What did he give you?' Dropping down to my knees, I searched through the folds of her skirt, my fingers shaking in anger.

Mr. Jaykar had been one of the clients at Falkland Road, and I remembered then that he worked as a porter at the Manama Hotel.

'He just gave me something to help me along, until we get set up,' she said.

'We're going to my parents' house in Avadi,' I said. 'The train leaves at eleven, so we can still make it.' I pulled at her arm, but Gloria wouldn't move.

'I'm not going.' She sank back against the wall.

'My parents will have pity on us. There are good doctors in Avadi who can save you.'

'I'm past saving now.'

'We were going to *be* something,' I said.

Gloria laughed. 'Do you think your parents want this on their doorstep?' She pulled at her own clothes. 'My father was right about me all along.'

'Stop this! You're Gloria, Queen of the Air.'

Gloria's laughter dissolved into tears, until her entire body was shaking. 'Help me, Muthu,' she cried. 'Help me.'

Instead of taking the train to Avadi, we made our way to Sankalp's drop-in centre at Mumbai Central.

'We have to know that you are committed to the programme,' the doctor said. 'You will be required to undergo counselling and opioid substitution therapy.' He held out a form towards Gloria.

'I'm ready,' she said. Her hand shook as she signed her name on the form.

The doctor offered Gloria a place on their seven-day programme, starting the following morning. 'Everything will be OK,' I told her as we left the clinic. 'Think of how Sanjay Dutt came through the same, and he's one of the biggest stars in Bollywood.'

While Gloria began her treatment, I made my way along Khar West and Juhu Church Road. The streets were lined with musicians, dancers, and mime artists, all hoping to be picked up by one of the entertainment businesses located there.

There was a place outside Apna Bazaar on Mehta Road, a busy thoroughfare, close to the hanging gardens and art galleries. For a while I stood there watching the poster boys with buckets of gum overlaying advertisements on lampposts and walls and handing out flyers for everything from discounted hotel rooms to wedding saris.

Using an empty Perspex box, I positioned myself outside the bazaar and stepped inside the box. It felt cool underneath my feet, like dipping down into the waters off Juhu Beach. All the worry about Gloria and what we were going to do dissolved around me as my body whorled up tighter and tighter, like a sea snail.

When I released myself from the box, there was a small group of people gathered before me, and a scattering of paise on the ground. It was only enough money for two cartons of chiwda, and when Gloria had finished eating hers, she retched into the empty foam box. 'This programme's going to kill me,' she complained, and all night long she shivered and moaned in her sleep.

■ ■ ■

To try to help her along, we used some more of the money from the pendant to move us into a hut behind the railway offices, paying the office manager ten rupees per week. It was pieced together with slices of corrugated iron, rice sacks, and cardboard boxes and smelt like the putrid yellow flesh of a durian fruit, but it was warm and dry. 'You're doing so well,' I told Gloria as she coughed and shivered each evening. 'Just three more days to go.'

But the following day when I turned up to collect Gloria, the doctor met me in the hallway. 'She disappeared midmorning,' he said. 'Just walked out and didn't come back.'

'But she'd almost finished.'

'These things happen. There are pushers from Mahdya Pradesh who come to this city to prey on the weak,' he said. 'It's too much temptation for someone like Gloria.'

She was in our new home by the railway, bent over, heating a lump of brown rock on a spoon. She didn't flinch when she saw me there but carefully placed the spoon inside a plastic bottle until it began to smoke, and then inhaled. Her eyes rolled, and she lay back onto the floor.

'You gave up on Sankalp's programme.'

'Yes,' she said triumphantly. 'I gave up.'

There was no stopping her after that, no matter how much I begged and pleaded. While I tried to make some money outside Apna Bazaar, Gloria hung around the station each day, coming back at night with droopy eyelids and itchy skin. The family who lived next door to us had a dog tied up outside. The skin hung off its scrawny body, and it licked noisily at its sores and wailed through the night. 'That's what you are like,' I shouted at her, my sympathy turning to anger. 'That stuff has made you worse than an animal.'

Gloria only laughed at me.

'How do you pay for it? We've no money left.'

'Just the way I paid for it with Mr. Iyer and all those other filthy bastards.'

I hated her for not being able to stop. It seemed that she didn't even want to try, but she had been there for me in the circus, saving me from Mr. Prem and then from Bubbles, so I couldn't let her down. There was no option but to take her with me everywhere I went. But without the hashish, she would convulse and vomit all over herself, and the other performers complained that she was driving customers away.

'You need to shake her off,' one of them said. 'She looks like a crazed hyena.'

'Join us instead,' the Potraj family said. They had brightly painted faces and bells on their ankles that rang when they danced in homage to Kadak, but they beat themselves with whips.

'No, we'll make it by ourselves once she's better,' I said.

But Gloria's downwards spiral continued, and by the time the festival of Chaturthi arrived in Mumbai to mark the end of the monsoon, we had nothing left. On the beach thousands of people converged, carrying idols of Ganesha into the sea. Drums beat loudly, and the crowd sang songs, before throwing luck coins into the water after their god.

'That money's going to waste; I'm going in,' I said to Gloria.

I removed my outer clothes, and leaving her there, slumped against the upturned curve of a fishing boat, I dived down into the murky waters. I felt my way around the feet of the men who carried the idols up over their heads. As the coins settled against the sand, I scooped them up into my grasp.

'Wicked girl,' one of the men shouted at me as I skipped my way over the gentle waves, my thin vest sticking to my skin.

Standing with the pickings from the sea I scanned the beach for Gloria. She wasn't at the station or in our home behind the railway offices, and when I asked one of the little girls next door if she had seen her, she looked at me blankly and then ran away, the dog limping behind her on a rope.

At the police station I filed a missing persons report. They did not ask me what she looked like: her hair, her eyes. 'How will you find her if you don't know what you are looking for?'

'Twenty-eight people go missing every day in Mumbai,' the officer said. 'It's impossible to find them all.'

I wandered the streets for days looking for her, up and down Metha Road, but nobody had anything to tell me. It seemed as though she had vanished into thin air. 'Maybe she was doing you a favour,' the doctor at Sankalp's drop-in centre said. 'Maybe she thought that you would be better off without her.'

Gloria had saved me again, and I could do nothing to save her.

Packing up what was left of my belongings, I made my way to the station, and by the time I reached the ticket booth, my face was red and swollen from tears.

'Are you running away?' asked a little girl in front of me, and then she nudged her bigger sister with her elbow. 'Look, look.' They both looked down at my tattered skirt and my torn sandals.

'We're going to the Badi Dargah shrine in Cuddapah,' the older girl announced. 'It's three hundred years old.'

'We're going to pray for a boy,' the smaller one added. 'Amma has to get her hair shaved off; it will itch and itch.'

'Chup Kar,' the mother snapped at the girls. She twisted them both by the arm until their backs were turned towards me.

As I thought about Belli and Safa, my body ached to reach out and hug them, but the queue moved forwards, and the girls were pulled along by their mother.

'Why didn't you get a baggage wallah, you stupid man?' she asked her husband.

'Do you know what those mongrels charge?' He leant down to help push the luggage along with his hands.

'Next,' the ticket seller called out from his booth, and the family moved on. The girls dragged bags along behind them, the little one turning towards me to stick out her tongue.

The aisles on the Mumbai–Chennai express were overcrowded, men and women hanging out of every window trying to catch a breath. By the time I located my sleeper, there were two men perched on the edge, one of them smoking a cigarette, the other eating an omelette from a paper wrapper. Too exhausted for an argument, I walked on past them, positioning myself instead between two carriages, the metal floors below me moving back and forth as we pulled away.

Through the narrow little window that looked out onto the platform, I could see men and children running after us, some of them clinging like limpets to the side of the train as it whistled its way out of the station. I wilted down onto the floor and wept again.

In my dreams I was back in Ambattur, bumping along on the front bar of dadi's bicycle, my hands curved around his. As we crossed the bridge, we could see below us the flattened houses on the lake, and then the ground below us began to shift and crack as dadi pedalled harder and harder to get away. 'Hold on!' he shouted, and the bicycle and dadi were tumbling through the air.

Waking with a jolt, I pulled myself up so that I was standing at the window. Outside there was nothing but darkness and the rumble of the train along the tracks, and then as the sky began to lighten, thick stretches of rolling forest appeared in the distance, some of the trees tipped here and there with bright-red flowers.

'Those are Tirupati Hills,' someone said. 'Home of the great Venkateswara Temple.' My stomach rolled as I realised that we were drawing closer to Avadi.

The platform had not changed from when dadi had taken me on the train to join the circus. There was the same yellow place sign, the white picket fence running the length of the station, and the blue concrete seats underneath the platform awning, all of them taken by waiting passengers. And beyond the fence there were houses, mostly pink and yellow, and looking at them I couldn't stop myself from smiling.

Outside Janaki Couriers I started to shake. What if he doesn't want to see me again? Or what if he doesn't even work here anymore?

'All collections through there,' a man behind me said. He was dressed in a blue short-sleeve shirt and blue cap, and he carried a stack of large brown envelopes underneath his arm.

'I'm looking for my father.'

'I'm not sure we deliver fathers,' he said, and then he laughed.

'Devesh Tikaram: he works here.'

'Ah, yes,' he said. 'The one with the radio.' He stepped ahead of me and opened the door. 'Always has an opinion on something, that one.'

Inside, the building was nothing more than a concrete box, with a counter running along one end. The air smelt of oil and dust. At the counter the man rang a bell, and we waited until someone appeared behind the glass hatch.

'As we say at Janaki, we always deliver,' the man beside me said.

Behind the glass the other man raised his hand to his head and took off his blue cap. He had a mess of black hair and a bulging nose, and when he raised his fingers up to press them against the glass, it was dadi's hand. 'Muthu,' he mouthed, but I couldn't hear his voice.

'He's forgotten to press the button,' the man beside me said. He pointed with his finger towards the counter.

'Muthu,' he said, again, and it sounded as if he was at the far end of a long tunnel. Then he disappeared down behind the counter, and suddenly a magic door opened up, and he squeezed his way out into the room. 'It's really you,' he said. When he opened his arms, I collapsed against him, burying myself into his chest. His grip tightened around me, as though he would never let go.

I wished we could have stayed in that little room forever.

'What will they say? After all this time?' he said

'You're not mad, about me leaving the circus?'

'You are home now,' he said. 'That's that.'

He pulled me through the corridors of Janaki Couriers and when he had removed his radio from his locker and hung up his cap, we collected his bicycle from a parking rack in the yard. 'I can't see over your head now,' he said. 'You'll have to take the seat.' I clung on tightly to his waist as we made our way through the streets, the radio playing *Unakenna*, violins and drums slicing past our ears in the midst of all the traffic.

The house and all those around it were pink. A row of washing hung in a line across the yard, and the windows and door were framed by white shutters.

'You like it?' he asked as he swung off the bicycle.

'I thought it would be yellow.'

We walked together through the small gate, and my father propped the bicycle against the inside wall. 'Muthu, there is one thing I should tell you.' He turned then so that we were only a few inches apart. 'Your grandmother is here; she is back staying with us now.'

'Aahnaji is here in Avadi?'

'You should stay out of her way,' he whispered. 'You know how she is.'

'She'll send me back.' My chest began to tighten. 'She won't want me here.'

Dadi removed his radio from the handlebars and started up the steps. 'Things will be different,' he said, but his face fell as he turned away from me and reached for the door.

25

From the hallway I could see Safa and Belli bent over at the table playing a game of billiards. Belli's face was rounder, her hair cut neatly to her chin, and Safa, who was now wearing glasses, was about to pocket her last carom when they looked up and saw me there. Neither of them said a word but looked towards our mother. She was dressed in a pink sari, and her thin hair was gathered in a loose little bun at the nape of her neck. We watched her as she dipped a slice of brinjal into a plate of egg and then placed it carefully on the grill.

'Amma,' Belli said finally. 'Look who has come home.'

When she turned around, the eyes that settled on me were large and dark, like those of a cicada insect, and there was something frightened in the way she stood with her shoulders all bunched up, and her hand raised to her mouth. 'Where have you been?' she asked, and for a second I thought that she had lost her mind.

'She ran away.' Dadi nudged me forwards into the kitchen. 'She didn't want to stay in the circus anymore.'

'We didn't hear from you,' she said.

'Look at her clothes,' Belli sniffed, coming up behind me. 'You look like a filthy Dalit.'

Amma nipped Belli hard on the arm and directed her back towards the table. 'You ran away? But where have you been sleeping?'

'Behind Mumbai Station.'

A small noise escaped from amma's throat as she turned back to the grill and flipped the brinjal off onto a plate with the end of a knife. 'Oh Shiva Parvati!'

'Aren't you happy to see me?'

And then she turned around, cupped my chin in her cool hands, and kissed my forehead. 'I never wanted you gone,' she said, her voice shaking.

'There, you see, everything will be just fine.' Dadi went and settled himself at the table, turning on his radio to Aahaa FM.

Amma took my hands and drew me towards the sink, running a cold flannel around my face and in between my fingers, and when she was finished, she held me back by the shoulders and looked at me. 'Did anyone hurt you, Muthu?' she whispered.

I shook my head. 'No, Amma.' She released a long, thin breath.

'Go and sit with your sisters; the food will be ready soon, and then you can get out of those rags.'

Belli and Safa couldn't take their eyes off me as I sat at the table and turned a carom over and over in my hand.

'You're not so little anymore, and your face is different, too,' Safa said.

Our father laughed loudly at something on the radio.

'Tomorrow I'll cut your hair,' Belli said. 'You know, I'm almost fully qualified.'

As they spoke I did not look at them but continued to turn the carom until it was sticking to my fingers.

'Did they have any pandas in the circus?' Belli tried again. 'What about tigers and rhinos?'

'They're endangered, don't you know,' Safa sniffed.

'The circus doesn't care about that,' I said.

'Was it horrible?' Safa asked in a soft voice, and the carom spun across the table and onto the floor. 'Do they treat the animals badly like they say?'

'They whip them and starve them.' When I looked up, Safa's mouth was hanging open.

Belli reached over and grabbed Safa's arm. 'They don't; do they, Safa?'

'They use hooks and electric prods to make them do tricks,' I said.

'People would report such things,' Safa said. 'The authorities would close them down.'

'Nobody knows what they do; we weren't allowed to tell.'

Belli and Safa sat back against their chairs and didn't ask me any more questions, and dadi turned the volume up on his radio to listen to the game show *Golmaal*.

'These guys come up with some funny situations,' he laughed.

'Nothing but rubbish.' Amma flicked a switch and the radio was silenced.

My father's scowl disappeared when she returned to the table with a plate of grilled brinjal, sambar, and curd rice.

'You must be hungry,' she said to me. 'Coming all the way from Mumbai.' She began to fill a plate with food.

Behind her there were jars of spices, two new matka water jars, and a potted cactus plant, and there at the end, pinned to the wall, was a poster for The Great Raman Circus of Chennai, the Wheel of Death circled in the middle. Underneath the palms of my hands, my knees began to shake.

Dadi was rolling a ball of rice and sambar around on his plate, and then he picked it up inside a slice of brinjal and popped it into his mouth.

'When did you come?' I nodded towards the poster. 'I never saw you there.'

Dadi swallowed the ball of rice and licked his fingers.

'That was from the time your dadi went to fetch you, when the house was ready,' my mother said brightly. She set the plate she was holding down before me. 'He said that you wouldn't come because you were enjoying the circus too much.'

It felt as though I had been sucked inside of myself. 'But nobody came, even after all the waiting and the letters; nobody came.'

Everyone looked towards my father. 'Devesh? You said that she wouldn't come.' Amma placed the spoon she was holding back into the bowl of rice. 'You said that you saw her climb inside a little glass box.'

'You saw me?' I was gasping at the air around me. 'Why didn't you come to me? Why didn't you bring me home?'

The room tightened, like the shift in the air before the monsoon, and then amma stood up and grabbed onto the back of her chair to steady herself. '*You did not go to her?*' she shouted at him.

'She seemed happy. Mr. Prem said that she was at a critical stage in her development, that it was best to leave her alone.'

'You were to bring her home.'

'You know it wasn't possible.' He clasped his hands together before him. '*Please.*'

Belli's sandal tapped against the leg of the table, and every mouthful of brinjal tasted charred against my tongue.

'What kind of man are you?' she said.

'My Devesh is a good son, who does what is right by his mother,' grandmother said. My body stiffened like a twig. She was standing in the doorway with a hairnet on her head, and she was moving back and forth, as if she was caught on the end of a spring. 'But here she is, back to poison us again.'

Amma brought her fist down on the table, causing the plates to shake. 'She's only a child,' she shouted.

'Shush now.' My father pulled out a chair for grandmother to sit down. 'This is supposed to be a happy occasion; the past is in the past.'

'Haan ji,' grandmother said calmly. She eased herself slowly onto the chair and sunk her fingers down into a plate of rice. 'But where is poor Safa now with the wedding? She reached out and put a hand on Safa's head. 'She is the one who will suffer.'

'Muthu is here to stay,' Amma snapped. 'You will not drive her away.'

■ ■ ■

The pink house in Avadi was all I had, so I buried everything that had been said that day down into the pit of my stomach, along with Gloria and Mr. Prem. At Preithaa Garden Pool I watched Safa perform the butterfly stroke. I accompanied amma to the farmers market on Saturday mornings and in the evenings cycled with my father around Avadi, delivering parcels on behalf of Janaki Couriers.

My mother returned to making roti again, and each day while Bella attended beauty school and Safa went to college, I stood outside the farmers market or the bus depot selling the breads, just as I had on the bridge. There was no more singing, no more tricks, and there was no more Maheesh to keep me company.

'What happened to Maheesh?' I asked amma.

'The chai-wallah? His family moved to Cuddalore.'

'That's where Gloria was from; she said it was nothing but a landfill site.'

'They will be rag pickers then,' she said. 'It serves him right for pushing you into that pool.'

'He didn't do it; it was Maheesh who tried to stop me.'

Amma placed a hand flat on the roti she was frying. 'You never said.'

'Nobody ever asked. Nobody ever asks me anything.'

But now and then they did ask about the circus, about the time that the maharani came, about the hippo that could dance, and about how Raja was killed by an elephant.

'I'm not sure why you'd ever want to leave such an exciting place,' Bella said.

It was impossible to tell them the truth, for they would say that it was my own fault, that I had brought such bad luck upon myself.

■ ■ ■

'You were screaming again.' Amma sat by the side of my bed and brushing back my hair.

'Do you think that I'm cursed, Amma?'

'Why would you ever think that?'

'Because bad things follow me everywhere, like a black cat.'

'You're just confused with all the change; it will take a while to settle in.'

'Grandmother always said it, and I hear her telling Safa and Belli things about me.'

'She's an ill-tempered old woman; don't listen to anything she says.' And she soothed me back to sleep.

But each night it continued. From out on the veranda, Belli and Safa's voices would reach me. Climbing up onto the roof, I could watch them there. Safa massaged the soles of grandmother's feet.

'She won't let me cut her hair,' Belli complained about me. 'I wanted to practise the bob.'

'It's the effect of the circus,' grandmother said. 'It has made her wild, like one of those caged animals.'

'She said that one of the girls was killed by a lion,' Belli said. 'Her neck snapped in two.'

'No such thing,' grandmother snorted. 'She's telling stories just to get your attention, like all the singing and dancing she used to do.'

'She could have been a star,' Safa said.

'But she's too small, like a mouse.' Grandmother raised her glass of milk to her mouth and took a long drink. 'Stars are tall and beautiful, like you.' She reached out and smoothed Safa's shiny hair. 'That is why you must marry Keshav.'

'Amma said that it will still happen.'

'You wait and see; now that she is home, Muthu will ruin things. That is the only talent she has.'

'How long is she here for?' I asked amma.

'She says that there is no one left to care for her in Pondicherry,' amma said. 'It's our responsibility now.'

As the days ticked by, I could see that grandmother had no intention of leaving. She had befriended the older ladies on the street, joining them each morning on their long walk around Avadi. Plus, she was on first-name terms with the local doctor, who came to check on her flaking skin each week. Through the gap in the bedroom door, I could see him unravelling the bandage around her leg.

'It's my nerves, Dakshi,' she complained to him. 'When I'm unsettled about something, it always flares up.'

'Then you need to deal with the problem,' he told her, and grandmother nodded.

Nobody else could see it, how she cursed at me when no one else was around. 'You will destroy everything for this family if you stay, just like you did at Kallikuppam and Ambattur,' she said.

I tried to keep out of her way, just as dadi had told me, hoping that she would forget I was there. My meals were taken in my room, and in the mornings I waited until she had gone for her walk before making my presence in the house. Everyone knew what was happening, that I was disappearing each day like the Elastic Girl, but nothing was said.

Still grandmother wasn't satisfied and would not settle until something was done.

'You never belonged here,' she said. 'It's time for you to leave.'

I was kneeling on a chair, watching amma through the window as she tended to her little vegetable patch. At the sound of grandmother's voice, my hands froze against the curved wooden back.

She had returned early from her walk and had planted herself firmly in the centre of the room.

'They wanted me home.'

'My Devesh has suffered enough.' Her face began to redden. 'Don't you see that he didn't want you anymore, that he left you at the circus because he couldn't bear to look at your face any longer?'

'It's not true. He took me to the cinema hall to perform for Mr. Prem.' A weight crushed down on my chest.

'No, he left you in the circus; it was all arranged,' she said.

Amma appeared in the doorway behind my grandmother, a basket full of vegetables now cradled in her arms. 'That's enough!' she shouted.

Grandmother stumbled backward, and then her eyes began to glisten with tears. 'She took him away from me.' Her voice quivered. 'My dear Samir.' She made her way down the dimly lit hallway, one hand stretched out against the wall to guide her along.

'Is it true?' I asked, my throat now dry. 'Did Dadi leave me there because he didn't want me?'

'Didn't I tell you to keep away from her?' Amma placed the basket on the table and then raised her hands in the air. 'Can't you do that one little thing for me?'

When dadi returned from work that evening, my grandmother called him to her room. 'I can't take it at my age.' She pressed her hand against her chest. 'She needs to go, or I won't last a single day more in this house.'

'Now, now, Maataa, don't upset yourself,' dadi said. 'You just need to take some rest.'

But she would not leave it, determined to turn them all against me, and the following day she played her trump card. 'Someone has taken my bangle,' she cried, appearing out of the room with her jewellery box. 'Look, it's not there.' She held the box out so that we could see the compartments inside.

'It must be in your room, under the bed?' dadi said.

'I've looked. Someone has taken it.' With one hand, she pulled me out of my chair.

'Leave her,' amma said.

Grandmother began to shake me hard, and then she reached down into my skirt. 'See, this little thief has been learning tricks in the circus.' She held the gold bangle up in the air. 'This was part of Safa's dowry, and now she is trying to upset her sister's happiness.'

'Why would she do such a thing?' my mother asked.

'She's full of jealousy and poison.'

Safa began to cry as amma gathered up plates of uneaten food. 'Go outside,' she told Belli and Safa.

They disappeared through the doorway out into the yard. I could see them through the window, Safa staring up at the washing on the line, tears still streaming down her face.

My mother lowered the plates down into the sink and then turned to face me. 'Did you take it, Muthu?'

'No. I promise, Amma.'

'She's a liar,' grandmother said. 'Someone like that belongs in the circus. Devesh—you must take her back straightaway.'

The muscles tightened down the length of my father's neck.

'Is it because you wanted a son; is that why you left me there, Dadi?'

'No, no,' he stuttered. 'You wanted to be a star, and we needed the money. You've never done anything wrong.'

'How can you say that? Everything that has ever happened to this family is all *her* fault!' grandmother shouted. 'Tell her how it was; tell her now.'

Amma folded back down onto her chair and placed her head in her hands.

'*Maataa*,' dadi whispered to my grandmother. 'She was never to know.'

'Know what?' When I looked at grandmother, there was blackness gathering in her eyes, like a storm.

'It was your fault that Samir killed that vile man, it was you who put him in jail, it was you who destroyed the life that we could have had in Kallikuppam.'

'No more.' Dadi placed his hand on grandmother's arm and tried to pull her out of the room, but grandmother wrenched herself away from him with the force of an angry bear.

'What do you mean? Grandfather killed Mr. Parthiban before I was even born; how can it be my fault?'

'Mr. Parthiban raped your mother,' she said.

'Dadi?' I looked at my father.

He dropped onto a chair beside amma, and spread his hands out on the table like the broad, veiny leaves from a banyan tree, and then his shoulders began to shake. 'Mr. Kalpak promised to look after you.'

'But, I'm yours? *I* was always yours?'

'You were never *his*, you foolish girl,' grandmother continued. '*You* were the sin that evil left behind; you were the one who drove us all into hell.'

Amma screamed as she leapt up out of her chair and reached for my grandmother, but I was running out of the pink house and past Belli and Safa, who were playing hopscotch, past the evening market and the marriage hall, where a wedding had just ended. After running as far as I could, my breath caught in my throat, and I dropped to the ground.

'Wake up, Muthu,' someone called to me. It was an old man leaning down over me, his white kurta trailing on the ground. 'You don't remember your neighbour from Ambattur?'

'Mr. Mody, it's you.' I began to cry.

'What is this?' he said. We were outside Murugan Temple, and it was starting to grow dark. 'What has upset you so much?'

'It's true what she said, that I was cursed all along.'

Mr. Mody helped me up from the ground. 'Sometimes things are not as bad as they seem,' he said. 'We will sort it all out.' He raised his hand in the air to hail a rickshaw.

He took me to his house; it was a small room up three flights of stairs. The walls were stained here and there with patches of damp, and all his belongings were packed away in cardboard boxes. 'Where are you going?'

'I'm still moving in.' He removed a bundle of clothes from the top of a wooden bench and nodded for me to sit down, then he set about making tea on a little gas stove in the corner of the room 'I've known your father for twenty-six years,' he said. 'We came from the same part of Pondicherry.'

'Then you know everything? That I was never his and that he sent me away because he couldn't bear to look at me anymore.'

'He raised you as his own.' He rifled through a box and produced two clay tumblers. 'Other men, weaker men, would have walked away, but not your father.'

'He's not my father.' When I said it, a hard little lump caught in my throat.

Mr. Mody stood up from the stove and handed me a cup. 'You have to understand, Muthu, your grandfather killed a man and then tried to frame someone else for the crime—it was a grave situation.' Mr. Mody sat down beside me on the bench. 'He was the *first* police officer in the state ever to be jailed for such a crime.'

'He went to jail?'

'He spent eighteen months in Puzhal Central and four years in Aashiana.' Mr. Mody took a long drink from his tumbler. 'Your parents were driven from their home by local goons, and when they arrived in Ambattur, they had lost almost everything.'

'Why didn't they get rid of me then?'

'Because despite everything they had gone through, they loved you, just as they love you now.'

I began to cry again. 'Then why did he leave me there?'

'It was your grandmother—she needed *someone* to blame.'

'She made him do it?'

'It's a strange thing between mothers and sons.' He drank the remains of his tea, rested the tumbler on the floor, and stood up. 'They will be wondering where you have gone.' He held out his hand to me. 'It's time to go home.'

26

'I'm doing your parents a great disservice,' Mr. Mody said as we pulled up outside the station. 'Leaving you here like this, allowing you to take off.'

'If you bring me back there, I'll only run away during the night, and they'll never see me again.'

'You could just talk to them. You might come to some understanding.'

'There's nothing else to understand.' Getting down from the taxi, I began making my way up the steps.

'Then what is the harm to stay a little longer, eh?' he asked, following me into the station. 'Just one more night?'

'It's not my home.'

'What is a home? Only four walls and a bed,' he said. 'You *belong* to your family.'

'Can't you see? They're not my family. That's why Belli and Safa always came first and why I was blamed for everything. Its clear to me now.'

'It is Mr. Parthiban who is to blame, not you.'

'I'm his blood.'

Mr. Mody gave me five hundred rupees. 'Buy a return.' He pressed the notes down into my hand. 'You might change your mind by the time you get there.'

I imagined him returning to my parents' house to tell them the news, and grandmother's mouth cracking into a smile. She had got what she was after.

As the train pulled out from the station, it all made sense; the circus had been my destiny all along. My mind gathered around this thought until something happened on the journey back to Mumbai; I thought about ending it all. What was the point in living with such misery, moving from one nightmare to another? It all seemed like such an exhausting struggle that I no longer wanted to live. One step off the train—that's all it would take—and my life would be over; nobody would even care.

Making my way down from my sleeper and to the end of the carriage to one of the doors, I placed my hand on the door handle. Outside, the morning sun was breaking over the Khandala Ghat, and as I looked down into the green valley, my mind wandered back to a time in the cinema with Maheesh when we were watching *Ghulam*. Maheesh's voice sang into my ear as though he were right there beside me on the train: '*What will we do after I come to Khandala? We'll roam, we'll move, we'll dance, we'll sing, we'll live a life of pleasure, what else?*'

When my eyes opened, my mind had cleared, and there was no more fear. Even when I returned to my sleeper, there was a bright light all about me, and my arms and legs felt as light as rain. I had decided to live.

By the time we arrived in Mumbai, it felt as though I had just been born and nothing that had gone before bore any significance. Stepping off the train, I marvelled at the smells, the sounds, and without knowing how I got there, I found myself outside the reclamation grounds in Bandra.

It had been over a year since the circus had arrived in Mumbai, so on seeing the red-and-yellow pickup truck with the advertising board propped up on the back, my legs gave way underneath me.

On waking, everything seemed familiar but more pristine: the green pitched roof, the curve of the bed underneath my back, the smell of the pillow, and when Shulisha and the two Nepalese girls leant down over me, tears came to my eyes, tears of complete joy.

'You came back,' the smaller one said. 'We knew you would.'

'You remember us?' the older one asked. 'Kamala.' She pointed to herself. 'And Priya.'

'Where's Gloria?' Shulisha asked. 'She made it?'

'She went her own way.' I sat up in the bed. 'There was nothing I could do.'

Shulisha drew a blanket up over my knees; it felt like silk against my legs. 'Go and fetch her something to eat and drink,' she told Kamala and Priya. 'She looks like she hasn't eaten in days.'

'How did you find me?'

'It was the gatekeeper; he said another stray had returned.' She propped me up against a pillow.

There were a dozen or so girls lying on beds on both sides of the tent, all of them staring at me with big dark eyes.

'You've been away for a whole year,' Shulisha laughed. 'Things have changed.'

'Where are they from?'

'They traffic them in from the villages in Nepal.'

'Their parents sell them too?' I asked.

'Some of them were taken without their parents even knowing, snatched when they were playing in the street.'

I looked around at the girls; some of them were as young as six years old. 'Why would they be so ruthless?'

'Attendance has been poor since you left, and these girls cost less.'

'So why has the circus stayed this long?'

'They've been looking for a new star to help draw the crowds back, and Mr. Prem is sure that he's going to find one in Mumbai.'

'That's why I've come back, why I didn't die.'

'You almost died?' Shulisha placed a hand on her chest.

'Several times, but it wasn't meant to happen that way; there is something left for me to do.'

'Mr. Prem said he would kill you both if he ever found you again.'

'This is my home.'

Shulisha stepped back and looked at me. 'You've changed,' she said. 'Everything used to frighten you.'

'My mind decided to set itself free, like the Giri Bala.'

'Then you must save us, Muthu,' she said. 'The place is in a terrible mess. The owners came all the way from Georgetown to see what was going on; they insisted on cutting costs.'

'So Mr. Prem needs me more than ever?'

'It's true! You should go to him now. Let him see that you are back and that you're not frightened anymore.'

'No, not yet; there's no hurry.'

Priya returned and lifted a cloudy glass of nimbu paani to my lips. 'I'll look after you,' she said, as the lemon and honey liquid soothed my dry throat. It was like nothing I had ever tasted before. 'I'm learning the hoop,' she told me. 'Mr. Kalpak says I'm almost ready.'

'Muthu needs to rest.' Shulisha shushed Priya away. She smoothed my hair until I could feel myself sinking down into a bath of warm ghee.

'You kept your promise to Gloria,' I whispered. 'You looked after the girls.'

My mind rewound like a film reel, taking me to Ambattur, swinging on the rope above the pool. Down below I could see my father and mother sitting at their kitchen table.

'Every time I look at her, it reminds me of what happened,' he said.

'Then what is it you want me to do?' amma asked him.

Dadi bent over and buried his face in his hands, and the rope gave way above me so that I was falling down into darkness, the sound of my grandfather's watch ticking in my ears.

When my eyes opened, the afternoon sun was disappearing into the dark. 'You have slept right through the night and the day,' Priya said. She was dressed in a bright-orange costume, and her hair had been scraped back tightly from her heart-shaped face. 'He knows the good news.' She looked down towards the end of the bed and Mr. Kalpak was standing there, one hand resting on the base of his back.

'Go and help Kamala with the props,' he said to Priya. 'I'll be along shortly.' Priya disappeared reluctantly from the tent.

When he stepped closer, I could see that Mr. Kalpak's hair had grown longer, softening his face, and that he had developed a dark little beard on the end of his chin. He stood there for a moment, examining my face. 'You're alive.' The cane in his hand began to shake. 'It was a foolish thing to do, running away in a city like Mumbai; what did you think you were doing?'

'We thought we could make it on our own; Gloria had plans.'

'Where is she?' he asked, looking about at the empty beds. 'I should whip her black and blue for putting such ideas in your head.'

'She was only trying to save me.'

'Then we will get her back and sort it out together.'

'Gloria is dead.' I was certain of it. 'It's too late for her.'

Mr. Kalpak reached out towards me, but I waved him away. 'I'm done with crying,' I said. 'I know everything now, and I'm not angry anymore, not even with you.'

He stepped back suddenly, as if he had just received a blow. 'You know?'

'Grandmother told me; it was her parting gift.'

His hand came up to rub at his grey head. 'I promised I would look after you.'

'Why did they bring me to *you*?'

Mr. Kalpak removed his glasses and took a long breath, as though he were about to take a dive from the end of a pier. 'It was something I owed your grandfather, the great Samir Tushar.' His eyes rested on the pocket watch hanging from around my neck. 'We met in Aashiana thirteen years ago. I was only a boy back then, in my early twenties.'

Rupa's words came back to me. 'So is it true—that you killed your wife?'

Mr. Kalpak settled himself on the end of the bed and rested his hands upon his knees. 'We were married only a couple of years when Hemaji took her own life,' he said. 'They called it bad karma. They said that she would wander aimlessly between Heaven and earth, and they tormented me until my mind couldn't take it anymore. Your grandfather was the only one who understood.'

'You were friends?'

'Your grandfather took me under his wing. He saved my spirit and I owed him something in return.'

'To protect me?'

Mr. Kalpak rested one hand loosely on my arm. 'Your father thought he was doing something good. He thought that I could look after you and that you would make something of yourself.' He removed his hand from my arm and stood up, his face full of sorrow.

'Now I'm back, and we both get a second chance.'

'Why?'

'Because fate brought me back here again; this is where I'm meant to be.'

'You listened to Niyama: endurance in difficult times.'

'And now I've had enough of running away, of being chased.'

'Mr. Prem is still here; what will you do about him?'

A feeling surged up from my feet, filling me completely until I knew what I must do. Removing the blanket from my legs, I made my way out of the tent.

'Maybe we should think about it for a moment,' Mr. Kalpak said, following behind me. 'You're tired; maybe tomorrow would be better.'

'All my life bad things have happened to me; I've let them happen, but not anymore.' I continued to charge ahead. The skirt around the big top looked as though it had been dipped in mud, and streams of torn bunting trailed carelessly from the peak. In the cages the camels looked uneasy, snatching on their ropes, and the elephants stood motionless in their own dung.

'Where are you going?' Shulisha called out to us, and when we didn't answer, she followed behind, as we wove our way in and out among the tents until we reached Mr. Prem's caravan.

The door was open, and we stood there for a while looking at the line of the unmade bed and the clutter on his floor, and then a pair of khussa slippers appeared before us.

'Ah, here she comes, crawling back on her belly like Rahu.' He spat a red line of paan down onto the ground.

The palms of my hands grew sticky, but I wiped them off on my skirt and straightened my back.

'You would do well to take her back,' Mr. Kalpak said.

Mr. Prem raised a hand at him. 'Does Rahu no longer have a tongue?'

'I'm here to perform as the Elastic Girl again.'

'Is that so?' He laughed. 'You want to come back, just like that.'

As he stood there sliding the gold ring on his little finger up and down, I felt nothing but pity for the man. He was finished.

'I'll tell them everything, about what you did to me and Rupa. Everyone will know what you are.'

'You can go back out onto the streets like a whore; this circus doesn't need you.'

'Then I will tell the men from Georgetown, and all this will turn to nothing.' I motioned behind me at the circus.

When I turned away, my heart was pounding, and it felt as though I was floating back across the grounds. Reaching inside the tent, I collapsed onto the bed.

'I could see it straightaway,' Mr. Kalpak said behind me.

'See what?' Shulisha asked.

'How she's found herself.'

It was the first night that sleep came easy, and when I awoke my eyes were dry and gritty, but outside the noises of the circus filled the air like music: the organ and chimes, the excited chatter of the audience as they made their way towards the big top, and the shouts of performers as they hurried back and forth in preparation.

'You're awake?' Shulisha asked, poking her head around the corner of the tent. She stepped inside cradling a stack of white spinning plates in her arms. 'He said you have one last chance,' she said excitedly. 'He wants you to stay.'

'You see; it is all as it should be.'

'Everything has changed.' She laughed. '*You're* telling *him* what to do.'

She was right, for something had changed. My mind had been stretched and tormented, but like elastic it had snapped back into place, and filled with new energy and determination, I returned to training.

Inside the ring, performers swung and high-wired their way across the space, and for a split second my breath caught in my throat when someone swung through the air. 'They had to replace her,' Shulisha said, when she caught me watching. 'They stole a girl from Kohinoor Circus—she's called Crystal.'

Pressing my hands together, I thought about the lumps on Gloria's palms, and then below the wire, I noticed Bose juggling clubs up into the air. 'What happened to Tulsi?'

'The men from Georgetown said that one clown was more than enough.'

'What about Sona and the Hula girls?'

'*Too old*, they said.'

Mr. Kalpak came and stood before us. His little beard had been trimmed, and he was wearing a crisp green kurta. 'Today we welcome back Muthu, our Elastic Girl.' He looked down at the floor and ran his cane through the dust.

'He hasn't been the same since you left,' Shulisha whispered. 'It was like he had lost all his fight.'

When it was my turn to take to the floor, it felt as though my bones had been filled with iron ore, and I managed to place only one leg behind my neck at a time.

'You've been away too long.' Mr. Kalpak shook his head.

'I'll practise all day, every day.'

'Any more than three hours of work a day, and you will pull a muscle.'

'It will take me at least a month at that rate.'

'You're not ready for the box,' Mr. Kalpak said. 'The man will *have* to wait.'

We started that day with a new conditioning programme, right back at the beginning again, practising backbends and elbow stands, and in the evening Mr. Kalpak made me balance lengthways between two chairs to strengthen my back. 'No tea, no meat, no sweets,' he warned me.

The gruelling schedule came as a relief, as there was no time to think, nothing to break my state of peace. Only at night did the dark thoughts come flooding back into my head: Gloria standing on the train tracks at Victoria Station as a train rumbled towards her in the distance, me trapped inside dadi's shoeshine box. But when daybreak came and my busy day began I was filled with happiness.

When the new flyers for the final show in Mumbai were printed, there I was: Elastic Girl, listed as the final act.

'That mongrel has put us on a deadline,' Mr. Kalpak barked. 'This show is only two weeks away.' He scrunched up the flyer in his hands.

'We can do it; I'll be ready.'

There was no longer time to worry about injury, and we did not stop until I was able to fold myself up without any effort at all. 'It's now or never,' Mr. Kalpak said. He led me towards the little glass box. It had been attached onto a metal clip that could raise me up into the air.

'It's not enough; they need to see what I can really do. Have them spin me around.'

'It's too dangerous,' he said. 'The chain could snap.'

'Do it.' I lowered myself down into the box. 'Nothing can go wrong now.'

Hoisted up into the air, they began swirling me around and around, until the big top disappeared into a wonderful dizzying haze. When the box was lowered to the floor again, Mr. Kalpak opened the lid. 'You're ready,' he said. 'It's time to be the Elastic Girl again.'

27

As the siren blew and performers hurried their way towards the back of the big top, I stood under the cover of my tent and watched the audience filtering through the gates. 'My Dadi came to see me, but I never knew,' I told Shulisha.

'You're lucky.' She pulled me back into the tent and began fixing the silver panels on my sleeves. 'My father wouldn't care if I were dead.'

'He didn't say whether he thought I was good; he didn't say anything about it at all.'

'Maybe he didn't know how to say it.'

'He kept the poster; that's something.' I thought about my dadi folding the piece of paper, putting it into his pocket, and then taking it all the way back to Avadi on the train. He loved me, I was sure of that, but I wasn't his. I could never be his.

I made my way out into the crowd. The show had already started, and one of the Nepalese girls was jumping on and off a running horse as the audience whooped and cheered. Mr. Kalpak was rolling back and forth on the balls of his feet. 'What kept you?' he said. 'I was about to send Priya to fetch you.'

'We were fixing Muthu's costume,' Shulisha said. 'I made it myself.'

Mr. Kalpak glanced down at the jewelled star motif in the centre of my chest. 'Let's hope you really are a star tonight,' he said. 'We're all counting on you now.'

A ripple of excitement passed through me as we continued to stand there together watching the acts.

'Get ready,' Mr. Kalpak said. 'You're next.' He nudged me forwards so that I was standing right at the entrance to the ring. The audience roared with laughter at Bose's cake-balancing act, and the women and children in the front row screeched as he squirted them with water from his plastic flower.

Then he was gone, and Mr. Prem was announcing my name.

Everything fell silent.

Under a single beam of light, I began to bend myself like the long, curved neck on a grey heron until I was whisked off into the air, spinning and whirling inside the little box, drumbeats thumping through the tent like a heartbeat. My mind was free, filled with total bliss. It came to me then that nothing else would ever feel greater.

Then the light fell away suddenly as the room came to a standstill, and I was lowered back onto the floor. A sound, like the first hard drops of rainwater against a metal roof—*clap, clap, clap*—and then a cloud burst, drowning me in the noise.

The *Mumbai Mirror* ran an article on the circus in the following morning's paper. It was printed below a picture of me performing my act. "A dazzling performance, not to be missed," Shulisha read. I stared at the picture for a long time; it reminded me again of the photograph Gloria had shown me of Ashwariya Rai when she was only a child. 'All of us come from nothing,' she had said.

■ ■ ■

By the end of the week, we were setting off on our return journey to Park Town, Chennai; we had come full circle. 'Now that you are back, Mr. Prem is done with his search for a star,' Shulisha said. 'There's no need to stay in Mumbai anymore.'

Apart from seeing him in the ring, Mr. Prem had kept his distance since my return, but each time he announced my act, the sound of his voice booming out through the speakers still made my stomach heave.

'It feels like I'm waiting for a lion to appear out of the long grass,' I told Mr. Kalpak. 'There's this feeling that something is wrong.'

'He won't come near you again,' Mr. Kalpak reassured me. 'Besides, he has too much to lose this time.'

Even though the sense of calm hadn't left me, something in the background was unsettling. I couldn't see what it was.

As we travelled back to Chennai, Mr. Prem was nowhere to be seen. 'I don't like it when he disappears,' I said to Shulisha. 'It's better to have him in your sights.' I stared out the window at the unending fields of millet and rice.

Sleep brought me to the Heavy Vehicles Factory in Avadi. My father was some distance away from me, dressed in a hard green hat, camouflage suit, and scuffed black boots, and when he reached the end of a line of tanks, he climbed up the hulking body of the last one, opened the driver's hatch, and disappeared inside. As the tank pulled out and trundled its way towards me, I could see a pair of eyes peering out through the viewing slot, staring straight at me as I screamed.

The bus was in darkness, and I was covered in a layer of sweat.

'I was going to wake you but didn't want to give you a fright,' Shulisha whispered. 'It's best not to disturb someone when they're in the middle of a bad dream.' She reached up then and pressed the switch on a reading light above our heads, and it flickered into life.

The bus had stopped in Tumkur, a small town nestling in the foothills of Devarayanadurga. Most of the men had wandered off in search of toddy shops, returning several hours later to urinate against the wheels.

'What happened to you?' Shulisha asked, raising her head from my shoulder. 'You've never said what happened out there, what it was that changed you.'

'It's like Mr. Kalpak said; I discovered who I really am.'

'You weren't the person you thought you were?'

'All my life, since before I could talk I believed myself to be cursed, to be a bringer of bad luck; that's the person I thought I was.'

'And now?'

'I've realized that bad things may have happened to me, but *I* am not bad.'

'I wish I could think like that,' Shulisha sighed. 'Forget how my father used to beat me and leave me to starve. If only I could believe it wasn't my fault.'

'You can; you just need to let it all go.'

'I always wanted to be a seamstress, like my mother.' She looked out the window. 'I had it all planned out in my head before he brought me here.'

'You can still do it,' I said. 'When the circus is gone, it could keep a roof over your head.'

'And what will you do then?'

Closing my eyes I tried to imagine myself stooped over at a sewing machine, but when I looked up again, the bus was rolling its way into Park Town, and from my window I could see the mound of earth where Raja had been buried, now covered in grass. 'This is all I know now,' I said. 'I think I will always be the Elastic Girl.'

■ ■ ■

As Mr. Prem predicted, within the first two weeks of our return to Chennai, the crowds were back. Mr. Prem took full advantage by increasing the ticket prices and selling new merchandise after each show: balloons, pens, and little key rings with the name of The Great Raman Circus etched along the side. And as the bright winter months returned, the circus began to look much sharper. But still the animals continued to go neglected, and the salaries for all the performers remained unchanged.

'What are they doing with all the money we are making for them?' Shulisha complained. 'We continue to suffer like the poor animals while those men in Georgetown grow fat.'

The only other person who appeared to be doing well was Mr. Prem, with his new range of brightly coloured shirts and shiny shoes, and under the glare of the spotlight, a gold watch shimmered and gleamed against his arm.

That feeling rose up in me again. 'He's stealing money from the circus,' I told Mr. Kalpak. 'Haven't you noticed all his fine things?'

'There's no point in stirring.'

'He's allowed to do what he wants? Take from everyone else?'

'One day it will come to an end for him, but for now, just be glad that he is keeping away.'

Mr. Prem's self-restraint did not sit easy with me. Something was going on; something much greater than the gold watch and fine clothes.

It was Priya. When I saw her playing at the back of the tent with a latoo made of polished lacquered wood, my belly turned. She wrapped a string around the lower part of the latoo and then tossed it out across the earth, watching it spin and spin. I'd never seen the toy before.

'A gift?'

She looked up at me 'I didn't steal it,' she said.

My chest grew tight. 'Is it from Mr. Prem?'

'My father gave it to me.' She wound the string around the top again and whipped it out into the dust.

That evening, while Priya was helping with the kitchen chores, I went to see her sister, Kamala. She was sitting cross-legged on her bed, massaging the calluses on the palms of her hands 'Here, show me.' I took her hands in mine and began to rub some turmeric paste into the toughened skin. 'If you let this soak in, after a few days they will settle down; Gloria swore by it.'

'My mother used turmeric for everything,' she said. 'Coughs, cuts, itching skin.' She looked over my shoulder and into the distance.

'You must miss home?'

'All the green,' she said. 'Mountains, trees, grass.'

'Your parents, too, your mother and father?'

'Our father died before Priya was one,' she said.

A shiver ran through me.

'She never knew him?'

'My mother couldn't afford to keep us after he died,' Kamala said. 'So she brought us to Mr. Prem, and he said he would look after us.'

When the siren blared for the evening performance, I waited until everyone was gone and then reached in underneath Priya's bed. There inside a little cardboard box was the spinning top, a thin gold bracelet, and several bottles of nail polish.

This was why I had come back to the circus; I was sure of it. It was my job to get rid of Mr. Prem.

'But she never leaves my sight,' Shulisha said when I told her that night. 'I'd know if something was going on.'

'No one has eyes in the back of their head.'

'She's only a child; how could you think he'd even do such a thing?'

'Because he did it to me.'

Shulisha's hand reached out to me. 'Why didn't you tell someone?'

'There was nothing anyone could do; that's why we ran away.'

'So, if it wasn't possible before, how will we stop him now?'

'We'll think of something.'

Over the next few days, I watched Priya carefully, and on the third night, while everyone was sleeping, I caught her returning to the tent. She removed a bundle of clothes from underneath her blanket, placed a trinket into her little box, and climbed in below her covers.

My body began to shake as I thought about Mr. Prem's mouth and about the smell of his skin, and I cried for Priya and all she had lost, as my mind searched in desperation for a way to stop him. It came to me as I slept, wading down into the waters at Palace Gardens, Bangalore. I could feel my hands reaching down into the water, pulling out Rupa's little trinket box. The lid was open, and inside, among whirls of pondweed, sat a gold watch and three gold and ruby rings. It was a sign from Rupa, and now I knew what I needed to do.

On Tuesday, the day of my fourteenth birthday, I asked Mr. Kalpak if Shulisha and I could go to the cinema. 'Just this once, please. We want to go and see *Krrish*,' I told Mr. Kalpak.

'Mr. Prem has forbidden you from leaving the grounds,' he said. 'If he found out, he would go crazy.'

'He plays cards on a Tuesday evening; he won't know we are missing at all.'

'How do *I* know you will come back?' he said, his face suddenly growing grey. 'You could disappear like before.'

Removing my grandfather's watch from my neck, I handed it to him. 'Keep this until we come back,' I said. He closed his fingers tightly against the watch.

Instead of going to the cinema, Shulisha and I made our way along Mount Road, stopping off at all the jewellery stores. 'Our father has mislaid his receipts,' we told them at each store. 'His name is Mr. Prem.'

Finally, at Utharikha Jewellers, the shop assistant wiping the glass surface of a display cabinet raised his head. 'Ah, yes, your father is one of our best customers,' he said. 'A man of very fine taste.'

By the time we made our way back to the circus, we had copies of receipts for the past six months. 'Count them up,' I asked Shulisha. 'Tell me how much they are for.'

She made her way through the receipts, marking out numbers on a piece of paper as she went along. 'It's over one lakh,' she said, underlining her final number. 'One hundred and forty-two thousand rupees.'

We sat there in silence. 'It's enough to buy a house.'

'If they knew that he was taking that kind of money from us, they would tear him apart out there,' Shulisha said.

'And if the men from Georgetown knew, they would finish him off.' I gathered up the receipts into a neat little bundle and placed them carefully underneath my pillow.

28

The following night we watched as Priya slipped from underneath her covers, drew her arms into a fresh kameez, and then stuffed the rest of her clothes underneath her blanket. She glanced about the room, bent down onto her knees and quietly crawled her way out of the tent.

'She's going to him,' Shulisha whispered across at me. 'We have to follow her.'

'It's time; we have to go.'

We were outside, clutching onto each other as we followed Priya, who was scurrying across the grounds like a mouse. Every now and then, we had to crouch behind a caravan and wait for the gateman to pass by, rapping his stick across the ground.

'We should get Mr. Kalpak.' Shulisha pulled me towards Mr. Kalpak's tent. 'We might need his help.'

'He'll only try to stop us.'

'Not now, not when we've come this far.' She drew back the cover on Mr. Kalpak's tent. 'You said it yourself; that man is like a demon; who knows what he will do?'

He was lying on his back, his hands resting across the curve of his chest. 'It's one of the girls.' I shook him gently by the shoulder, causing him to jump.

'Muthu?' He reached his hand over to the little table by his bedside and fumbled about for his glasses.

'It's Priya; she's in trouble.'

'What kind of trouble?' He fixed the glasses onto the bridge of his nose and then propped himself up in the bed. The top buttons on his pyjama were undone, and I turned away.

'Mr. Prem has her, and we are going to fetch her back.'

'That monster.' The bed creaked as he sat up and bent over to put on his slippers.

Shulisha poked her head into the tent. 'She's gone into the caravan,' she said. 'We'll be too late if you don't hurry.'

'We're already too late for Priya; it's the others we have to save now,' I said.

Lamplight flickered against the net drapes of the caravan, and underneath, an empty beer bottle rattled back and forth in the slight breeze.

'It will be his word against ours,' Mr. Kalpak said. 'There is a very great chance that we will be causing problems only for ourselves.'

'This time there is no escape for Mr. Prem; we have him caged.'

'I hope you know what you are doing.' Mr. Kalpak stepped up towards the caravan and opened the door.

For a second we could see Priya's legs dangling over the edge of the bed, and then Mr. Prem appeared in the doorway. 'You bloody kutta,' he spat at Mr. Kalpak and then grabbed him by the throat. 'What are you snooping after, huh?'

'Stop it!' I shouted, pulling on Mr. Prem's arm.

'Ah, little Miss Elastic Girl,' he said. 'Come to see who is keeping your bed warm?'

Mr. Kalpak swung his fist up and punched Mr. Prem on the side of the head, sending him toppling backwards onto the floor. Behind them Priya screamed.

'Priya, come here,' I called. 'Everything will be OK now.'

When she did not come, I stepped up into the caravan. Mr. Prem was crouched up in the corner nursing a bloody ear, and Priya was still sitting on the edge of the bed, holding a new hair comb in her hands. She stared at me, as if she was in the middle of a dream. As I pulled her out of the caravan, the comb dropped away to the ground.

'I'm sorry.' She began to cry in soft little sobs, burying her head against Shulisha's chest.

'Are you going to call the police?' Mr. Prem laughed, returning to the doorway of the caravan, one hand still pressed against his ear. 'I'm sure they would be very interested to hear your stories.'

'There is no need to call on your friends in the police,' I said. 'It's the men from Georgetown I'll be talking to.'

'Hah, who do you think they will believe?' Mr. Prem said. 'A little whore like you or the man who made this place a success?'

'We'll tell them how you have lined your own pockets with their profits,' Shulisha said.

Mr. Prem swatted a hand in the air. 'Take them away,' he said to Mr. Kalpak. 'Or you will all be out on the streets in the morning.'

Mr. Kalpak did not move.

'We have copies of all your receipts—watches, rings, necklaces. It all adds up to quite a sum.'

'One hundred and forty-two thousand rupees, to be exact,' Shulisha said.

Mr. Kalpak's breath whistled through his teeth.

'What is it you want from me? Your own share, too?' Mr. Prem patted the pockets of his trousers. 'Is that it?'

'We want you gone by the morning, or all this will go to the owners.' I held the receipts up in the air.

'You should be thrown in jail,' Mr. Kalpak said. 'That's what they would do.'

'Name a sum.' His voice was now filled with gloom.

'You can keep all the money; just go and never come back.' I turned and walked away, Shulisha, Priya, and Mr. Kalpak following behind.

When we reached Mr. Kalpak's tent, Priya began to scream. 'The comb, we dropped the comb!' she shouted, pulling away from Shulisha and kicking her feet against the dust.

'You don't need those things,' Shulisha said. She tried to draw Priya towards her again. 'Why didn't you tell me what he was doing, huh?'

'He was going to make me a star,' Priya whispered. 'Now I've got no one.'

'You have Kamala,' I said.

Suddenly she collapsed onto the ground. 'Don't tell Kamala,' she pleaded. 'Or she'll leave me, too.'

Mr. Kalpak lifted Priya from the ground and placed her on his bed, and we all sat around and waited until she fell asleep.

'She's like a little fly.' Shulisha began to cry.

The following morning Mr. Prem had gone.

'He's off to one of those bigger shows,' Bose said. 'He was always a selfish bastard.' He joined in with the others as they squabbled over the stash of magazines and cigarettes left lying in his van. He had taken all the new jewellery, his collection of shoes, and the colour TV.

In his absence even the air about us seemed to relax.

'There's no boss, so why should we kill ourselves?' the men said. They set up card tables in between performances and had too much to drink. Even the Nepalese girls began to take advantage, turning up late for training and not bothering to help with the chores.

'It's only a matter of time before the numbers drop again,' Mr. Kalpak complained. 'Everyone needs a boss, no matter how bad they are.'

'You should take charge,' I told him. 'You've been here long enough.'

'I'm an acrobatic trainer; that's all I am.'

■■■

When word reached Georgetown of Mr. Prem's mysterious disappearance, the owners, the two Chandhok brothers, came at once.

They stalked around the circus in matching pinstriped suits, inspecting the tents and the animal enclosures and then shaking their heads. Between them walked a slim man with his hair pulled back into a ponytail. He was dressed in light-coloured slacks and a short-sleeve shirt, and each time one of the performers passed by, he nodded his head.

'That one with the hair, he's probably going to buy it over,' someone suggested.

'Nah, he's from the bank; they're putting a price on everything, so they can sell it all bit by bit,' Bose said. 'We're too much bother for them now.'

The Chandhok brothers called a meeting that night, and everyone gathered in the big top to hear what they had to say. The wider of the brothers took to the floor, brushing down the arms of his suit. 'You must all be wondering what has happened to our friend Mr. Prem.' He coughed loudly into his hand. 'Indeed, *we* have been left wondering, too.'

Some of the men laughed, and Mr. Chandhok raised his hand. 'The point is, he has gone, but The Great Raman Circus will always remain.'

Beside me Mr. Kalpak released a sigh, and some of the men whooped and whistled loudly.

'There will be some changes, including the appointment of a new troupe master, Mr. Rankumar.' He held out a hand towards the man in the light-coloured slacks.

Mr. Kalpak removed his glasses, and his eyebrows dipped into the furrow of his brow, as though he hadn't quite heard what had been said.

'They should have picked you,' I whispered.

'They will retire me soon.' He put his glasses back on and shook his head. 'I'm like a bullock no longer fit to pull his plough.'

Mr. Kalpak was not much older than Mr. Rankumar, but he had a worn look in his face, like he had seen too much. While he rubbed at his bristly chin, the Chandhok brothers continued to talk about reducing costs and bringing new talent to the show, and then they left, leaving Mr. Rankumar behind. He leant back against the fence, one leg crossed over the other at the ankles, and nodded his head calmly as questions were fired at him from the floor.

'They said they will cut costs, so how many of us will lose our jobs?' someone asked.

'You won't lose your job if you perform well,' he said. 'Not if we keep the numbers up.'

'Will we get the pay we deserve?'

'Profits will be shared, but it's too early to say what will happen,' he said. 'Let's concentrate on getting things back to normal first.'

■ ■ ■

By the following morning, Mr. Rankumar had settled into Mr. Prem's old caravan. He sat on the step holding a cup of chai and watching us as we made our way to training. 'He's handsome, don't you think?' Shulisha dug me in the ribs with her elbow.

'Who?'

'Mr. Rankumar; he looks a little like Akshay Kumar, with his heart-shaped face.'

He came during training and stood watching us from a distance. 'I can't concentrate,' Shulisha said. 'What is it that he's looking at?'

Several of the Nepalese girls began to giggle.

'Is there something we can help you with?' Mr. Kalpak asked him.

'As troupe master, I'd like to get to know everyone.' He hopped over the fence and joined us. 'You don't mind?' He ran a hand through his thick dark hair, which was now loose about his shoulders.

Mr. Kalpak instructed us to get in line, and then he made his way along, pointing at us one by one with his cane. 'Govindi, the hoop; Ambi, hand-walking; Kumud, the wire,' he called out.

Mr. Rankumar held up his hand 'I'd like them to speak for themselves,' he said.

Mr. Kalpak nodded at Shulisha, who was next in line.

'I'm Shulisha, a plate-spinner.' Her face grew red as she lowered her gaze towards the floor.

Some of the Nepalese girls giggled as they tried to find the right words, and Priya refused to speak at all. When he came to me, he stood up straight. 'Ah, yes, the Elastic Girl; you're the one who has caused such a stir.'

'Chop, chop,' Mr. Kalpak called, rapping his cane loudly off the edge of the fence. 'We'll never get any training done at this rate.'

'He's got an eye for you,' Shulisha said over breakfast. 'He didn't even stop to look at me.'

'He looked at me no more than anyone else. Besides, I've no interest in Mr. Rankumar or any other man.'

■ ■ ■

Mr. Rankumar continued to pop in and out during our training, making suggestions to Mr. Kalpak every now and then on things he might wish to improve. 'Their training is too rigid. You shouldn't have every day the same.'

'These girls need stability and discipline,' Mr. Kalpak told him, 'without it the show wouldn't succeed.'

'They don't look like they're enjoying themselves,' Mr. Rankumar continued. 'The audience will pick up on their mood.'

It continued that way, with Mr. Rankumar insisting on changing things to suit his ideas. 'They must have breakfast before they practise; how do you expect them to focus without food?'

'With food in their bellies, their minds and bodies slow down,' Mr. Kalpak told him. 'It's better to loosen up first thing.'

'Those are old-fashioned ideas,' Mr. Rankumar said. 'We have to move with the times; Jumbo Circus, Gemini—they are all getting bigger, while we are being left behind.'

'Sometimes things can move too fast,' Mr. Kalpak warned him. 'Too much change can send everything out of control.'

'You worry too much.' Mr. Rankumar laughed, and he went about his way.

For several weeks the mood between Mr. Kalpak and Mr. Rankumar tightened like a wire. Everyone else was pleased with the changes, clapping for joy when Mr. Rankumar bought in proper cricket equipment and installed a basketball hoop. 'Leisure time is essential for health,' he said. 'Without it we might as well be machines.'

He encouraged the girls to enroll in classes at USHA Institute. 'Two hours per week for each girl to study what she wants,' he said.

It was freedom we had never imagined.

Mr. Kalpak went out of his way to avoid the new troupe master, remaining in his tent during the weekly meetings and refusing to join the rest of the performers for dinner.

'You're being rude,' I told him when I brought him something to eat. 'It's not Mr. Rankumar's fault that he is here.'

'That man will be the downfall of this place. Replacing training with ball games will not get us very far.'

'He thinks that it would be good for our soul.'

'And what do *you* think?' he asked. 'Do you believe what he says?'

'No. Of course you know what's best.'

Mr. Kalpak reached across the table and patted my hand. 'I knew that you would not turn your back on me,' he said.

■ ■ ■

'There's a seamstress class,' Shulisha said that evening. She was flicking through the brochure for USHA. 'Do you think Mr. Rankumar would allow us to join a class?'

Some of the girls had already signed up for pot-modelling and painting.

'Mr. Kalpak doesn't think it's a good idea; he thinks it would interfere with our training.'

'He's only afraid that you will run off with Mr. Rankumar.'

'Mr. Kalpak is my guru; he doesn't think about those things.'

'He's in love with you. The man is afraid to let you out of his sight.'

'You're a fool.' I began to flick through the brochure for USHA, my fingers sticking to the pages as I went.

29

Mr. Kalpak wasn't happy when Shulisha and I signed up for a tailoring class at USHA. 'You told me that you didn't agree with his fancy ideas; I thought you had more sense,' he said.

'What's the harm in a little freedom now that Mr. Prem has gone?'

'But don't you see? He will open up all these possibilities. He will turn your head away from here.'

'Why's that so bad?'

'It will ruin everything.' He turned away from me and began gathering up hoops from the ground.

'You don't have to look after me anymore.'

'No, you don't need me now.' He threw the hoops into a trunk and left me there in the big top.

It was the first time that I felt a spark of anger again. After everything that I'd been through, he wanted to deny me that one piece of happiness, and vowing not to let him win, I began to sew.

Every Tuesday evening Shulisha and I attended our class. It was made up of middle-aged women, all chopping their way through yards of cloth and battering away on their Umbrella machines until they had produced a pair of curtains, a cushion cover, or a salwar suit.

While Shulisha quickly remembered what her mother had taught her about the backstitch and the slipstitch, the teacher, Mrs. Achari, laughed when I struggled to thread a needle into one of the machines. 'You will need to stick to hand-stitching for now,' she said.

'It's pointless; I'll never get so far as sewing on a button,' I complained to Shulisha. 'Mr. Kalpak was right; it's a waste of time.'

'Please.' Shulisha grabbed my hand. 'If you leave, Mr. Rankumar will not come to collect us anymore.'

Mr. Rankumar had insisted on collecting us after each class. 'It's on my way back from Talwalker's fitness studio,' he had said. 'It makes sense for us to share a taxi.'

'You never speak to him,' I said to Shulisha. 'Each week he asks us how we are enjoying the class, and all you do is nod.'

'Arms up.' Shulisha began to wrap a measuring tape around my chest and my waist.

'He will think that you don't like him.'

'I don't know what to say.' She placed the tape along the length of my shoulder. 'He makes me shake.'

'Then you must be in love.' Mrs. Achari poked her head in from behind us.

'It's nothing.' She bent down low over the table and began to write out measurements, her lips pressed together tightly.

As the rickshaw took us back along Mount Road, I pulled out the blouse Shulisha had been working on. 'Don't you think this is good, Mr. Rankumar? Mrs. Achari says that Shulisha has a very steady hand.'

Shulisha snatched the blouse back. 'It's not finished; the arms are all wrong,' she said.

'You're enjoying the class?' he asked.

Shulisha only nodded again, but the following day, Mr. Rankumar presented us with a white, wicker, sewing-basket. Inside, it was lined with red silk and neatly filled with coloured spools of thread, needles, scissors, and a measuring tape. Shulisha was beside herself with joy. 'It's wonderful.' She clutched the sewing box to her chest like a baby.

'Only something to get you started,' he said. 'I was thinking that you could do the repairs in the circus.'

Shulisha looked at him, wide-eyed, and said nothing. 'Yes, we could do that,' I offered. 'We'll give you a very good price.'

'Good, then I'll send someone over with the costumes,' he said.

'So, he's just trying to cut costs,' she said when he'd gone. 'It's all part of his plan to save the circus.'

'It was a gift; he was thinking of you when he bought it.'

Shulisha ran her fingers over the lid of the box. 'My father said that no man would ever look at me,' she said.

'Then he did not know Mr. Rankumar.'

Just as he'd said, Kamala came that evening with a stack of clothes in her arms. 'Mr. Rankumar says that you are to do the repairs this week,' she said, and she lowered the clothes onto the bed.

'We'll never get through all this; you heard what Mrs. Achari said about my stitching.'

'I'll show you,' Shulisha said brightly. She began to feed some yellow thread through a needle.

All night we worked, Shulisha humming along happily as we repaired hems and added sequins and motifs to costumes, but by the end of the week, my fingers were pricked purple and my hands stiff. When Mr. Rankumar came to pay us for the work, Shulisha smiled at him, and a loneliness rose up out of my belly.

When we had saved up two hundred rupees, we bought an Umbrella sewing machine. 'It can do up to three thousand stitches per minute,' Shulisha read from the instructions. 'I'll be able to do five times the work.'

'Now you can start your business; some of those women in the class earn three hundred rupee for a suit.'

So, from inside the circus grounds, Shulisha set up an enterprise called Star Creations, and every Thursday evening Mr. Rankumar would take her to Egmore, a small side street lined with stalls of bright stacks of unfinished cotton and silk. They returned laden with stacks of material, which Shulisha busily began to transform into salwar suits.

When she had finished one dozen suits and covered them all in plastic wrapping, we took them to Gupta Market. Mr. Rankumar's prediction was right; the first batch of 'Star Creations' sold out within three hours, and by the following week, Shulisha was looking for new premises in Ashok Nagar.

'You see, this is what happens,' Mr. Kalpak complained when Shulisha announced that she was leaving the show.

'Shulisha has a great talent for tailoring; you haven't seen what she can do.'

'Do you know how many tailors operate in Ashok Nagar? Some of them have been there for generations.'

'She wants to make her own way in the world.'

'And you? Will you go, too?'

'I can't stay here forever; my contract will be up in one year, and then I'll have to move on, just like everyone else.'

He stood there looking upward, as if there was something that he wanted to say.

'They're all gone.' I looked about me at the empty tent. 'I'll have to go and help Shulisha with repairs.'

'Yes.' He straightened himself. 'You have to go.'

■ ■ ■

Once Shulisha had found premises in the basement of a grocery store, there was no stopping her, and Mr. Rankumar used his own money to have the place cleared out. He helped her in the evenings, drafting in men to fit lights and fans and to partition off the room to create a workspace and some sleeping quarters. In less than one month, the shop was ready to open for business, and a pooja was organised the night before the doors opened. Shulisha invited some of the women and men from the circus. They wondered how it had all been possible. 'All this from nothing,' they said. 'Like magic.'

'You can do anything you set your mind to,' Shulisha told them. 'I was only a plate-spinner, and now I'm a businesswoman.'

Everyone began to talk about what they might do, how they could make it without The Great Raman Circus of Chennai. Instead of dreaming of walking tightropes and flying the trapeze, the acrobats wanted to become hairdressers and bookkeepers. 'At USHA there are courses for everything,' Kamala said.

Before long the younger girls were struggling to maintain their acts, and several of the audience members booed when Ashmita faltered on the tightwire.

'They've lost all concentration,' Mr. Kalpak complained to Rankumar. 'You must stop all this nonsense at once, or the numbers will start to fall.'

'It will help them in the long run; you will see.'

'Just like it helped Shulisha,' he snapped. 'Is that what you want: to develop a business empire and have everyone leave the show?'

'They have their own minds,' Mr. Rankumar replied. 'What they do is up to them.'

'You will destroy them, and you will destroy The Great Raman Circus,' Mr. Kalpak warned him. 'Then we will see what the Chandhok brothers have to say.'

■ ■ ■

Mr. Kalpak appeared to be right; the numbers dropped for the second month in a row, and everyone began to talk about how things were beginning to fall apart, but Mr. Rankumar seemed oblivious to it all, continuing to go to the shop each evening to check on Shulisha's progress. 'She won a contract to supply twenty-five suits to Gyan Fashions,' he told everyone, and then he began staying over with her at Ashok Nagar, returning in the morning like a man who had caught a lion.

'See, now you know what he is like,' Mr. Kalpak tutted.

'You don't want anyone to be happy, do you?' I snapped. 'You think everyone should be miserable just like you.'

Mr. Kalpak's face dropped, and he disappeared back into his tent. For a whole week he didn't look at me during training and began staying in his tent each evening, ordering in his food. 'He doesn't say much,' Priya said, heading towards his tent with a plate of dahl and rice. 'All he does is pray.'

He seemed to have given up on trying to make the circus work, no longer shouting at the girls when they performed badly or seeming to care that the numbers continued to drop.

'If it continues like this, we will all be out on the street,' Kamala said. 'Someone needs to get through to him.'

When I went to him, he was slouched over on the end of the bed. 'I've been waiting for over an hour.' He stopped when he saw that it was me. 'I thought that you were Priya.'

'I came to see what it is that you are doing in here.'

'Mr. Rankumar will wonder where you are,' he said.

'What are you talking about?'

'He's a young, good-looking man. I wouldn't blame you if you were attracted to him.'

'He's devoted to Shulisha; you would see that if you ever left your tent.'

'There is nothing for me out there.' His face was filled with sadness, and there was nothing left in him of the man I'd met the first day in the circus.

'Why have you given up?' I sat down beside him on the bed.

'What have *I* to give?'

'You were the one to teach me about inner strength, about the resilience of the myna bird; where has that spirit gone?'

'Nobody needs me anymore.'

'Mr. Rankumar's not working out as expected, and the circus is suffering. We still need you out there.'

Suddenly he took my face in his hands, and my blood pounded at his closeness. 'Do *you* need me?' he asked.

I remembered what Shulisha had said about him being in love with me, about him not wanting to let me out of his sight.

'You're like a brother to me.' I pulled away, and he slumped back onto the bed.

'I'm a fool,' he said. 'Just go.'

The circus continued to suffer, and when Mr. Rankumar announced that he was leaving to join Shulisha at Star Creations, everyone began to worry.

'The Chandhok brothers have appointed you to take over as troupe master,' he told Mr. Kalpak. 'It's time for you to do things your way.'

After three more days, Mr. Kalpak emerged from his tent. He had shaved off his little beard and got rid of his cane.

'Thank God Mr. Kalpak has returned,' Kamala said. 'Now we are saved.'

During training his eyes lingered over me, and when he spoke to me, his voice was different, softer. Something about it made me feel awkward, so that I struggled to look at him without blushing.

He turned the circus around, taking on new acts and advertising to entice people back to the show. His energy and determination were palpable.

He called me to his caravan one day.

'I've something for you,' he said. 'It's a poem that belonged to your grandfather; we shared a love for Bharathiar.' He handed me a slip of paper. 'It's called *Praying the Mother Goddess*.'

'Read it to me,' I said, pressing the paper back into his hand.

We sat on the bed together, our knees touching as he read. '*Should all my wishes be fulfilled, should I wish only that is good! Should I possess a heart that is strong, so should I acquire a knowledge devoid of doubts.*' He paused for a moment, and I closed my eyes. '*All my sins like the mist before the sun, in your graceful presence disappear, should all they be! Oh! Mother!*'

With my eyes still closed, his lips touched mine, and it felt like a thousand fireflies had landed on my skin at once. It stunned me completely.

'It's not possible,' I said, opening my eyes.

'You forgot that the human spirit can achieve anything, that we can make the impossible possible.'

I'd never have imagined it, but somehow it happened.

It was nothing like the way Mr. Prem had treated me. It was gentle and sweet, and Mr. Kalpak didn't force himself on me in any way. But sometimes, when he touched me, I froze with terror and he would stroke my arm, telling me, 'Everything is OK; I'll never hurt you.' I believed him.

But then Shulisha and Mr. Rankumar returned to the circus to announce that they were to be married, and it came to me that I could never have those things with Mr. Kalpak. He was too old and a widower; it was not allowed.

'We're going to close the shop for a week,' Shulisha told me. 'We've booked a honeymoon in Goa.'

'I could help out at the shop, keep things moving.'

'And leave Mr. Kalpak on his own?' My face burned as Shulisha leant towards me. 'I could see the way you look at each other.'

'It's nothing.'

'He will never marry you,' she said. 'You need to think about that, about what you will do after you leave here.'

'He looks after me.'

'Like a father?'

'He cares for me.' Tears began to fill my eyes.

'Be careful what you are getting into, Muthu.'

30

Soon all the women of the circus were looking at me like a cracked pot.

'They're whispering about us.'

'Ignore them,' he said. 'They will soon find something else to talk about.'

We continued to spend our nights together, our feelings for each other deepening during the hot summer months. I convinced myself that this was happiness.

But our moments together remained behind closed doors, both of us pretending to everyone else that we were nothing more than friends. We knew that closing ourselves off from reality couldn't last forever, and when it reached December, the cracks started to appear.

On my sixteenth birthday Mr. Kalpak asked me to call him Raksha. 'It means protection, for that's what I was born to do; look after *you* Muthu.' He gave me an orange silk scarf.

'It suits you,' he said, removing my grandfather's watch from over my head and tying the scarf in a knot to the side of my neck.

It reminded me of Baba and the pendant.

'It looks expensive; you shouldn't have spent so much.'

'It belonged to Hemaji,' he said, and a shiver ran through me.

There was no way to tell him that I didn't want to wear his dead wife's clothing, that the colour did not suit my pale skin, and more than that, it troubled me that he couldn't see my annoyance.

Other things began to annoy me; in the evenings he no longer read me poetry but spent all his attention on the upcoming elections. 'Listen to this,' he said, flicking a page of the *Indian Express*. 'The cabinet want to ban opinion polls; they say they influence the outcome of the elections.' He rose out of his chair and began to pace the length of the tent. 'Bloody hypocrites want to take away our fundamental right to free speech and then pretend we are living in a democratic country.'

As I wasn't eligible to vote, it didn't interest me, but with every passing day, Raksha continued to get more and more worked up about the state of things, and everything between us seemed to change.

Maybe Shulisha had been right. I stopped going to him at night, sending Priya to deliver his dinner instead. If he spoke to me at rehearsals I turned away.

'You and Mr. Kalpak have fallen out of love?' Priya asked.

'We were never in love.'

'They say that he can't be with you because it's forbidden by the *Gita*.'

'You listen to too much gossip. If you ever want to make it as a Hula girl, you should focus on your training instead.'

■ ■ ■

But, forbidden or not, with every passing day, I missed him. I missed watching the way he slept with his hand on mine, the smell of bergamot and clove oil on his skin, so when he found me alone one evening and sank down beside me on the bed, my heart began hammering in my chest.

'I've missed you,' he said, with tears in his eyes. 'Why aren't you happy?'

'I'm never going to be married like Shulisha or have a family, and one day I will be left all alone.'

'If I could give you all these things you wish for, I would.' He drew me in against his neck. 'You can't leave me. I'd rather die.'

■ ■ ■

It was true; I couldn't leave him, not then, because the following morning I stood looking down at the brown, viscous mass in the toilet bowl, waited for the wave of nausea to pass, and then leant forward to heave and retch again. Calculating the dates, I figured out that my menses were two months late; I was pregnant. 'I would not leave such things to chance; you can trust me, Muthu,' he had said. He had convinced me to have the coil removed. 'It's not necessary now; it will only remind us of the past.'

Sobs racked my body as I realised he had trapped me, just like Baba and Mr. Prem.

'I've always wanted a child,' he cried when I told him. He bent down to kiss my belly. 'Hemaji was never blessed with one.'

'I want to get rid of it,' I said. 'I'm only telling you because I need two thousand rupees for the doctor in Poonamallee.'

'No,' he said. 'You can't destroy it.'

'You told me it couldn't happen.'

'It's a blessing; can't you see?'

'What kind of life would this be for a child? You would bring it up here, in a circus?'

'We'll leave,' he said. 'I'll take care of you both.'

'It wouldn't work.'

'There's nothing else to do,' he said. 'We have been given this by god; it's a sign that we're meant to stay together.' He reached out and pulled me towards him.

If it hadn't happened that way, I may have left him. My fate may have taken a different path, for two days later I received a visitor.

'Your mother is here,' Kamala announced. 'She's waiting for you, just outside.'

I did not look up, continuing to stitch the fallen hem of a skirt.

'Muthu, did you hear me?' Kamala asked when I failed to move. 'Your mother is waiting.'

Taking the needle, I stuck it into my hand until I drew blood. 'She has come too late.'

When I stepped out into the yard, she was standing with her back towards me, face tilted in the direction of the elephant enclosure. Everything about me seemed to buzz and hum: the flies hovering over the animal dung, the pair of quarrelling white-throated munias in the tree overhead, and the whirl of colours coming and going under the flap of the big top. Suddenly the munias shot off into the air, alerting amma to turn around and face me.

'Beti.' She moved forwards and embraced me, her bones pressing against me.

'Why have you come after all this time?'

'To bring you home.' Her voice began to shake.

'To that woman?'

'Your Dadi sent her away; he couldn't stand to be in the same house as her anymore, not after all she had done.'

She followed me into the tent.

'It was he who brought me here.'

'It was your grandmother. She wanted to get rid of you at the start, but he wouldn't hear tell of it,' she said. 'He always wanted you, despite everything.'

We sat on the bed, and I lay my head against her shoulder.

'So, you will come?'

'It's too late, Amma; you've come too late.'

'Mrs. Tikaram, you've come to visit.' It was Raksha, standing awkwardly in the width of the opening, moving from one foot to another.

'I've come to take Muthu home,' she said brightly, as I raised my head wearily from her shoulder.

'Home?' Raksha asked, stepping inside. 'It's not possible.'

'It's been five years; her contract is up.'

'She's not told you her news?' He glanced down towards my stomach.

My mother's face grew pale as she stared at the gentle curve of my belly. 'You're mistaken,' she said. 'How could it happen?'

'We're in love,' he said, straightening his back.

Amma shook her head. 'We trusted you to look after her!' She stood up and began to pull at his kurta. 'She's only a child; what kind of man would do this?'

'She's staying with me,' he said calmly, and my body stiffened.

Amma collapsed back onto the bed. 'Is it true, Muthu—is this what you want?'

'This is where I'm meant to be.'

My mother fell to her knees and clasped her thin arms around my legs. 'You can still come home; we will look after you,' she cried.

Raksha turned his back to us and I reached out my hand to help amma up from the floor. 'I still love you,' I said. 'You can tell Dadi that.'

'Then we can try,' she pleaded, her voice now a whisper. 'We can make it work.'

'I can't go with you, not now,' I said. 'Too much has happened.'

'He will be waiting.' She looked around her. 'What will I tell him?'

'Give him this.' I reached underneath my pillow and handed her my grandfather's pocket watch. 'I kept it for him.'

She leant forwards and kissed my head, and then she was gone, Raksha walking her to the gate. When he returned, he gathered me into his arms. 'It's time to go,' he said. 'It's time to leave this place, Elastic Girl.'

31

We moved into a flat in Adambakkam. It was a cramped two-bed flat, miles outside the centre of the city, and every morning the three of us would walk to Guindy Station, Kautik's little feet carrying him as fast as they could. Raksha would wave to us from his carriage. 'Don't forget to come at four o'clock,' he would say. When he returned from the circus that afternoon, he would thrust little wooden toys and trinkets upon Kautik, who at one, was not old enough to play with them and, to Raksha's dismay, would toss them to the ground.

'Of course, he's too bright for such things,' he would say, lifting the toy from the platform and examining it as though he had simply found it lying there and had not been responsible for the foolish purchase.

His love for Kautik made me want to make our little family work, and while Kautik played with his building blocks and his red fire engine, I began to rearrange our small apartment, brightening the walls with white paint and sewing cushion covers in reds and greens.

'See, with a little bit of work, it is so much better,' Raksha said. 'Everything in life requires some effort to be at its best.' He would settle himself with Kautik on his lap and begin to tell him about his day in the circus, Kautik squealing with laughter as his father mimicked the sounds of the monkeys and elephants.

At the market I picked up handfuls of okra and chillies and slowly learned how to cook some of the dishes that my mother used to make, and at night when Raksha reached out to me, I would turn to him like a wife.

Contentment grew out of our little flat like fragrant starry jasmine, and for a while we were happy in Adambakkam, browsing through the new Thangam department store, taking the bus out to the coast on a Sunday, where I would watch Raksha show Kautik how to fly a kite, and eating ice cream as we strolled through Guindy Park.

'Just one moment,' a lady called, running up from behind as we made our way through the park one day. She caught up with us and tucked Kautik's bear back into his stroller. 'Your grandson dropped this.' She looked at Raksha.

'She thought you were my father,' I whispered to him so that Kautik could not hear.

'Let her think what she wants.' He leant over to kiss my lips, and behind him the woman's eyes widened in recognition of what we really were.

'You're wicked; that poor woman almost had a seizure.'

'I love you, and I don't care what anybody thinks.' He took my hand to head on through the park, and together we watched Kautik run ahead of us chasing a butterfly, the citrus scent of wood-apple fruit enveloping us as it was crushed beneath our feet. The peace that I had found on the train back from Avadi returned to me.

We knew happiness for a while.

■ ■ ■

But then the monsoon came, filling Raksha with dengue fever. 'It's the trains,' he coughed. 'In this heat the germs spread like wildfire among the passengers.'

He lay in bed for days, his muscles aching and his chest covered in a bright-red rash. Still he would not allow me to call upon a doctor. 'It will pass in a day or so. A doctor will only tell me to drink more fluids; I don't need to pay someone to tell me that.'

I tried to nurse him, laying cold towels on his face, but he insisted that we stay away. 'Take Kautik out somewhere, before he too gets ill.'

When we returned in the evening, Raksha was lying on his back, one hand resting across his face.

'I bought you some fresh ginger; it's good for fever.' I reached out to waken him up, but he didn't move, and I saw then a trail of saliva down the curve of his chin. 'Raksha, wake up!' But still he lay there, and when I pushed at his arm in desperation, it fell away from his face. His eyes stared blankly up towards the ceiling and in that instant everything shattered around me.

'Dadi?' Kautik asked. He was standing in the doorway, holding out his father's glasses in his hand. 'Dadi, see,' he said.

I began to sob, Kautik coming to cling onto my heaving body.

Things happened around us: the simple little pyre arranged by Mr. Butra, the flower seller who lived upstairs, and the concerned visits by mothers from the Golden Lotus Club. They had helped me when Kautik was born, they had shown me what to do, but they could not help me now. 'You have to eat for Kautik's sake,' they tried. They filled the kitchen with Tupperware containers of food and cleaned the house, clearing all of Raksha's clothing into plastic bags. 'Do you want to keep something?' they asked, but I told them to take it all away.

During the night a smell or a sound would rise up in the flat suddenly and fill me with utter dismay, and I would go to Kautik and rouse him from his sleep just to press his damp forehead against my aching chest. But mostly I didn't feel anything; for I had slipped down into the ocean, deep down where everything was cold and black.

■ ■ ■

It was Mr. Butra who came to our rescue, reading stories to Kautik in the evenings and cooking us dinner on my little gas stove.

'What am I going to do?' I asked him one evening.

'Time will pass,' he said simply. 'Time.'

He taught me how to make ladoos and burfi and finally coaxed me out of the flat to accompany him and Kautik to the flower market at Pondy Bazaar. As I walked behind them, amongst the flower carts, he taught Kautik the names of all the flowers and plants, explaining when was the best time to plant lotus bulbs, and how the marigold was most popular for weddings. And then when we reached the wedding garlands, strung up in rows on either side of us, the smell of jasmine filled me, and I began to sob.

Kautik rushed towards me and clung to my legs, and Mr. Butra continued to stand at a distance, his hands clasped behind his back, like he was in no great hurry. It was there in the midst of the flower market that I began to rise up through the water, like a piece of soft coral that had broken free.

EPILOGUE

Like Kakudmi, the Lord of the Ocean, I travelled back through the depths of time, looking for truths and answers about my existence. Now, having returned to Earth, so much time has passed, and the landscape and the air about me have changed so that it's as if I am seeing everything for the first time.

We are outside the gates of Ponmalligai Hospital, Adambakkam, and before me Kautik is playing. He's dressed in a pair of navy shorts and a white shirt, like a little man rather than a five-year-old. 'Shoo, shoo,' he cries out, clapping his hands at a cat and then squealing with laughter when the cat takes a leap up onto Mr. Butra's flower stall, knocking over a bowl of pink-and-yellow gerberas and sending Mr. Butra into a rage.

I continue to watch them, all the while rolling the mixture of coconut, sugar, and fried flour between my oiled palms.

'One kilogram of coconut ladoo and a mixed bouquet!' Kautik calls out to the flow of hospital visitors. He cocks his head to the side and smiles at them in a way that prevents them from passing him by without making a purchase. Then he gives half of the money to Mr. Butra, who is too old and cranky to sell the flowers himself.

When Kautik returns to the rickety little table I'm working at, he hands me his earnings, and together we begin to fold away the table and repack the unsold boxes of sweets, placing them onto Mr. Butra's wooden cart.

'Amma, can I have one?' Kautik asks, his eyes resting on a plate of coconut ladoos. When I nod, he pops one into his mouth, his cheeks puffing out in his round face. My heart swells with happiness, and I pull my son to me and hold him tight.

Mr.Butra leans over and spills the water from an empty flower jug out into the road. 'You're back,' he says, smiling at me.

Kautik looks up, his dark, wide eyes searching my face. 'Where were you, Amma?' he asks.

'Nowhere,' I tell him. 'Nowhere.'

ACKNOWLEDGEMENTS

My debut novel, *Elastic Girl*, has been a work in progress for several years, and there are many wonderful people who have helped me along the way. The life of this novel started out whilst I was undertaking a Masters in Creative Writing at Queen's University, Belfast. I would like to thank all those within the Seamus Heaney Centre at Queens for their support, and I am particularly indebted to Carlo Gébler, former lecturer and adviser, who helped me immensely in shaping this book.

I extend my thanks also to Mary-Jane Holmes from Fish Publishing, and to the lovely Jane Harrison for their editorial advice. Appreciation to my first-draft readers and advisers, Sheena Wilkinson, Kathleen Quinn and members of the Yellow Door writing group for their friendship, book discussions and guidance.

Thanks to the late Mary Ellen Mark for her inspirational photography, and to Child Rescue Nepal for bringing this issue to my attention. I wish Joanna Bega and Child Rescue Nepal continued success with their work in rescuing and rehabilitating children who have been trafficked.

My appreciation also to Joanna Lumley, OBE. Amongst her many roles, Joanna is a human rights activist and a strong campaigner against the injustice of child trafficking and child poverty. I am indebted to her for taking the time to support my book.

I was incredibly lucky to receive a bursary award from the Arts Council of Northern Ireland (Support for the Individual Artist Programme), and I am thankful to the work of the Arts Council in supporting emerging artists in Northern Ireland.

Sincere thanks to my entire family, who have continually encouraged me in the pursuit of this project. In particular I would like to thank my mother, whose love and guidance is always with me, and also my sister, Frances, for her eagle eye and her support when I most needed it.

Most importantly, I wish to thank my loving and supportive husband Rajesh, without whom this book would not have been possible, and my two wonderful children, Lucia and Marcus, who inspire me each and every day.

LOTTERY FUNDED

arts council of Northern Ireland

ABOUT THE AUTHOR

Olivia Rana was inspired in part to write *Elastic Girl* by the work of photographer Mary Ellen Mark, who documented the struggles of child circus performers in India, and Child Rescue Nepal (formerly the Esther Benjamins Trust).

Rana received a writer's bursary award from the Arts Council of Northern Ireland for *Elastic Girl*. Her work has been both long-and short-listed for a selection of other awards.

Rana holds a master's degree in computing and information science, as well as one in creative writing. She spent many years in project management before devoting her time to writing. She also teaches a novel-writing course at Queens University.

Rana is married with two children. She lives with her family in Belfast, Ireland.

Printed in Great Britain
by Amazon